*He could think of a dozen reasons to avoid attraction, let alone sex, with her.*

Not the least of which was the fact that she was a government agent, secretive and probably paranoid, schooled in deception.

Not the girl next door she appeared to be.

And she thought he was engaged to be married. Why did she make him keep forgetting that? His mind needed to be on their common goal— stopping New Dawn. This dicey situation called for focus and restraint.

He would ignore his companion. In fact, he would avoid her except for when they had to appear in public as lovers.

Anything but icy control might blow this whole charade.

Dear Reader,

Welcome to the New Year—and to another month of fabulous reading. We've got a lineup of books you won't be able to resist, starting with the latest CAVANAUGH JUSTICE title from RITA® Award winner Marie Ferrarella. *Dangerous Disguise* takes an undercover hero, adds a tempting heroine, then mixes them up with a Mob money-laundering operation run out of a restaurant. It's a recipe for irresistibility.

*Undercover Mistress* is the latest STARRS OF THE WEST title from multi-RITA® Award-winning author Kathleen Creighton. A desperate rescue leads to an unlikely alliance between a soap opera actress who's nowhere near as ditsy as everyone assumes and a federal agent who's finally discovered he has a heart. In *Close to the Edge*, Kylie Brant takes a bayou-born private detective and his high-society boss, then forces them onto a case where "hands off" turns at last into "hands on." In Susan Vaughan's *Code Name: Fiancée,* when agent Vanessa Wade has to pose as the fiancée of wealthy Nick Markos, it's all for the sake of national security. Or is it? Desire writer Michelle Celmer joins the Intimate Moments roster with *Running on Empty*, an amnesia story that starts at the local discount store and ends up…in bed. Finally, Barbara Phinney makes her second appearance in the line with *Necessary Secrets*, introducing a pregnant heroine and a sexy cop— but everyone's got secrets to hide.

Enjoy them all, then come back next month for more of the best and most exciting romantic reading around.

Yours,

Leslie J. Wainger
Executive Editor

Please address questions and book requests to:
Silhouette Reader Service
U.S.: 3010 Walden Ave., P.O. Box 1325, Buffalo, NY 14269
Canadian: P.O. Box 609, Fort Erie, Ont. L2A 5X3

# CODE NAME:
# FIANCÉE

## SUSAN VAUGHAN

Silhouette

INTIMATE MOMENTS™

Published by Silhouette Books

America's Publisher of Contemporary Romance

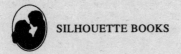 SILHOUETTE BOOKS

ISBN 0-373-27412-2

CODE NAME: FIANCÉE

Copyright © 2005 by Susan Hofstetter Vaughan

Visit Silhouette Books at www.eHarlequin.com

**Printed in U.S.A.**

**Books by Susan Vaughan**

Silhouette Intimate Moments

*Dangerous Attraction* #1086
*Guarding Laura* #1314
*Code Name: Fiancée* #1342

---

## SUSAN VAUGHAN

Susan Vaughan is a West Virginia native who lives on the coast of Maine. Battles with insomnia over the years fired her imagination with stories. Living in many places in the U.S. while studying and teaching gave her characters and ideas. Once she even lived with a French family and attended the Sorbonne.

With her husband, she has kissed the Blarney Stone, canoed the Maine wilderness, kayaked the Colorado River, sailed the Caribbean and won ballroom dancing competitions. Susan's first Silhouette Intimate Moments book, *Dangerous Attraction*, won the 2001 NJRW Golden Leaf for Best First Book. Readers may write to Susan at Saint George, Maine 04860, or via her Web site at www.susanvaughan.com.

To my friend Beth Chamberlin, who gave me
my first romance novel. Little did you know.
As always, to my husband, Warner,
my once and future hero.

# *Prologue*

"You will return the money your brother stole from us, or we will take action."

"It's three in the morning. Who the hell is this?" Nick Markos slammed down his half-empty glass. Glenfiddich splashed onto the mahogany desk that dominated one end of the library.

*Damn.* A waste of single malt Scotch.

He'd spent the day torn in two directions—running his own business long-distance and trying to sell another. Sleep eluded him this autumn night, but he had no patience for demands in the wee hours. He didn't know the voice, but recognized the Middle Eastern accent and the menacing tone.

The quicksand of his brother's dirty dealings was sucking him deeper and deeper. Would he ever be rid of the muck?

"My name is not important." The sly smile in the man's unctuous voice scraped Nick's nerves. "Are you not the brother of Alexei Markos? The *late* Alexei Markos?"

*Regrettably.* Although they hadn't spoken in years until

Nick had visited Alexei in the District of Columbia jail, he did regret his younger brother's untimely death—for many reasons. This phone call among them.

"Who wants to know?"

"You are conducting his affairs at present?"

"If this is about business you had with my brother, call the office tomorrow. Markos Imports, on O Street. *During business hours.*"

The cordless headset at his ear, he paced the length of the library. Books on antiques, history, art and artifacts filled the floor-to-ceiling shelves. Their musty odor permeated the room.

He stopped at the modern globe in the Victorian oak stand. Though Alexei'd lacked integrity, he'd known value and he'd had taste. Nick spun the globe, stopping it with his finger on a tiny Middle Eastern country—about as far from suburban Chevy Chase, Maryland, as you could imagine.

If, as he suspected, the caller was the leader of an ultra-extremist group from that land, no records of those transactions were in the office or anywhere else Nick had searched. His temporizing tactic would serve only as a chance for more information.

If he were given more luck than he'd had lately.

"Your brother conducted transactions for us, but he kept ten million dollars that is ours. It matters not where you get it." The falsely pleasant tone vanished. His caller fired the words out hard and clipped, bullets. "You know who we are. It is not wise of you to feign ignorance, Mr. Markos."

"Ignorance is all I have to offer," Nick said, forging the steel in his own voice. "Alexei and I weren't close. He didn't confide in me. He left no money and no investments. Only debts, which will be paid as much as possible once his business and this house are sold. Get in line."

He stalked back to the desk and downed the rest of his drink. The Scotch, smoky and rich, slid warmth down his throat. He'd rather have savored it slowly.

There was a pause at the other end of the line. Would the bastard give up so easily? Not bloody likely.

"Mr. Markos, I see you do not yet understand the precariousness of your position. Your brother also thought he could cheat us and get away with it. Alas, the warrior sent into the jail to persuade him otherwise went too far."

The chill meaning of the words sank into Nick's bones. The D.C. jail was notoriously overcrowded and dangerous. A knife fight had broken out during a recreation period. After the scuffle, Alexei had been found stabbed although he hadn't been anywhere near the two men fighting. The strange altercation made grim sense in light of the caller's words.

Nick had hoped to settle his brother's estate quickly and quietly and return to his business in London and New York. He wanted no breath of the scandal to reach their ailing father in Greece. The depths to which Alexei had sunk boiled his blood and sickened him.

But redeeming the family honor seemed impossible in the short run.

First Alexei had sullied the family name by dealing with these scum calling themselves New Dawn Warriors. To help them fill their war chest, he'd sold valuable imported art and artifacts. He'd murdered two people and tried to kill a third. Four jurisdictions had charged him with crimes. Enmeshed in greed, Alexei had stolen from the extremists and gotten himself killed. More than anything, Nick wished he could erase the whole sordid affair.

"Are you admitting to murder?"

He should've agreed to the wiretap suggested by the Anti-Terrorism Security Agency, but at first, he'd hidden his head in the sand and denied the need.

The man barked a laugh. "I am merely saying that the few who cross the New Dawn Warriors often meet with unfortunate accidents. We are the chosen, the enlightened ones who will lead the way. No one thwarts our ordained path."

"Sounds like a threat." He fished through the desk drawer for the card from the ATSA officer. "It won't work because I don't have your money. Goodbye."

Nick was about to tap the disconnect button, but the caller's next words stilled his finger.

"You have a fiancée, do you not?"

*Danielle.*

Fear squeezed Nick's throat.

Without waiting for a reply, the caller continued, "A lovely, flame-haired young woman, the warrior in London said. You had your chance, Mr. Markos. Do not bother to meet her flight. She will not be on it. We will be in touch."

A quiet click severed the connection.

# Chapter 1

The next afternoon, Vanessa Wade entered the ATSA director's office.

"Sorry I'm late, General Nolan. Getting this report together took a while, and time got away from me." She held up a thick black portfolio with the agency's seal in the center.

The director beckoned her closer to his desk, a battered oak monument to his career in the U.S. Army.

"Fine, Wade, your thoroughness is worth waiting for. Relax while I glance at those files." He leaned back in his swivel chair and chomped on an unlit cigar.

She scooted back into the enveloping comfort of a leather chair and waited. Though her last mission had been a success, their quarry had died in jail before he could spill information about the New Dawn leader. This development eased her disappointment, but the idea of another undercover gig so soon tightened the muscles in her stomach.

When undercover work meant cozying up to the bad guys,

staying detached was a piece of cake. The challenge—and the adrenaline rush—came from immersing herself in a persona while remaining vigilant.

But recently she'd mingled with the innocent, involving herself in their lives. This last time she'd befriended an inn full of good people, including the woman ATSA had protected.

Slamming the door afterward had felt like amputating a piece of herself without anesthetic.

Duty and responsibility were important, but her naturally gregarious personality needed people. Commitment to friends and family nurtured her soul. Away from her real family in New York, she embraced ATSA as her family.

But undercover work cut her off even from her colleagues. In a false persona, she couldn't help but develop friendships undercover. When the assignment ended, so did those connections. Sometimes painfully, with the sudden force and finality of a guillotine. People resented being deceived.

She'd come to hate deception herself. No more. She couldn't, wouldn't do undercover work again.

She had to convince Nolan that she wasn't the woman for the role recommended in the portfolio. Especially not with Nick Markos. She'd participate in another capacity.

*Any* other capacity.

Maxwell Nolan fixed her with a steely-gray gaze the same color as his hair. After maneuvering the obscenely large cigar from one side of his mouth to the other, he tucked it in a pocket and laced his fingers on top the file.

"So it looks like a break in the New Dawn Warriors op."

She leaned forward. "Yes, good news. The trail didn't end with Alexei Markos's death. Early this morning we had a phone call from his brother, Nicolas Markos."

The general listened raptly to her description of Markos's dilemma. For months ATSA had been searching for Husam Al-Din, the New Dawn leader, and the phone call implied he might be not only in the U.S. but nearby.

Nolan sat and patted his pocket for his cigar. "The money's not our concern other than what it means to New Dawn. If ten million's what Alexei Markos skimmed, they must have a hell of a big war chest. What are they planning?"

"Stratton's unit's working on that one."

He flipped open one of the folders and tapped a photograph with his index finger. The grainy faxed picture showed a sleek, elegant woman about thirty.

"And the woman?"

"One of our London officers and a couple of FBI agents found her safe in her flat, sipping tea with two Scotland Yard detectives. Since she's an American citizen, ATSA took over from the Brits. We have her under protection at a safe house."

Mouthing the soggy tobacco, he closed the file as Vanessa continued. "Danielle LeBec was supposed to fly here this morning to help her fiancé with funeral and business arrangements. On her way to the airport, two swarthy men speaking an unidentified foreign language tried to force her into a car. She hit them with pepper spray and ran like hell."

"Bully for her. Al-Din wants his money. You think he'll try again?"

"As you see in the files, sir, intelligence reports indicate Al-Din sees Markos's fiancée as his Achilles' heel. We'll place an ATSA officer in the house and post several others nearby for surveillance. More security might ratchet up the violence level. We don't want to endanger civilians. A soft target should lure in our bad guys."

"Logical. A harder target leads to a harder attack. How will this deployment catch Al-Din?"

"Nicolas Markos is running his deceased brother's import business and trying to sell it. He'll be out in society at VIP dinners and receptions. New Dawn is bound to try again to kidnap or harm Ms. LeBec, and we'll be ready to grab them."

"You think one of the flunkies'll lead you to his boss."

"Exactly, sir."

She hoped they could get at least one New Dawn flunky to talk. The rest of their plan was loose, improvisation the watchword.

The cigar rolled across the director's lower lip. "Then you'll need to pack for a round trip to London."

Not sure she heard him correctly, she blinked. "I'll be happy to act as control officer or surveillance coordinator. I should stay in the background on this one, sir. Nicolas Markos and I met a few years ago. It's in the file."

Nolan leaned back. "I saw that, but I don't see the problem. You concerned about the society parties?"

She was, but not for the reason he thought. Nolan didn't need a peek at her insecurities. Danielle LeBec was beautiful and elegant. No one had ever used those words to describe Vanessa. "Upper-crust galas are no sweat. I may be a uniform cop's daughter, but I know which fork to use."

"I can always trust your instincts, Wade. That's one reason I want you on this. The other is this aura that invites people to confide in you. They don't call you Vanessa the Confessor for nothing. You're the best officer for this. If the fiancé objects, we'll deal with it."

Her heart sank into her stomach. No way out of it now. *Yes, sir, general, sir.*

"And what about Markos? Can he be trusted? Says in his file he was Special Forces in Kuwait and Somalia."

She cleared her throat. She shouldn't think of Markos as anything but an assignment. "Right. He distinguished himself on special ops duty in Iraq, and Special Forces recruited him. After Somalia he quit and started his business. Our security check says he's clean. He learned of his brother's criminal dealings when the first murder charge hit the press."

"I wonder about his reliability. It says here he refused to help ATSA until the threat to Ms. LeBec forced the issue. His international restaurant-supply business has made him a fortune. He has the means to pay off New Dawn and be done with them while we protect her for him. And who knows what powerful connections he has in society?"

"Those are legitimate reasons for skepticism," she said. "We'll dig deeper and keep a close eye on him." Just so she wasn't that close eye.

The intercom buzzed, and the general picked up the phone. Her gaze drifted to the file her boss still held.

Nicolas Markos. The name conjured up an image of a domineering Greek tycoon out of a novel. The idea both fascinated and repelled her.

Born in Brooklyn, one of his merchant-ship-captain father's many residences, self-made multimillionaire. She ignored the sexual tug evoked by visualizing his proud, handsome face.

The kind of man not to be taken lightly. The kind of arrogant man who thought money and power gave him carte blanche, who went for cover models like her sister Diana. Or sophisticated fashion-magazine editors like Danielle LeBec. The kind of man Vanessa avoided like the plague.

Whoa.

Ye gods, where had all that animosity come from?

Granted, the man was the cold-hearted, calculating type Diana drooled over. Vanessa drooled, too, but hunky guys usually thought of her as a pal, not a femme fatale.

Glamorous? Not her. *Cute* and *girl-next-door* fit her better. Then there were the major chunks anti-terrorism work chopped out of her social life. Social life. For her an oxymoron. Home on Saturday night without even a cat.

Whether Vanessa approved of or liked Markos didn't matter. Her past resentments and insecurities should slink back into her mental attic and stay there for the duration. And a mission like this could last months. She tamped down her dread with professional duty.

And she would be nothing but professional. She'd prove—if only to herself—that she could do the job without personal involvement.

When Nolan replaced the receiver, she said, "I'll arrange to fly to London today, sir."

"The sooner the better. I've just had an urgent message."

"General?"

"There's a deadline on this mission."

"What's the deal?"

"Intelligence reports indicate New Dawn's plotting some sort of attack here in D.C. on Veterans Day. We have to roll up Husam Al-Din and disrupt their plan by November 11."

"But that's four weeks from now!"

Early Saturday afternoon, Nick waited in Baggage Claims at Dulles International Airport.

A polyglot cacophony of greetings surrounded the international-arrivals luggage carousels. On his left an Italian couple in Calvin Klein hugged and kissed a teary old woman in peasant black. On his right a Japanese tour group clicked cameras and chattered with excitement. And somewhere in the waiting crowd lurked three or more ATSA officers.

At first he'd been reluctant because keeping a low profile distanced him from the slime. The kidnap attempt and learning that New Dawn had engineered Alexei's death had forced him into action. He wanted none of his brother's dirty money, but capturing Husam Al-Din and stopping the terrorist plan went a long way toward redeeming the family honor.

And his personal honor, lost in what seemed another lifetime.

Nick had spoken on the telephone with Danielle since her aborted kidnapping. Knowing she was protected eased his mind about cooperating with ATSA. He figured she was giving her minders holy hell. In three languages. He grinned.

She'd sure given him the devil for placing her at risk. Second on her list, or maybe first, was the danger to her damn reputation for the connection to crooks and terrorists. Before slamming down the phone, she'd ended the engagement.

Not revealing his broken engagement had seemed wise at

first. Now he wasn't so sure, but the relationship allowed ATSA to set up this trap. He'd keep up the pretense for the mission's sake. He'd convinced Danielle to keep mum about the engagement until the kidnappers were caught. The sudden breakup might not deter them at all.

So how did he feel about being dumped?

Angry? No. Hurt? Sort of. He felt the disappointment of a lost account rather than the pain of a broken heart.

Brief affairs that went nowhere had palled. Danielle and he had things in common—friends, ambition…. Marriage had seemed like a good idea at the time.

Too much heartbreak and turmoil with his father's serial marriages had taught him he wasn't cut out for true love. No forever and family for him. He'd thought good sex and a tight prenup would yield a marriage with few strings, so no one got hurt when it ended. Still, he'd had misgivings.

He shifted his feet. Glanced at his Rolex.

An hour since the London plane had landed. The woman playing Danielle should be finished with Customs. He wanted to get this initial meeting over with and hustle her to the house.

He shouldn't be anxious. He knew the drill, but he'd put cloak-and-dagger ops behind him ten years ago after his last, disastrous op. These days he was a simple businessman. No intrigue outside the board room.

His spoiled younger brother had changed that.

Activity in the corridor from the International Arrivals Building caught his attention. Among the group of tourists and business travelers came the woman he awaited. The designer sunglasses hooked in the breast pocket of her jacket identified her. Bulging tote and slim black Prada purse of the type Danielle favored swinging from her shoulder, she walked with purposeful grace.

Close behind her strode a copper-skinned man in sunglasses and a denim jacket. Too close.

Alarmed, Nick started toward the advancing crowd. As they drew nearer, he saw that Denim Jacket wore an owl lapel pin.

The ATSA pin of the day that they wore to ID each other.

Of course. ATSA had arranged guards to protect her during her trip. He deliberately relaxed the tension in his shoulders and turned his attention to his "fiancée."

The tailored jeans, fitted leather jacket and heeled boots were right on target. About the same diminutive height as Danielle, but curvier. Yes, curves where there should be curves. Very nice. Red hair, but a softer rose-blond than the fire-engine tone the salon regularly painted Danielle.

The overall look and her oval face would match any description or photographs New Dawn possessed. On her ring finger winked the two-carat stone he'd bought Danielle to seal their bargain.

Odd. He had the feeling he'd met this woman before. Impossible.

Intelligent green eyes searched the lounge with candor and warmth, not the guarded coolness he expected from a spy.

Just as well she wasn't his type. Too wholesome. Too open. Too…cute. But as he perused her parted lips and ripe curves, his blood stirred.

Bad move. Hell, what was he thinking?

Wholesome and open was an act. She was an undercover agent, probably more expert in deception and betrayal than any jet-set babe. The downside of wealth was that women wanted him for his money or his connections, not for himself. Danielle had been no exception.

Plus the situation precluded sex. She had to do her job as Danielle. He had to do his part. He had to stay alert if they were to stop New Dawn.

*"Nick!"* the pretend Danielle called, threading her way through the crowd. A warm smile curved her lips. She halted in front of him and turned her cheek for a kiss.

Danielle had coached this woman well.

She leaned close, her breasts pillowing against him.

Her subtle scent, not calculating perfume or cloying hair goop, but something like rain-washed spring flowers, triggered traitorous urges. The errant urge to taste her lush mouth temporarily derailed him.

With a mental kick in the butt, he gave her the expected quick buss. "Danielle, I'm glad to see you."

Her un-Danielle-like, bubbly laugh elicited a smile from him, the first he'd managed in days. Weeks.

"*You're* glad? I felt as though I was in a bad movie. Let's get out of here."

Nodding at the uniformed porter alert for his signal, he started to lift the tote from "Danielle's" shoulder.

With a firm grip that surprised him, she held on to the strap. "I can manage this one."

Nick understood her independence. He would've done the same. But Danielle was used to being catered to. He covered her hand with his and spoke low enough so only she could hear. "My fiancée would have the porter handle *all* the luggage."

Without so much as a blink, she released the tote to his grasp. The pink flush on her fair cheeks was the only sign of her chagrin at the slip.

Buttery freckles on her nose. She might be a true redhead. The notion pleased him. The image of her on his bed, naked, the proof before him, popped sweat on his brow.

A few minutes later, the suitcases on a cart, they headed outside to his waiting Mercedes.

Nick preferred to do his own driving. He didn't want to forget that at one time he didn't have the wherewithal for even a junker. But ATSA'd inserted an officer as driver and bodyguard. After New Dawn's threatening call, the terrorists would expect him to hire protection.

Denim Jacket and the local ATSA surveillance team entered a second sedan ahead of them. The lead car would take the same route, but remain separate and unobtrusive.

Unless they ran into trouble.

Green eyes glinting with good will, the woman he was supposed to call Danielle smiled at him. "That went fine back there. I think this will work."

Her voice was low and sexy, without the hint of twang that sneaked into Danielle's speech. He couldn't put out of his head—and his body—the feel of her breasts against him when he'd kissed her cheek.

No. Kissed *Danielle*.

Hell.

"It'd better work," he said, irritated at his unwanted attraction. "You do your part, and I'll do mine."

They pulled away from the curb behind the lead car. He subsided into the plush upholstery. Damn. He was protecting the woman he'd planned to marry, and here he was lusting after a stranger. And being deliberately rude to her. He saw no honor in any of that.

Snow, the driver, steered the car into the terminal departure lanes. Heavy traffic slowed their progress toward the exit.

Vanessa glanced sideways, speculating. "Of course," she said. "A lot is riding on our success."

He merely nodded and gazed at her solemnly. As his dossier had suggested, Nick Markos fit the self-made tycoon type.

Decisive, domineering and direct.

In his silver-gray silk T-shirt and hand-tailored sport coat that molded to the hard planes of his chest and shoulders, he exuded confidence and male power. His cool confidence bespoke his Special Forces experience.

Late thirties. Eyes the color of the Mediterranean, even bluer against his olive skin and raven hair. A blade of a nose, cleft chin. A face of hard, masculine beauty. Drifts of Brooklyn and the Continent in his deep voice added to his undeniable appeal.

Her heart throbbed an extra beat. Just the anticipation of this mission. No big deal.

In London, Danielle had described Nick as principled, but in charge and inflexible. The definitive way he'd phrased his statement bore that out. But why was he angry? No, she shouldn't even think the question. *Detachment, remember?*

She leaned forward. "Snow, all clear to head directly to the house?"

"No problem. Straight up the fairway," the officer said, with his typical golf allusion. He kept his eyes on the traffic as he nosed the Mercedes onto the Dulles Access Road.

Conscious of Markos's azure gaze on her, she kept her eyes forward. He might be a handsome devil, but he was an arrogant one, had to be to get where he was. She didn't have to like the man to do her job, and she'd ignore her hormones.

Dislike and sexual attraction. Ironic, but she could use both. Her attraction to him would enhance her role as his fiancée, and her distaste would help her project the cool disdain she'd learned was characteristic of Danielle.

Her persona's aloofness would work to maintain her detachment, her distance.

Now to focus on the other part of her job. She extracted a mirror from her purse. In the reflection, she observed the scooped roof of the Dulles terminal receding in the distance.

At closer range, a black Durango with Virginia plates. Two men in the front. One more behind, maybe two.

"Snow," she said.

"Roger. Got 'em," Grant Snow replied. He spoke into a tiny microphone hooked around one ear, then to her. "Here. You take the map. Alternate routes are marked."

Vanessa unbuckled her seat belt and leaned up to accept the folded chart.

"Are we being followed?" Nick said. He, too, unbuckled and twisted around to peer behind him.

"Maybe. Or the Durango might contain a bunch of guys coming home from a Vegas weekend." Vanessa didn't want to alarm him unduly. She unfolded the map of greater D.C.

Nick placed the flat of his hand on the maze of streets and highways. "Don't cut me out of the loop…*Danielle*. This charade won't work if you do. I'll shut it down."

Surprised at the heated tone in such a cool customer, Vanessa angled her head at him.

His eyes blazed blue fire at her. Anger. And something else. Did he recognize her? She didn't think so. Fear? Mr. Macho feared losing control?

Reluctant to touch him again, she hesitated. Being pressed against that hard body in a chaste embrace had heated her from the inside out. She didn't need that complication.

But he needed reassurance.

She patted his hand, then snatched hers away. "I understand your concern. I didn't mean to ignore you. We're just into the standard drill."

"License plate's a rental," Snow said. "This could be a shot over the bow."

"So following us could be just a warning?" Nick asked.

"Exactly. To make you nervous."

"Let's let them know we're on to them," Snow suggested.

"You got it," Vanessa said, studying the map and the alternate routes on yellow stickies.

When they pulled onto I-495, the Beltway, the SUV was still with them. Vanessa watched the tail with her mirror.

"Sucker them," she said to the driver. "They're probably expecting us to exit at River Road. Take the one before it instead, onto the George Washington Parkway."

"Roger that." A moment later, Snow veered from the left lane across two lanes of traffic. Horns blared and tires screeched as they careened down the exit ramp.

The SUV tried to follow, but a tan Hummer cut it off.

The sudden turn slid the map to the floor. Vanessa landed in Nick's lap. They lurched sideways into a corner. His arms went around her. One hand clamped her shoulder. The other brushed her breast before sliding to her waist.

Fiery tingles shot through Vanessa. Male heat and the scents of cedar and sage filled her senses.

So much for cool disdain.

When the car straightened out onto the Parkway, she realized how intimately she was draped across Nick's lap. And how the contact had affected him. A hard ridge poked her ribs.

*Ye gods.*

Heart pounding, she flew back to her side of the seat.

"Fasten your seat belts," Snow ordered.

His words reminded Vanessa of an old Bette Davis movie. The rest of the famous line popped into her head.

*It's going to be a bumpy ride.*

# Chapter 2

Nick straightened his jacket and buckled his seat belt. His trousers pinched, thanks to his body's reaction to having this woman's breasts imprinted on his lap.

Apparently oblivious, her expression was neutral as she refastened her seat belt. Her cheeks glowed pink, but her transparent complexion probably reacted to any stimulus.

"Yo, Grant," she said to the driver, "you took ten years off my life, but it was worth it. We lost them."

"Anytime. V12 power. Yowza! All-wheel drive. Room for clubs in the trunk. Do much off-roading, Mr. M?"

His brush cut was all Nick could see above the headrest, but he heard the grin in the man's voice.

The powerful German machine sped eastward along the highway following the Potomac River's meanderings.

"Not lately. Remember who owns the car. I'd like to be able to drive it again once this is over." The S600 was an indulgence, one he deserved for working his butt off the past several years.

The man gave a chastened nod. "Yes, sir. Will do."

Nick muttered an inarticulate grunt. Famous last words. That's exactly what Alexei had said before he'd totaled their father's Alfa Romeo in a rocky field.

Snow adjusted his earpiece. "The other car's following the Durango on 495. Just a bunch of goons, but we'll set up surveillance on them. CO says to keep our original route."

"They followed us. We saw them. Now they know we saw them. What's next?" Nick said.

"Probably nothing today," the woman answered. "They'll have to regroup. One thing we know about this bunch—they don't give up."

She directed Snow to take the next exit. In a few minutes they were rolling along Gouldsboro toward Bradley Boulevard, a direct route to Alexei's house in Chevy Chase.

Now that Nick's body had subsided, he settled back. Why'd he have such a strong sexual reaction to her? Even now his libido was prodding him with the fantasy of peeling her out of those tight jeans and easing her beneath him on the plush leather. He'd put his lips on the delicate skin of her throat, just there, where a blush—

He went still. What the hell was wrong with him?

He could think of a dozen reasons to avoid attraction, let alone sex, with her. Not the least of which was the fact that she was a government agent, secretive and probably paranoid, schooled in deception.

Not the girl-next-door she appeared to be.

And she thought he was engaged to be married. Why did she make him keep forgetting that?

His mind needed to be on their common goal—stopping New Dawn and keeping Danielle safe. This dicey situation called for focus and restraint.

He would ignore his seat companion. In fact, he would avoid her except when they had to be in public as lovers. Anything but icy control might blow this whole charade. He kept his gaze on what passed for scenery—strip malls and new brick McMansions plopped on treeless lawns.

"Approaching choke point," Snow said from the front as they headed left on Connecticut Avenue.

Apparently ATSA and Special Forces used the same jargon for a blind spot prime for ambush. "Choke point? You expect another attempt?" Nick turned to his "fiancée."

The car turned off Connecticut into the neighborhood streets that led to Alexei's house.

"These narrow, winding streets are funneling us to our destination," she replied. "ATSA did a sweep earlier, so it should be clear. Caution's a good idea anyway."

She combed her fingers through her long hair, and then let it fall across her shoulders in cognac-colored waves.

Nick wondered if her curls felt as silky as they looked. Something about the hair… A memory stirred, amorphous and distant, but he shook it away as irrelevant.

Stately old homes in Tudor and Colonial styles sat in repose like dowagers at the end of a banquet table. Privacy fences or stone walls shielded some estates, and expansive, landscaped lawns distanced house from street. Graceful old maples and beeches shaded decks and porches. Driveways curved to garages. Only a few vehicles were parked on the street.

"Most of these belong to employees and visitors." Nick nodded toward a truck with Zeno's Lawn Care painted on the side. "That's the same company that mows Alexei's lawn."

The woman cocked her head at him. "It's your lawn now. He left everything to you, didn't he?"

He nodded ruefully. The property, the business, the debts. The trouble. Until he could unload it all.

"*Everything.* More than I bargained for."

The Mercedes made a left onto Park Boulevard, a street hardly wide enough for the landscaped median between the lanes. Ahead of them, a tan pickup truck pulled from the curb at an angle and stopped, blocking their way.

"*Snow!* A stopper, up ahead." The woman withdrew a small pistol from an ankle holster. She looked out the rear window. "And a plug to box us in."

Nick saw the green sedan behind them.

Adrenaline surged in a rush that threw him back more than a decade to a Somali village and a snatch-and-grab that had gone sour because of an ambush. Remembered smells of sweat, dust and cordite filled his senses. Dread raked his spine.

Time slowed and perceptions sharpened. Gasoline fumes and the woman's fragrance flared his nostrils. Her piece was a Smith & Wesson 640. He could distinguish individual grains of dirt smearing the pickup's license plate.

Long-suppressed battle instincts kicked in.

All in an instant of real time.

"Stop the car!" Nick barked. "I know this street. You can cut across by that driveway on the left."

The pickup's driver's door opened. A man stepped out, shielded by the door. He wielded a long-barreled handgun.

The woman's green eyes glittered with skepticism as she weighed Nick's suggestion.

"Snow, here's your chance for off-roading. Hang a left across the median. See the driveway?"

Without a word, the driver swung the big sedan onto the median strip. It powered between two trees and across a bed of yellow fall flowers.

The pickup man stepped away from his vehicle, but he didn't fire. The rear car roared toward them.

The Mercedes bounced across into the other lane.

"Go straight through to the street in back." A 3-D map of the neighborhood in his mind, Nick was in combat mode.

A uniformed maid ran out of the house and yelled at them as they sped across the yard and onto Park Lane.

"They're not following," "Danielle" said, replacing her S&W in the ankle holster. "Turn right."

She looked to Nick for verification.

He nodded. "Affirmative."

In less than thirty seconds they were speeding along Oakdale Terrace. Snow zipped into the driveway of a massive Tudor-style house. The property sloped to the garage at basement level. He pressed the remote clipped on the visor. The left garage door swung up and open and then closed securely behind them.

"I'll check the house," Snow said as he cut the engine.

Vanessa exhaled a relieved breath. Her pulse lowered to an inaudible level. "That was close. We misjudged their readiness. The guys in the SUV must've figured out we'd go back to plan A. We wanted to have officers ready to roll them up when they tried that. That mistake won't happen again."

"The E&E worked."

*E&E. Escape and evasion.*

She glanced sideways. He sat erect and still, his gaze on the door from the garage to the basement. The jargon and the hunting hawk's wary alertness in his blue eyes would've told her he was military whether or not she'd read his file.

He was a dangerous man in more ways than one. Awareness prickled her forearm.

And he hadn't even touched her.

She gathered her hair and yanked it upward into the black scrunchie from her pocket. Now that she could relax a little, she needed the mass out of her way. She shook her head to tumble the curls around the top of her head.

"Nessa. No, *Vanessa*."

Startled, she gaped at Markos. "You know my name."

"You're Diana's sister." His black brows bunched. The sculpted mouth thinned to a razor blade. His voice held its sharpness. "The painter. You ruined my best suit."

Ye gods. He remembered her. "I hoped you'd forgotten."

Not only was Nick Markos the urbane CEO type her sister had dated, but he actually *had* gone out with Diana. At the memory of their previous encounter, Vanessa couldn't contain a groan. If he hadn't recognized her, she wouldn't have had to deal with the embarrassing episode.

Or with her less-than-professional reaction to this strong and sexy man. Oh, how could she stay detached and cool while acting undercover as his fiancée? How could she stay uninvolved? Her stomach clenched at the nerve-racking challenge.

Snow appeared at the doorway. "All clear."

Not quite.

While Grant Snow showed Vanessa—no, *Danielle*—to her room and oriented her to the security setup, Nick retreated to the sunroom in the back of the house. He strode across the terra-cotta floor and the beige-and-green Tabriz—another of Alexei's damned extravagances—and around the cushioned bamboo sofa and chairs.

He stopped at the bank of tall windows overlooking the flagstone terrace and backyard. Staring out blindly, he sucked in calming deep breaths.

Damn. His hands still shook from the adrenaline rush.

For years he'd successfully avoided E&E situations and all physical confrontations outside a gym.

He'd avoided anything that reminded him of why he'd left the army.

And all it took to slam him back into the zone was two cars of bad guys in an ambush.

He wouldn't go there again. ATSA had a full backgrounder on him. They knew of his failure. They wouldn't trust him, shouldn't trust him. They sure as hell wouldn't want him to straphang on their operation. Insert himself where he wasn't wanted. He was Alexei's heir and Danielle's ostensible lover, the go-between with the bad guys.

That was all.

His shoulders relaxed as calm returned. He turned and passed through the door to the terrace. Earthy smells of drying leaves and bare soil in the planters hung on the warm October breeze.

A wooden privacy fence extended from the sides of the house around the back to enclose stands of maples and shrubbery gone wild. Not very secure.

Too many places for an intruder to conceal himself.

But that was the idea, to let the terrorists think kidnapping Danielle was possible.

At the terrace edge sat a pile of flat rocks next to the half-mortared low wall—part of his brother's now-aborted landscaping plan. He lowered himself to a stone step and stretched his legs out.

The wall was a reminder of what else he needed to focus on—liquidating all Alexei's properties. The real Danielle was safe. Let ATSA take care of the extremists. From what he'd just witnessed, their people were prepared for contingencies.

Their people included a hell of a shocker—Diana Wade's overly protective sister. That relationship was another reason to stifle his hormones around her. His turned-on reaction to her five years ago—in spite of what she'd done to him—was what had cooled him on Diana.

He'd ignored the attraction then, and he'd ignore it now. He needed to redeem his family's name, to regain his own honor, not sully it further with a libido lapse.

Besides, she was a professional government agent involved in a potentially dangerous situation—with him. Undercover meant a mask, subterfuge, deception.

He shook his head. Danger in his hormonal reaction to her. Danger in the situation. Danger in female deception.

Good reasons to keep secret his broken engagement. To prop a wall between them. She'd be too professional to breach that barrier. He could use it to shield himself.

He did admire Vanessa's cool competence. Her decisiveness and intuition in the car ambush told him why she was on point for this op.

*On point.* Damn. He had to squash the Special Forces mode.

* * *

"This equipment is better than that at ATSA headquarters," Vanessa said.

The large basement room had been converted from a rec room to a gym, complete with stair climber, two treadmills, free weights and a Bowflex machine.

Snow grinned. "Alexei Markos sure spared no expense on this country club."

"More like a palace."

Vanessa mulled over the cost of Alexei's renovations. Nick had speculated that his brother had spent New Dawn's skimmed money on the house. That might not be far off.

She followed as Snow continued the grand tour through the laundry and utility rooms. Humming softly, the central air system kept Washington's sultry climate at bay.

They'd begun on the second floor. The Tudor-style house had five bedrooms, not including a private basement suite for a nanny or chauffeur. Three baths upstairs and two and a half down. The master suite—*his*—boasted a dressing room and a sitting alcove as well as a Jacuzzi and a separate shower.

Decadent, she thought. Just what she expected of Alexei.

What did Nick think about the house and his sybaritic brother's expensive tastes?

Ye gods, she was an idiot. She didn't know the man. He was CEO of his own company. From offices in three countries, he oversaw importation of exotic décor, equipment, foods and ingredients. He wore hand-tailored silk sport coats and Gucci loafers. He probably thought nothing of living among Persian rugs, Chinese screens and brocade draperies.

His tastes made no difference to her. She would have to know more about him for the role, but her interest was professional, not personal. In spite of her sensual reaction to the man, she had to remain professional from here on out.

No personal involvement, she vowed. Detachment. That was the key to her survival undercover.

They mounted the stairs to the marble-floored foyer, a three-story sweep with a balcony, beamed ceiling and mullioned clerestory windows. She expected Queen Elizabeth I to sweep down the long staircase and order her to go dress properly.

Tough, Queenie. She wasn't taking off five hundred dollars in designer silk and denim.

Vanessa grinned at her flight of fancy. This was just playing dress-up. She didn't care much about fashion.

"Living room's there on the left, dining room right." Snow gestured ahead of them. "Kitchen and sunroom in the back. Markos is probably in the library, here to our right over the garage. He can show you the in-house security system. I need to report in."

"Who's control officer on this mission, Gabriel Harris?" She'd seen him driving the escort car.

Snow shook his head. "Simon Byrne pulled CO. Hero Harris's tail's in a twist, but he's in the unit."

Gabe Harris had seniority on Byrne, Vanessa knew, but his tendency for grandstanding, the reason for his sobriquet, made him a risky CO. Byrne was brash and unconventional, but a good man. She didn't know why, but the two men seemed to be in constant competition.

"You all set?" Snow asked.

Her pulse kicked up a notch. *All set? You're leaving me alone with him?* she nearly said. She'd known all along she'd be alone with Danielle's fiancé, but that was before her embarrassing past had been resurrected.

The ATSA command post was set up in the empty house next door. The owners, away on a two-month trip abroad, had approved it. Snow could go unseen through the fence to the CP.

"I'm good to go," she said. "Wearing my GPS tracking button and communicator." She reached up to adjust the receiver in her left ear. She'd brushed her hair and left it down to conceal the miniature device.

"No mike?" Snow lowered his voice. "Aiming to keep things private between you and the Greek tycoon?" Poker-faced, he hiked a thumb toward the library door.

Vanessa lifted her chin. "The mike's in my pocket, turkey. It'll stay off while I use the ladies' room." She'd take time to unpack, too.

She turned and walked up the stairs with Snow's chuckle resounding in her ears.

"Hi. May I come in?" Vanessa rapped lightly on the open library door. "Snow said you'd show me the security system."

Nick rose from his chair at the gleaming wooden desk and closed the lid of his laptop. "Come in, Vanessa. The security command station's over there." He indicated the console on a library shelf.

"Don't stand on my account." She strolled over to examine the console, but her gaze kept veering to the man.

His guarded expression and stance—on the balls of his feet—said soldier. The sport coat was gone. Its removal didn't diminish the power in his shoulders or the breadth of his chest. He didn't return to the leather desk chair, but hooked a hip on an edge of the desk. The position stretched the worsted fabric of his trousers across muscular thighs.

Vanessa ignored the flip of her pulse. Learning a predator's killing skills in Special Forces probably paid off in the business world, she speculated as she examined the console's small screen and keypad.

She knew this wireless security system—keypad operation, audible or on-screen feedback, window sensors, motion sensors and a battery backup. "Ibex makes a good home system."

"Alexei wanted thorough protection for his precious antiques." His words held an edge of bitterness.

Setting aside Alexei's descent into criminal activities, did Nick disapprove of his brother's lifestyle?

"This setup would do under normal circumstances. But I'm sure you've already been told that."

"And about the outside cameras ATSA has installed to compensate for its inadequacies." He didn't return the smile. "Did you get settled all right?"

The expensive, layered businessman's cut didn't suppress his glossy hair's rebellion at being tamed. Crisp curls here and there softened his severe features.

The intensity of his gaze beneath the raven brow rattled her. Was that heat in his incredible azure eyes, as though he were mentally undressing her?

No, only her imagination. No.

She cleared her throat. "I'm in the bedroom beside the hall bathroom." Only the bathroom between her room and his. Too close. She swallowed. *Detachment, detachment.*

The black brows crinkled again. "Danielle would be sharing my suite with me. Janine, my housekeeper, will wonder about our…relationship."

At the humor in his eyes, Vanessa felt the heat color her cheeks.

"I took the liberty of placing some of my things—extra cosmetics and some clothing—in your suite. Your housekeeper will understand that a high-maintenance woman like Danielle would want her own bathroom and dressing area."

"I see. If you don't find towels, I'll have to search. This house is a maze, and Janine's off weekends."

His mocking tone slid into a courteous one, but artificial, as though he pretended she was his invited house guest instead of a government operative on duty.

As though he didn't want to confront how they'd first met.

She'd like to forget that brief encounter, too, but the time to face the firing squad had arrived. She trailed a finger along a bookshelf as she perused art history titles.

"Um, about that episode five years ago…"

"Ah. How is Diana these days?"

White teeth gleamed against his olive skin, but somehow the expression didn't project good humor. And yet his heated gaze still raked her. Was it male arrogance or attraction or anger? He folded his arms. Below the T-shirt sleeves, dark hairs swirled over sinewy forearms.

"Fantastic! Couldn't be better," she said with forced brightness. "She's doing television commercials and magazine spreads for L'Oreal. And she's engaged. Whitley's the ad exec on the cosmetics campaign." Finally Diana'd found a man who appreciated the real woman behind the beautiful facade.

One day Vanessa, too, would find a man who appreciated her as a real woman, not just a buddy or an undercover persona. Definitely not undercover, where no one saw Vanessa at all. She could dream, couldn't she? She shored up the corners of her smile, which had begun to sag.

His jaw firmed. "Either he sneaked by her sister the pit bull or he passed muster better than I did."

Bookshelves reached to the high ceiling. Afternoon sunlight streamed through a wide window to the desk at the far end. But the room seemed to shrink to a closet as Vanessa closed the space between her and her steel-jawed companion.

She hated confrontation and dealing with angry people. In most of her FBI career, she'd played the good cop, a role ATSA had capitalized on when she transferred. Honesty and compassion suited her better than deception and smoothed most bumps.

"Look, I apologize for getting paint on your suit that day. I never meant to do that."

His unblinking blue glare told her he wasn't buying. "That's what Diana said when she hustled me out of there. What *did* you mean to do?"

"Diana was just getting over a painful affair. I came over to paint the bedroom in her new apartment. I saw you as the same type of controlling, high-powered executive who'd used and dumped her. I didn't want to see her hurt again."

Philip had romanced Diana and moved her in with him.

When he'd met someone new, Diana'd come home one afternoon to find her bags packed.

"So you were warning me off."

"Not exactly. Advising you to be gentle. Considerate."

"Sounded more like back off. Or else."

Ye gods, had her clumsiness paint-rolled over a potential
relationship between him and Diana? They'd had only that
single whitewashed date. Diana'd reported an enjoyable evening at the theater. Then he'd simply never phoned again. Vanessa couldn't tell from his poker face, but did he still have a
thing for her stunning sister?

But he was engaged, she reminded herself.

She didn't like the pang either thought gave her.

A dark ring outlined his irises and intensified the blue. His
sage-and-cedar aftershave teased her senses, and she backed
up a step instead of burying her nose in his chest.

"I let my temper get the best of me. I shouldn't have
lumped you in with that rat bastard Philip."

But like Philip, he was smooth and urbane. His male
confidence and exotic looks had sent a current of electricity through her that scrambled her circuits. Out of self-defense as well as sibling loyalty, she'd gone extreme on the
attack.

"Forget about it. I'm lucky you were wielding a paint roller
and not that deadly Smith & Wesson." His voice and gaze softened. His mouth twitched, but didn't curve into a smile.

Just as well. If he smiled, her heart might not be able to
survive the impact.

"I won't be carrying the 640 again. Danielle wouldn't have
a firearm." Vanessa grinned. "Back then, I was an FBI special agent. I had a Sig-Sauer 9mm." She saw no reason to mention that on paint duty, she hadn't been armed.

His mouth thinned and one ebony brow arched. "I'm intrigued. How did a redhead from Brooklyn—"

"Queens."

"Queens, then. How did a redhead from Queens get to the FBI and ATSA?"

"Don't tell me you're one of those sexist pigs who think women should be secretaries or socialites."

"Not me. Two of my company's top executives are women. In spite of your militant defense of your sister, you don't seem the cop type."

Vanessa shrugged. She'd heard that before. "I come from a long line of cops. My dad's a desk sergeant in Queens now, but he walked a beat for years. Jason's a detective in Manhattan. Troy's a uniform cop."

"Where does Diana fit? Youngest? In the middle?"

Ouch. So he was still interested in the cover girl. So what had happened? Somehow she couldn't bring herself to ask. "Jason. Then me, Diana a year later. Troy's the baby."

"So why the FBI and not NYPD?"

Defensive anger heated her cheeks. Was he checking her qualifications? "New York City seemed to have enough Wades on the job. And I wanted to leave home." Observing an FBI negotiator at a bank robbery when she was twelve had led her to the Bureau and their use of her people talents. Talents that seemed to fail her with this enigmatic man.

He sat as implacable as Buddha, awaiting the full story.

Another memory constricted her throat with sorrow. "I joined ATSA when it was formed under the Homeland Security Department. Some of the cops who died in the 9-11 attack were friends. I had to do what I could to prevent more carnage."

Nick nodded solemnly. "I'll bet you never expected to trap terrorists by living in a Chevy Chase mansion."

"And you never expected to be in the midst of a terrorist trap." When he didn't react, she said, "I'm glad we've cleared up the past. But our having a past causes a small problem."

"And what's that?"

"You know my real name. You can't call me Vanessa even

in front of Officer Snow. Thinking of me as Danielle must be a habit. One slip could jeopardize the entire mission."

His features hardened, his expression closed and cautious. The soldier—or the CEO—was back.

"I have no problem with you as Danielle. Trust me to play my part, or find another woman to be Danielle." He paused. "Ah, is that it? Do you want out—*Danielle?*"

Here was her chance.

Vanessa hadn't wanted this undercover gig to start with. She had come to hate pretense and deception, immersing herself in someone's life only to leave in the end, struggling to remain detached when indifference went against her nature.

She felt as false as the fake rock that weighed down her third finger, left hand.

Director Nolan didn't see this glitch as a legitimate out. He'd said she was the best one for the job. And finding a new Danielle double would take time they didn't have. Stopping the terrorist attack was of prime importance. Her reluctance counted for nothing in the scheme of things.

Surely her awareness of Nick as a very attractive, sexy man was a complication she could avoid acting on. But could she ignore the other complication her intuition nagged her about—the troubled soul that lurked beneath his strong facade? She had to. For the duration—four weeks, tops—she could remain neutral, uninvolved and play her role.

"I don't want out. If you have no problem, neither do I."

"Then that's settled," Nick said. His smile, a lethal curve of sculpted lips and blinding white teeth, zinged straight into her bloodstream.

Her earpiece crackled to life. *"Yo, Wade, we have a problem. Intruder on the grounds."*

# Chapter 3

Nick was just opening his mouth to offer congratulations to Diana and her new fiancé, when Vanessa held up her hand.

She clicked something in the breast pocket of her blouse. "I'm in the library. Intruder location?"

He realized she'd heard a surveillance report in her earpiece and activated a microphone. Just as well it hadn't been turned on during their trip down memory lane.

ATSA eavesdropping wouldn't have mattered. No equipment was sensitive enough to pick up his fascination with her. Without the leather jacket, her silk blouse revealed the curves he'd brushed in their back-seat scramble. She listened intently, an apricot-pink painting her cheeks.

Cute and incongruous as hell.

She turned to him, green eyes glittering as though she'd discovered the mother lode.

"African-American male, late teens, short dreadlocks,

backpack. Entered by the garden gate on the far side of the house. Headed toward the back."

"Not one of New Dawn's finest, then," he said as he headed out the door toward the sunroom.

Vanessa caught up to him at the door to the terrace. She grabbed his arm. Her strong grip surprised him, but didn't halt him. The sizzle from her touch did.

He glanced at her slender hand on his dark forearm. How small she was, only about five-four, but professional and self-assured. The contrast between her girl-next-door appearance and her terrorist-hunting profession intrigued him. He didn't know what to think. Or what she'd do next.

She was tough, frank and quick-thinking, all qualities he admired but observed rarely. Danielle had those qualities, but in her they were like a stabbing blade, not a reassuring hand.

Vanessa's glorious rose-gold hair was down, Danielle-style, yet was nothing like hers. Her milk-white skin was nearly translucent, as if passion waited just beneath the surface. Her big green eyes, the stray curls licking her temples and a slightly pointed chin made her oval face pixieish.

*Pixieish.* He'd never used that word before.

What the hell was the matter with him? *Focus, man. Remember, you're engaged and she's government.*

"What? You intend to go out there instead of me and confront him? Danielle wouldn't do that."

She shook her head, let her hand drop away. "If we need backup, the surveillance unit will take care of it. I just wanted to advise you not to be a hero."

Guilt sliced his gut at her absurd statement. She shouldn't trust him with her safety. No one should.

At his sides, his hands had curled into fists. He forced them open. "Honey, the last thing you can expect *me* to do is play hero."

She tipped her head at his admittedly odd reply, but didn't comment. He watched her studying him with apprehension.

He didn't need her concern, though ATSA must know what had happened in Somalia. He'd led men to their deaths. Didn't she get it?

Something in her lured him, a siren song that beckoned him to trust her, to spill the details of that shameful episode in his past. And more. But unlike Ulysses, he needed no ropes to restrain him. He'd kept his counsel for ten years. Whining about his failure now would serve no purpose.

"Besides," he continued, "this sounds like Janine's daughter's boyfriend."

"The housekeeper? What's her daughter's boyfriend doing here on a Saturday?"

From what Alexei'd told him, he could think of several reasons, none of them legitimate. "Shall we go find out?"

"So we're on the same page, what *would* Danielle do?"

"Danielle might be aloof and cynical, but she's a journalist, curious as ten cats. She'd be right next to me."

Her smile caught him off guard. The beam of pleasure was a spill of sunshine from his father's native Aegean isles. Its warmth curled around his chest. He shrugged off the impression and opened the door.

As they emerged onto the terrace, the young man rounded the back corner of the house and neared them. Baggy gangsta pants and layers of shirts, the hot brand of basketball shoes, earrings. No tattoos in view, but the kid probably had those, too. Nick knew the rebel uniform. He saw it often enough on New York streets. D.C. was no different.

When the kid spotted them on the terrace, surprise opened his mouth before caution—possibly guilt—closed him up tight. Challenge defined his walnut-colored features. He slouched, affecting a cocky and defiant demeanor.

"You must be Ray," Nick said. He sat on the finished part of the low stone wall. Unthreatening, casual.

"You must be Mr. Markos's brother." Ray adjusted the bulky pack hitched over one shoulder and came to stand in front of Nick. The slope of lawn and the terrace exaggerated his lowered position. He flicked a curious glance toward Vanessa, who stood behind Nick.

Nick judged him to be about six feet and fit. Probably a dirty street fighter, but no match for Special Forces training. Nick hoped they'd never need to find out. He hadn't the heart for it anymore.

"I'm Nick Markos. This is my fiancée Danielle LeBec. The house is mine now."

Vanessa said nothing, but offered Ray a cool nod. She ambled to the left, flanking the kid.

Nick gave himself a mental slap. He'd automatically positioned himself to protect a woman who didn't need it.

Intelligent brown eyes assessed the two adults on the terrace. Ray might dress and walk the antisocial street-thug part, but he met a gaze directly. Nick awarded him a point.

"I ain't done nothin'."

"That's good, Ray. Real good. So why are you here?"

"I come to see Lise. Ain't she here helping her mom do the cleaning?"

"It's Saturday, Ray. Janine works here Monday, Wednesday and Friday. I'm surprised you don't know that."

"Reckon I forgot." He bobbed his head in a servile manner Nick recognized as crap. "I be outta here then."

Vanessa meandered to a stone fountain. She trailed her fingers in the water and smiled. "Ray, isn't there something you want to ask my fiancé? The *other* reason you came?"

Nick slanted her a questioning look.

"The gloves?" she added.

Worn brown cotton work gloves peeked from an outside pouch on the pack's side. Nick suspected a less benign reason for those gloves, such as fingerprint prevention. Was he more of a skeptic than the ATSA officer?

Vanessa's smile had a disarming effect. A ruddy hue infused Ray's dark cheeks, and he nearly smiled back before he caught himself and twisted his mouth to tough-guy sullen.

"Miz Janine, she said you might have odd jobs for me sometimes. Like some yard work. Or that sad-ass wall."

Either Ray thought fast on his feet or Vanessa had hit it right. The job excuse allowed the kid to save face. Why not?

"Zeno does the yard work, but if there's something extra, I'll tell you."

Ray jerked his chin toward the terrace corner where the wall ended in a tumble of odd stones. "Ain't nobody worked on that wall in months. Too bad to leave it half-done."

Alexei's grandiose designs would've buried him in debt. Unless that mysterious ten million existed after all.

"I agree," Nick answered. "My brother stopped paying the landscaping company, so his plan crashed. Are you a mason?"

Ray shrugged. "I helped a guy build a couple walls." He toed a stone. "This one don't look too hard."

"I haven't decided how much of Alexei's renovations to complete. We'll see."

"I be goin' then." He hitched up the pack and started toward the corner.

"One more thing, Ray."

Ray turned, eyes opaque, mouth tight.

"I'll take the gate key. Next time you come to see Lise, ring the bell by the garage walk-in door."

Without demur, Ray extracted a brass key from a deep pocket in his shorts and handed it over.

A moment after he disappeared around the house, Vanessa said, "Snow reports he's out. Jogging down the street toward Connecticut Avenue. They put a man on him."

She listened again. "Roger that. Out."

She clicked off her mike. For the first time her gaze held no warmth, only the green ice of emeralds. "Nick, what's Ray's last name? He wasn't on our list of possible visitors. We'll find him, but a last name would speed identification."

"All I know is Ray. When I saw Alexei in jail, he said he'd ordered the boyfriend not to come around again. I didn't expect to see him."

From Vanessa's tone, he gathered ATSA was suspicious of his motives for neglecting to mention the kid.

They wanted the household to appear normal, so Janine and her daughter continued their routine, but under ATSA eyes. The government distrusted the two women because of Alexei. Nick scoffed at that, but he'd insisted the surveillance also be protection. In case New Dawn got new hostage ideas.

But Nick had forgotten about Ray.

Let ATSA suspect the hell out of him. He had enough to deal with. Ray was the least of his worries.

He levered to his feet and walked to the stack of building stones and picked up a flat granite circle the size of a dinner plate. On one side he observed an intricate design in relief. Another similar stone was mortared in the finished part of the wall. The stack contained enough of the circular medallions to form a pattern around the terrace.

Nick laid the medallion down. "The pool and tennis courts Alexei dreamed up are out of the question, but I like the wall. And these stone medallions."

"A finished terrace will help sell the house."

"I'll see about having it finished. Ray was right about that. What makes you think he came ready to do honest labor?"

"He had the gloves, and his hands are callused. You don't think so?"

"Maybe. Alexei suspected him of casing the house for what he could sell. He found Ray skulking around outside exactly like today. That's when he ordered him off the property."

"So why'd you say he could come back to see Lise?"

If Ray *was* honest after all, he shouldn't be punished because Alexei'd acted the lord of the manor, something he'd learned at his mama's breast. Those were family affairs Nick shouldn't get into with this perceptive woman. But the more he explained to her, the more he wanted to spill.

Before he crossed his self-imposed line, he had to get away from her. And stay away.

"Beats the hell out of me. Dinner's at seven." He turned and walked into the house.

Dinner at seven? Not exactly.

On Monday, as she browsed a computer at Markos Imports in Georgetown, Vanessa was still mulling over what had happened.

Nick had disappeared to his room and then to the gym downstairs. She'd showered and napped for a couple of hours. She never napped, but whisking to London and back in three days had skewed her body clock. How did the jet set do it?

When she'd found her way to the hangar-sized, gleaming granite-and-stainless-steel kitchen, no Nicolas Markos. Only a scrawled note with a salad and the menu for what to nuke. A chicken breast and some sort of bean-and-rice dish Janine had prepared. Nick hadn't appeared the rest of the evening.

And she'd seen little of him on Sunday, come to think of it. She'd spent some of the day going over strategy with the surveillance guys.

When they were alone, Nick seemed to find somewhere else to be. ATSA needed her to dig out more about him.

Background checks had uncovered nothing concrete, but ATSA still wondered if he'd been involved in his half brother's dirty dealings. His Special Forces experience and his overseas business and social connections made him a potential risk to the mission. And there was that missing money. She needed proximity to coax out information.

But Nick was making himself as scarce as that ten mil. The director had chosen her because people usually talked to her.

But not Nicolas Markos.

Was he just working or had she alienated him? They'd cleared up her past transgression at Diana's apartment, hadn't they? Was it the encounter with young Ray?

She'd observed Nick going into soldier mode, but then he'd shut down and shut her out. His harsh comment about not being a hero kept repeating in her brain like an annoying tune. She'd noticed nothing unusual in his file.

What was going on?

Whatever it was, his suspicious actions didn't bode well for this operation.

She had to find a way to spend time with him, so he'd open up. That plan would exacerbate her other problem—hiding her inconvenient awareness of him. She would be her usual friendly self, and keep things on a professional plane.

As long as they were alone, anyway.

In public, that was another story. Would he have his hand on her? His arm around her?

How could she ignore the lure of his woodsy scent mingled with salty male? Or forget the solid feel of his arms? Or the controlled burn in his eyes? Or was it the lure of the forbidden and the mystery she sensed in his soul?

*Think of him as your brother, like Jason or Troy.* She tried to imagine Nicolas Markos scouring her face with mud after she'd doused him with the garden hose.

Dream on. *Professional interest, not personal involvement. Detachment.* She repeated the mantra.

She sighed. Her mind wasn't on the task at hand. She'd been at this computer too long. She hit Page Down.

She and her so-called lover were spending the day at Markos Imports on O Street in Georgetown. Nestled among antique shops and galleries, the old brick building housed a retail shop and offices on the ground floor and more offices and warehouse space in a second story.

Across the street, in an upstairs storage room, was another ATSA surveillance unit. During the night, they'd secreted electronic bugs throughout the business. Cameras and micro-phones covered the entrances, front and back.

Since she was supposed to be a magazine editor and savvy with computers, Vanessa aka Danielle had the task of examining the electronic books. She figured that was Nick's excuse to stash her out of the way.

Accounts were straightforward, up to date, but so far contained no hint of Alexei's transactions for the New Dawn Warriors, let alone a couple of million spare bucks.

Even with the smattering of econ theory she remembered from college, Vanessa didn't think it took an economist or even an accountant to see that Markos Imports was sinking, not as fast as the *Titanic,* but as inevitably.

Without an infusion of new stock and without Alexei's contacts, clients and vendors were abandoning ship.

When the numbers on the computer screen began to blur, Vanessa left the cramped office and went in search of Nick.

She found him in the executive office that occupied the entire back of the shop.

The lavish suite dazzled with a kaleidoscope of patterns and colors—burgundy-and-navy Persian rugs, black-lacquered cabinets and tables, gold-framed paintings and Japanese brush drawings. A cobalt-blue porcelain vase stood on a low hammered-brass table. A black-and-gold enameled dragon guarded one end of a mahogany desk, the twin of the one at the house.

She waited quietly at the doorway while he conversed with the manager and assistant manager.

Nick's burnished-olive skin contrasted with the snowy white of his band-collared shirt. He'd opened one button, and the ebony hairs curling above the opening caught Vanessa's gaze. She had yet to see him in a tie, but he looked every inch the CEO in a navy pinstripe Hugo Boss.

All day he'd spent in negotiations. Sessions with the employees, who didn't want him to sell, and with importers, who might buy the shop, meant walking a tightrope. He was in command, quiet but firm and decisive, putting Vanessa in mind of a conquering knight.

Or the Greek tycoon of her first impression.

The shop manager was an elegant, wand-slim Chinese-American woman named Celia Chin. "The rugs are no problem," she was saying, "and the small decorative pieces. We sell a few every day. We could continue if we could obtain more."

Emil Alfieris, the assistant manager, stabbed the air with an emphatic index finger. "Alexei traveled abroad on buying trips. If—"

"But Alexei is gone, and that won't be happening." Nick spoke softly, but in a tone that brooked no argument. He sat in a matching chair, not in the executive throne behind the desk, but his authority suffered not an iota for it.

Celia cast an anxious look at her assistant. "For the screens and the friezes, the more ornate cabinets, the market is specialized."

"Alexei knew how to bring in certain buyers," Emil added, drumming his manicured nails on the brass table. A slight, dapper man in a bow tie, his Greek extraction totaled his only kinship with Nick.

"Danielle and I are slated to attend a reception at the Washington Cultural Museum on Friday," Nick said. "Networking could line up more prospects for the business."

"If *I* could make the buying trips to the Orient that *he* used to do, new imports might breathe new life into the business." Celia sat still as ivory on a blue brocade chair, with her folded hands in her lap. Her knuckles gleamed white.

Nick sighed. His hands on his knees looked relaxed, but a muscle twitched in his jaw. "Ms. Chin, it's too late for that. Selling is the only option. In the meantime, I'll write up that reference for you. For you both."

Vanessa ducked from view. Time to retreat.

All five employees—the clerks and warehouse attendants

as well as the managers—were wound as tight as harp strings with anxiety. No evidence tied them to Alexei's nefarious dealings, but they bore watching.

The background report said that after Alexei had disappeared, Nick had paid the utilities and the housekeeper. He'd also kept the import business afloat, but he refused to do anything to keep it flourishing. He wanted out.

Why?

His international restaurant supply company was diverse. This was just another kind of import business. With a little effort, it could be profitable again. Why was he so determined to sell? Was he as rigid and inflexible as Danielle had said?

Or was it something more?

After the shop closed and the employees had left, Nick found Vanessa reading through Alexei's business e-mail.

Her freckled nose wrinkled as she studied something obscure. Her glorious hair seemed to contain the sun's rays even under the office's ugly fluorescent lighting. He longed to run his fingers through the fiery waves. Would they feel cool and silky or would their heat warm his hand?

Idiotic thoughts like that had kept him away from her over the weekend. Damn, but he'd thought he'd hardened his internal armor against her gentle warmth. What was it about her wholesome beauty that drew him so?

Studying the business's books and chatting up the employees, she'd played the role of Danielle well today.

Except for her personality.

Besides her red hair, he could see why ATSA'd chosen her. The employees talked to her easily. All she'd had to do was ask a simple question here, make a comment there, and they blathered away. Her skill at drawing them out amazed him.

From the snatches of conversation Nick had overheard, he inferred their complaints were endless.

About him.

For them, he hated to close up shop, but keeping reminders of Alexei's filth was like being flayed alive daily.

"Didn't ATSA and the cops go all through those e-mails ten times already?" he asked.

Turning, she rolled her shoulders. The movement lifted her breasts against the soft fabric of her beige linen dress.

Heat kindled in his belly.

She laughed, a cynical chuckle.

The sensual sound stoked the flame.

"I've found nothing new yet, mostly chitchat about objets d'art I know little about. But I can't help myself. In there, in that extravagant office is where he choked a man to death. I was part of the unit that trapped and captured Alexei, and I want closure."

"I want closure, too. I want this damned mess out of my life!" *Damn Alexei!* Nick slapped the door frame.

Vanessa rose from the swivel chair and placed a hand on his forearm. Muscles bunched at her warm touch. Her sorrowful gaze tugged at him.

"I'm sorry, Nick. That was thoughtless. I shouldn't have spoken so coldly about your brother. No matter what he did, his death is a tragic loss to your family."

He turned, breaking the physical contact, but not the spell she wove over him. He strode into the showroom. There he had more space, more control.

Stopping beside an ivory chess set, he lifted the black queen's knight. "What do you know about my family?"

Great. At last Nick was talking. Vanessa threaded her way through the display cases to him. Strangely nervous now that they were alone in the shop, she circled her index finger on the white king's crown.

"I know what the ATSA file contained. Your father, Dmitri Markos, was a merchant marine captain for a Greek freighter line before he retired to his villa in Greece. You're the oldest of his three offspring, by his first wife."

"My mother was Spanish. Zita died when I was two. I grew up in Brooklyn, Athens and Marseilles."

"Sad to lose a parent at such a young age. But Alexei's mother came into the picture a year later, I believe." She waited quietly, her hand cradling the king. She rubbed the smooth ivory as if it were a worry stone.

Nick lifted his gaze from the carved figure. "Father is never long without a woman." He dropped the queen on her side.

Vanessa approached, her gaze trying to reach inside him, to grasp what demon knotted him up. "Each child had a different mother. You, then Alexei. You have a half sister, Mikela, who lives with your father and his third wife."

"After the divorce Alexei lived with his mother. He visited when Father was home. He was the spoiled son, and I was the responsible one. We were too... We were opposites."

She lifted her chin, caught by his emotion, but not afraid. He seemed to surround her, filling her with his intense gaze, with his heat and male scent.

"What are you trying to tell me, Nick?"

Unnamed turmoil swirling in his stormy blue eyes, he clasped her shoulders. For support or in frustration, she didn't know. His grip was tense and firm, but not painfully so. The force of his emotion trembled through her as though an earthquake swept them up.

He was going to kiss her. Her pulse raced.

But she must've been mistaken. His expression hardened as he seemed to subdue his internal tempest.

"I'm saying your expressions of sympathy are misplaced. Alexei trafficked with terrorists and committed two murders. He deserved what he got. If my father knew the truth about his precious, pampered son, it would kill him. The only tragic loss I grieve for is our family honor."

\* \* \*

After midnight, Nick lay awake in the dark, staring at the white ceiling.

He had to get a grip. What was it about that woman that brought out the worst in him?

Her unwanted sympathy had only exacerbated his self-loathing for being glad Alexei was gone. First he'd vented his temper by grabbing her and shaking her. Then he'd nearly succumbed to the urge to kiss her until neither one could stand. At the last moment, he'd reined himself in.

She was going to be here for weeks as his fiancée.

His fiancée, for God's sake.

In public he had to treat her as his fiancée. In private he had to pretend he still had a damn fiancée and deal with her in a businesslike manner.

Danielle was safe. Stopping New Dawn was the goal. Punishing the damned murderers. Maybe he could let go of his anger once the Markos name was cleansed. Maybe. His lost personal honor years ago placed that outcome in doubt.

Closing his eyes, he began consciously relaxing his muscles, focusing inward, calming himself. He was aware only of the faint moonlight leaking between the curtains, of the banjo clock ticking, of the lemon tang of furniture polish.

*Of the footsteps on the stairs.*

Muscles taut, he rolled out of bed.

Had New Dawn infiltrated the house without the alarm's warning? Where the hell was ATSA surveillance?

He glanced at the portable security monitor. No breach. The damned thing thought everything was secure.

Then who was sneaking around the house?

Holding his breath, Nick opened the door a crack. From

the master bedroom, he had a clear view of the staircase and the hallway to the other upstairs rooms. High windows let in enough moonlight to illumine movement in the dark.

A dark-clad figure reached the top step and stopped. Apparently listening.

Hell. ATSA should be handling an intruder. Not him. A damned failure who'd sent men to their deaths.

But he couldn't let them take Vanessa.

The figure took a tentative step. He turned to go down the hall. Nick lunged and grabbed him in a choke hold.

The guy heaved a kick at Nick's knee.

Nick twisted enough to deflect the worst of the blow. He yanked the intruder's right arm behind his back.

Then reality hit him— *Small. Soft, sweet scent.* Hell. *Vanessa.*

Without realizing, he relaxed. Mistake.

A foot behind his calf sent him tumbling. At the last moment, Nick took her with him, and they fell to the hardwood floor together. He managed to take the brunt of the impact before rolling and trapping her beneath him. He pinned her hands beside her head.

"Van— *Danielle!* It's me."

She twisted beneath him. Soft, rounded curves rubbed against him. With every stroke, the friction made him harder.

"Nick! What are you doing tackling me?"

"What are you doing skulking around in my house?"

"I wasn't skulking. Snow and I did a perimeter check."

"Danielle wouldn't be out there in the wee hours." Danielle wouldn't be here at all. He shouldn't be here either, plastered against this delectable woman who thought he was engaged to another. Maybe he should tell her the truth.

Another wriggle. This one was an attempt at a shrug. "I needed to know the layout. A little night work. It didn't blow my cover. I apologize if I woke you."

Hell. His arousal reached the point of pain. He nearly groaned. If he confessed his broken engagement now, she wouldn't believe him. It was a bad idea anyway. The artificial barrier between them should remain.

A tangled web indeed. "I wasn't asleep."

She wore a commando-style jumpsuit, thin and clinging to her curves. With each panted breath, her breasts rose and fell against his bare chest. Autumn leaf and dew scents mingled with her unique fragrance.

If he lowered his head, he could bury his nose in her hair. Or taste the soft skin on her neck.

Or kiss her.

And find respite from his torment.

"You have that little mike turned on?"

"No. Why?" The breathy tone said she knew the answer.

If he thought any more, he'd remember why he shouldn't do what he longed to do.

So he didn't think.

# Chapter 4

Vanessa could see little of his face in the dark. She didn't need vision to know his intent.

Although the danger of attack had receded, adrenaline hyperpowered her senses. Every pressure point where his muscled body touched hers tingled—fingers, arms, breasts, belly. Massaged by his burgeoning erection, the sensitive nub at the apex of her thighs pulsed. Desire rolled off him in waves. Her erratic heart thumped in time with his so they seemed to possess a single heartbeat. Awareness burned into her, melting her very bones.

"Nick," she whispered, her mouth as dry as sand, "this is a bad idea."

"I know."

The deep velvet of his voice thrilled through her. He lowered his head. His chiseled mouth took hers with surprising warmth and softness. As he savored her with his lips, his tongue, his entire body, passion built to the same burning intensity with which he did everything.

She felt feminine and desirable, consumed by his passion. *I can't. This is wrong. Not this man.*

Common sense managed barely a whisper, but her body fairly shouted.

*Let go. Let the feeling take you.*

His heat poured into her body, rich and drugging, and she yearned toward him as she tasted and savored. His kiss, powerful and thorough, claimed her as his own. His hand skimmed the length of her throat and her cheekbones.

Was that her voice murmuring pleasure against his mouth? She didn't know. She was aware only of him, of him surrounding her with his scent and intensity and hardness.

He pressed gentle kisses to the corners of her lips, to her temples, then pulled away. "Ah, Vanessa, I knew you'd be hot like this. Night work with you should mean tangled sheets, not tackling terrorists."

When he brushed his thumb across her lower lip, moist and still yearning, she realized her hands were free, had been free for some time. She was clinging to his broad shoulders—his broad, naked shoulders. As he rolled away from her, her fingers slid, bereft, against muscle and bone. He was breathing as hard as she.

Willing herself to resist the powerful chemistry between them, Vanessa scooted away. She pushed to her feet on legs made rubbery by desire.

Her heart raced as though she'd just completed a marathon. In a way she had.

She shook her head. "Nick, no night work for us. No distractions that could jeopardize the mission. There can be nothing between us. I gave in to the heat of the moment. I admit it. But how can a man who puts so much stock in honor forget he belongs to another woman?"

"Apparently I need reminding." He rose to his feet as fluidly as the panther he resembled in the shadows. He padded on bare feet into the faint light cast by the gallery windows.

Her gaze skated over layered slabs of muscle and a flat belly dusted with dark hair that trailed down to the waistband of his pajama bottoms. The thin silk outlined his corded thighs and rampant masculinity.

Ye gods, she knew his pajamas were silk because she'd run her hands down his sinewy back to his taut butt.

Desire slammed her again, and her mouth went dry.

"I'm going to pull on some sweats and have a brandy. Join me downstairs?" He disappeared into his room and left her alone to decide.

Was he giving her a gentle out? Or was he so supremely confident of his masculine appeal that he knew she'd agree?

She shouldn't. If she knew what was good for her, she'd toddle off to her cool sheets and barricade the door.

To keep herself in, not to keep him out.

He was rich and influential, a man women threw themselves at, a man used to having anything and any woman he wanted. He didn't want her. Not really. Attraction, at least on his part, was due to proximity.

She'd spoken the bald truth. Intimacy could jeopardize the mission. The larger mission of trapping the New Dawn leader and her secondary mission of making sure Nicolas Markos stayed on ATSA's side. Her personal mission of staying out of his life. And keeping him out of hers.

Intimacy would compromise her impartiality and her emotions. Emotions blurred the line between an unwanted masquerade and her identity. Was she too burned out from all the deception to keep her emotions in check?

Emotions, sensations, drives were sure running amok inside her at this very moment. Her belly quivered with unfulfilled need. Her heart bloomed with foolish hope. And her soul longed for what could not be.

Damn the man for being walking temptation.

He was engaged, for goodness' sake. What kind of man hit on one woman when he was promised to another? So what did his indiscretion mean? Would her male colleagues see it as another reason to suspect Nick's integrity? She doubted it from guys who constantly thought with their anatomy.

If he tended to forget he belonged to another woman, she wouldn't. She didn't poach. She wasn't that kind of woman.

But she'd use her resentment and latch on to suspicion as a talisman to protect her. The flutter in her stomach told her she needed all the protection she could muster. The list in her mantra was growing.

*Suspicion. Detachment. No intimacy.*

If she knew what was good for her… She did, but this wasn't about her.

She'd go have that brandy. For her reasons, not his. Hadn't she bemoaned the fact that he wasn't talking to her?

Earlier he'd exploded with anger at his brother. Raised in many ports of call by a Greek ship-captain father, he had an old-world view of honor.

That outburst wasn't nearly enough of a peek at what made him tick. She needed a cozy chat to open him up about his life, his business, his family.

Cozy, or intimate? Didn't intimacy lead to confiding? No, she'd stick to cozy.

*Suspicion. Detachment. No intimacy.*

Right.

Nick left his room a few minutes later, dressed in a gray T-shirt and sweatpants but barefooted. He found the hallway dark and empty. No light beneath Vanessa's door.

Damn.

He'd gone too far and chased her away. Already in bed and done with him.

She was too professional to be snared by his impulsive seduction. Once he'd felt her beneath him—sweet with buried fire—and sensed the same elemental need in her, his blood had surged with such wild need he'd barely been able to stop.

He was thankful her breathy moans had thrown him back to reality or he'd have taken her there on the hall floor.

She was right that anything between them might endanger their operation. Danielle was safe, and he, like ATSA, wanted the terrorist leader caught and his dirty business stopped.

Only then would he feel he'd restored family honor…and to a lesser degree his personal honor and pride.

How ironic that Vanessa believed he'd beggared his honor to cheat on his real fiancée with his pretend one. That was something he'd never do if he were still engaged. Guilt writhed in his belly.

He could tell her the truth. Let the chemistry sizzle between them. See where it led… But she was a capable, experienced government officer. Why would she want a former soldier with a shameful disaster in his past?

Besides, any hint that he'd lied might arouse suspicions and endanger Danielle. Might endanger the entire operation. Better to ice down his libido. His relationship with Vanessa would be professional only.

But damn, somehow, holding her had eased his grief and anger. Her sweetness both soothed and aroused him. He wanted the fresh-faced, passionate agent in his bed, naked and—

Hell. Angry at his continued heated thoughts, he stomped down the stairs.

He stopped in the doorway of the formal living room. A single brass lamp burned on an end table. Vanessa sat curled up on a red brocade-upholstered wing chair. She still wore the black jumpsuit, but now he could see—but not feel—the thin fabric hugging her body. Her hair was tied back in a braid, with small curls at her temples where his lips had touched.

His heart kicked from exasperation to pleasure that she hadn't run to her room after all.

"Ah, good, you're here. A man shouldn't drink alone at this

time of night." He rubbed his hands together and strode to the Chinese puzzle chest that served as a liquor cabinet.

"I decided brandy would help me sleep after my little adventure."

He turned to her with raised brows and a sly grin he couldn't prevent.

"*Outside.*" Cheeks turning pink, she hurried to correct herself. "My little foray with Snow. To check the perimeter."

All right. He'd flustered her.

Grinning, he pushed the correct sequence of inlaid ivory leaves on the cabinet front, and the doors opened, revealing decanters and bottles on a shelf. "I had to talk Alexei into giving me the code to this thing."

She chuckled. "I'm surprised he told you."

"So am I. A secretive and possessive son of a bitch." He selected a bottle of Benedictine and two glasses. "My half brother had his faults, but he knew good liquor. I think you'll like this better than brandy."

"Thank you." She accepted the snifter with its serving of dark amber liquid.

He sprawled on the curve-backed sofa, the only comfortable piece in the room as far as he was concerned, and tossed the decorative pillows. He sighed as the liqueur slid smoky warmth down his throat. He watched her as she took tentative sips.

A careful woman. Both restraint and pleasure at the alcohol's effect. She'd like to be spontaneous, but her professional training—and something else—prevented her from letting go. Intriguing, but he should let it pass.

*Professional only, remember?*

"I have to tell you about the perimeter check." She started to set her glass on the end table, but instead clutched it in her lap. Her features stayed calm, but excitement glittered in her eyes.

Taken aback, he sat more erectly. Hell. She'd returned

from facing danger, and he'd jumped her bones. "Something happened. Are you all right?"

She waved away his concern with a flutter of one hand. "We found a breach in the fence."

"Where?"

"Southwest corner—back corner—behind the overgrown shrubbery. The fence backs onto a park with more shrubbery. Someone sawed partway through the boards. That's it so far."

"A point of insertion not likely to be discovered under normal circumstances. What will you do?"

"The techs have set up another camera and some motion sensors. All we can do now is wait. Snow and the others will snatch whoever comes in."

"Not you," he said, mentally heaving a sigh of relief. He swallowed a long gulp of Benedictine. Not the best way to enjoy the fine liqueur, but he wanted its punch.

She smiled. "Not me. I'm the target. Remember?"

"Sometimes it's harder to sit in the background unable to take part in the action." He knew firsthand what torment that inflicted. Unwanted memories knotted his shoulder muscles.

"Yes, you feel anxious and helpless though you're not responsible for that aspect of the operation."

"Or you *are* responsible and still you can do nothing because it's too damned late!"

His hand clenched, shattering the glass. With a ringing pop the bulbous bowl flew apart in a fireworks starburst that sprinkled tiny crystal shards and amber droplets onto the sofa and Oriental carpet.

*"Damn!"*

"Ye gods, are you hurt?" Vanessa flew to him and grabbed his hand.

Blinking away the painful memory, Nick looked down at his hand. He felt no pain, but blood welled from the pad of his thumb where a needlelike shard protruded. He dropped the rest of the glass's stem and plucked out the offending sliver. "Looks like I am. I'll go take care of this."

Vanessa clucked and tsked at him, herding him to the other end of the sofa. "Here, scoot down this way, away from the broken pieces. You'll cut your bare feet."

Once he was vertical, she cradled his wounded thumb in her small hands. Her warmth and gentleness seeped into him. "Let's get this cleaned out and disinfected."

He wanted to yield, to let her pamper him, but he dug in his heels. She was *not* going to bandage him like a little boy who'd fallen off his bike. He'd already allowed her to glimpse too much of his private pain. Coddling him would mean more intimacy. Intimacy meant questions.

He firmed his mouth. "A minor cut. Nothing. I'll manage."

He watched her expression flash from concern to hurt, then recognition. Recognition of what, he couldn't fathom. What did her perceptive green eyes see? He almost caved and let her nurse him.

She released him, her expression neutral. "Yes, you go ahead and bandage that. I'll clean up this mess." She turned and strode down the hall toward the kitchen.

Uncertain, Nick stood in the same spot for a moment. What the hell had just happened? One minute, she'd been Nurse Vanessa, all mother-hen worry and kiss-it-make-it-better tenderness. The next she couldn't wait to get away from him. Did she see his determination? Or did she remember that they ought to steer clear of togetherness?

Shaking his head, he padded toward the stairs.

Vanessa emerged from the back of the house with a hand vacuum, broom and dustpan. "Nick."

He halted on the second step.

"Before you come down, put something on your feet. In case I don't find all the bits of glass." With that she breezed into the living room.

She cared after all. Unaccountably pleased, he took the stairs two at a time.

\* \* \*

After clearing away the broken glass, Vanessa stowed the cleaning tools in their places in the utility closet. She returned to the living room. What had just gone on? What torment had built to critical mass inside Nick?

It wasn't about his half brother. Not this time. All that anguish about responsibility and helplessness had sprung from another source. Add his sardonic comment about not being a hero, and it had to stem from his military service. Some hidden trauma.

Well hidden.

Nothing in his file was suspicious. Whatever had happened churned inside him. His emotional reactions might affect this mission, so she needed to know. Pulling it out of him would mean delicate moves on her part. He'd already raised new barriers against her seeing his physical pain.

Many times she'd seen the same tight jaw and closed expression on her brothers when they'd come home from basketball or soccer games with cut eyebrows or banged-up shins. The male code: show no pain; show no weakness. Her mom had ignored their protestations and cuddled them anyway. Stoic Troy'd endured the pampering, but Jason, ever the sybarite, had milked it for all it was worth.

Vanessa figured Nick to be more the stoic type. Except for that inner volcano that had erupted just now.

Besides, treating his cut in the closeness of the master bathroom might have been dangerous in another, more personal way. No, she'd wait here for another window into what made Nicolas Markos tick.

"Danielle," Nick yelled from upstairs.

She hesitated a second at the unfamiliar name, then smiled at his attempt to put her in her undercover identity. She scurried into the hallway. "Problem?"

He appeared at the railing, a washcloth pressed to the injured thumb. "Yes, dammit. The cut's deeper than I thought, and I'm too right-handed to do much with my left. I need your assistance after all."

With a nod, she started toward the stairs.

"Would you bring me another drink on your way up?"

To his suite. His bathroom.

His bedroom.

Her face heated at the possibilities.

"On second thought," he called, "bring the bottle."

She was a professional. She could handle this situation. Besides, he wanted the drink for medicinal purposes. And a little more liqueur might ease the tension humming along her nerves. But no, if she hoped to elicit more from her complicated companion, she needed all her wits and defenses about her.

She collected the bottle and one snifter before climbing the stairs.

The master suite was every bit as decadent as Vanessa remembered from her quick tour with Grant Snow. A bedside lamp illuminated a mirrored ceiling, silken covers and drapes and an ankle-deep white carpet.

Averting her gaze from the rumpled jade-green sheets on the two-acre bed, she looked beyond to the sitting area, which she knew led to closets and a dressing room as big as her studio apartment. A few days' worth of newspapers littered a sea-green upholstered settee. A tray laden with dirty dishes sat on a small table.

So that was where he retreated to to escape sharing meals with her.

"I'm in the bathroom. Turn right," he called.

Nick sat on a stool to the right of the sink, the washcloth pressed to his wounded thumb. Impassive demeanor in place, he extended his left hand for the liqueur glass.

"Sure I can trust you with this one?" Irritated, she couldn't help the biting tone.

A wry expression canted his mouth, and humor glinted in his eyes. "Unless you want to hand-feed me."

She pictured herself holding the goblet and pressing the rim to his lips. The lips that had kissed her so thoroughly only moments earlier. Then tipping the liquid into his mouth and watching the strong column of his throat work as he swallowed. *Don't go there.*

Dry-mouthed, Vanessa poured him a generous amount.

He drank down the Benedictine in one gulp. "That's better. Damn thing stings like the devil. Bandages and antiseptic are there on the sink."

The bedroom's color scheme extended into the bath with white tiles and forest-green cabinet and towels. The spacious room boasted a shower stall separate from the Jacuzzi-equipped bathtub. No antiques except in the design of the brass towel racks. Heated, of course. Alexei'd enjoyed his luxuries.

"Let's see that cut." Determined to be businesslike, she cradled his hand in both of hers. "You washed it out?"

His strong, lean fingers dwarfed hers. His heat seeped into her, softening her insides and threatening her composure. Hard calluses on his palms surprised her. Running an international import company didn't entail physical labor.

He nodded. "Washed it, rinsed with peroxide. You probably heard me howl."

Pleased at his rare show of humor, she replied, "I thought a tomcat was serenading on the back fence."

She lifted the blood-soaked washcloth and peered at the cut. "Deep, but small enough that you don't need stitches. You'll have to keep pressure on it for a while."

"Wrap it good and tight, doc. I don't want to get blood all over those fancy silk sheets."

Intrigued at the disapproval in his voice, she cocked her head at him. "You don't like Alexei's bedroom decor?"

He snorted. "Most of his choices tick me off. The extravagance in this house reminds me every day of the greed that led to more than one death. Including his own." A muscle twitched in his jaw, and his shoulders jerked.

"Hold still."

"Sorry." He clamped his mouth into a tight line and lowered his gaze as she worked to treat his thumb.

Vanessa eyed him as she squeezed out antiseptic cream on the cut. "The anger that crushed the glass wasn't about your brother, was it?"

"No." The finality of his tone didn't invite questions.

She had to think how to draw him out.

But his nearness made it hard to think at all. The liqueur's rich scent mingled with Nick's soap to lure her closer. She applied a sterile bandage while fighting the urge to run her fingers through his tousled sable hair.

When she bumped up against his knees, she blinked and stepped back. "There, all wrapped up like Tutankhamen."

She busied herself with stowing the first-aid materials in the medicine cabinet.

"If King Tut'd had some of this fine liqueur, he might still be alive." One eyebrow quirked up as he held out his glass for more.

Vanessa restrained herself from pointing out that Nick liked that particular extravagance of his brother's.

She picked up the Benedictine bottle and poured. "Your wound will need the bandage for a day or two, but after that, opening it up will allow oxygen to promote healing."

He mumbled a growl as he swigged from the snifter. "Now you even sound like a medic. Medical training or ATSA?"

"You'd be surprised at the variety of undercover roles I've played. Yes, doctor was one. I've also been a barmaid, a banker and a secretary."

"Doctor, lawyer, Indian chief. Is that the kids' rhyme?"

Was he a little drunk? "Lawyer yes. Indian chief no." She handed him two ibuprofen tablets and a glass of water.

He ignored the water and downed the tablets with liqueur.

He probably wasn't in the mood to be warned about mixing pills and alcohol. Watching him, she chose her tactic.

"A wound can fester and turn to poison if it's kept covered for too long. Fresh air can heal all kinds of hurts, even old, buried ones."

# Chapter 5

Nick looked up to see her watching him, a gentle smile on her face. Her quiet, calm and clear honest gaze implied she cared, but probing his mind was probably part of her damn job. She was making sure he didn't flip out and scuttle the mission.

ATSA must have a file on the Somalia strike. Though she didn't act like it, she probably knew the worst. Knew why ATSA wouldn't want him involved except as the fiancé.

Why the hell did she want him to spell out his shame?

He rose from the stool, nearly kicking it over. "Old wounds never heal if you keep opening them up." He stalked into the bedroom and to the window beyond the bed.

He didn't hear her follow. Just as well if she left him alone. The nearer she was the more irresistible he found her. She was strong and savvy, warm and comforting.

With a body he ached to possess.

On the stool, he'd had an eyeful. He'd inhaled her sweet

scent and barely resisted nuzzling her full breasts. The erect nipples poking the thin jumpsuit had begged to be tasted.

"Something happened to you in Special Forces," she said, coming up beside him. The direct look in her brilliant green eyes offered encouragement, inspired confidence.

"Something. Yes." He set his glass on the windowsill. No more mind-fuzzing. His edges were blurred enough that he could face it. "What does my file say about Somalia?"

She tilted her head as if considering her answer. Small furrows appeared between her eyebrows. The freckles on her nose invited kissing.

"You were a sergeant with the third Special Forces group sent as security for the humanitarian relief."

He worked up an encouraging expression, but his attempt at a smile was probably more of a sneer. "Right so far. Go on. What else?"

She gazed upward as if trying to remember. "There's mention of an op to secure a weapons cache in a remote village. Something went wrong and men were lost."

"Then you know everything. My screwup killed four men. End of story."

"But surely—"

"You have enough without me rattling the skeletons." He'd tortured himself enough for one night.

His gaze snagged on her sweet mouth, a much better alternative to think about. He slid a hand behind her neck and tugged gently until he closed the space between them to barely an inch. Her silken skin and fresh scent lured him to forget everything else.

The bed was only a foot behind her. He began edging her backward. "Instead, let's talk about how hot you look in that slinky commando gear."

Her feathery lashes fluttered in uncertainty and she swayed toward him.

*She wanted him.* Knowing that stoked the coals inside him to a blaze.

Only inches to the bed now.

He danced one hand down her back, closer to that pert round bottom he ached to hold. They could be on the bed, wrapped around each other. He went from aroused to hard in a nanosecond.

But before his lips could touch hers, she sidestepped, the furrows again between her brows.

She scooted around the bed, out of reach. "Clever job of derailing, but a dangerous detour. For both of us. You want the real Danielle. I'm just a convenient warm body. And I don't trespass." Her voice shook.

He'd rattled her. Good, Somalia had flown from her head.

"And such a sexy, warm body. You're off base about who I want. I know exactly who I was about to kiss." He trailed after her on her escape route.

She stopped at the bedroom door and faced him. "Sexy? Me? Now I know you're merely trying to change topics. You have to pretend in public, but in private allow me my pride." Temper infused high color in her cheeks and flared her nostrils.

"No pretense. You're damn cute when you're angry."

"Cute. Exactly. Not sexy. Not seductive. Wholesome. The cute sister. The good buddy, the best friend. That's me."

Puzzled, he scratched his nape with his good hand. She had some strange ideas about herself. "I apologize for stepping over the line. Honey, you make me forget I'm supposed to be engaged."

"Give it up, Nick. Good night."

He stood in the doorway until he heard her door close. Confusing female, but weren't they all?

Fascinating. Bright and competent, witty, confident in her profession, but insecure as a woman.

Maybe having a cover model for a sister was to blame. But they were nothing alike. Vanessa had her own beauty. Anyone with testosterone could see that. He sure as hell didn't think of her as his buddy.

But damn, he'd better try, or he'd blow his cover story of the engagement.

He stretched out on his rumpled sheets and tried to ignore his thumb and another throbbing need caused by that particular confusing female.

As soon as she'd secured the motion sensor on her door, Vanessa stripped off the black jumpsuit. She'd considered the garment only protective cover until Nick's ogling had turned it into seduction fashion.

She slipped on her comfortable, dowdy cotton nightgown. The garment was one of the few items of her own clothing she'd brought. No one but her would see it. Although the housekeeper knew she kept her toiletries and clothing in this guest room, Vanessa made the bed carefully every day to keep up the pretense that she spent her nights in Nick's bed.

*Nick's bed.*

She could've spent tonight there if she'd yielded to temptation. And his blatant invitation.

He seemed to have no compunction about betraying his fiancée and expected her to have none. That incongruous lack of principle in a man bound to regain his honor worried her.

His final words as she left came to her: *You make me forget I'm supposed to be engaged.*

*Supposed* to be engaged? What an odd choice of words for a man in love! Or was he?

She heaved a tired sigh. She was being overly picky and suspicious, the default trait of her profession. A man of the world like Nick, with a glamorous fiancée, didn't really want plain girl-next-door Vanessa. He simply needed distraction from the demons plaguing him.

Demons, oh yes, she thought as she climbed into the four-poster bed. Demons of guilt for what he believed he'd done or not done years ago. What had happened in that Somali village ate at him like a cancer.

That incomplete confession increased her insight into Nick. His anger at his brother's crimes stemmed from a strong sense of responsibility—and a need to redeem his own honor as well as his family's.

Her heart squeezed in sympathy. If she could banish the demons, she'd be tempted to go to him.

But taking him in her arms would be dangerous. It would be wrong. Wrong for him, wrong for his real fiancée. And wrong for her. Sex would compromise her duty and jeopardize the mission. She had to ignore her attraction to him while she acted the fiancée role. And while she spied on him to ensure he didn't deviate from ATSA's program. She could be objective and do her job. She had to be.

She punched her pillow and turned over. Chasing sleep was a losing race.


Vanessa saw Nick only briefly the next day. She found him in the study on a conference call with New York and London.

He punched the speaker button off and growled, "My restaurant supply business is going down the tubes. One disaster after another, and all I can do is delegate."

She made sympathetic comments. When his expression softened, she said, "I'll be working next door on security arrangements for the Friday reception." She didn't mention she'd also search for information about that Somalia mission.

Leaning against the closed door, she thought he seemed grateful for the cooldown after the night's heated encounter. He was probably regretting coming on to her. Better all around. Better that they could avoid each other in the house. Alone, they didn't have to pretend an attraction that was all too real for her. All too dangerous for her.

Safer for her to be the pal. And more professional.

*Suspicion. Detachment. No intimacy.*

Heaving a sigh, she pushed off and headed next door.

Ah, just once, she wanted a man to mean it when he said she looked hot and tried to seduce her. She wanted him to want her, not her undercover persona. She wanted him not to have an ulterior motive, like an introduction to her hotter sister. Or like a detour from his problems in sweaty sex.

She wanted a man who didn't already have a fiancée.

That night, the ATSA cameras and motion sensors recorded no intruders. No burglars, New Dawn or otherwise, attempted to enter through the severed fence.

On Wednesday morning ATSA officer Grant Snow drove Nick and Vanessa to Markos Imports, where Nick fought another round with the employees about selling the business. Vanessa was beginning to understand that his determination to sell arose from his aversion to anything of Alexei's.

Later Snow drove them to the suitably gloomy Georgian structure housing Falstone and Drumm Funeral Home. The authorities had only just released Alexei's body for cremation, so Nick had to schedule the service. When Snow stopped the Mercedes beneath Falstone and Drumm's portico, Nick hesitated, his hand on the door.

Snow turned around. "All clear, Mr. M. Unknown vehicle parked down the block, but our guys have them boxed in. If it's New Dawn, they're ours."

Vanessa recognized Nick's taut jaw as tension about arranging a funeral for his disgraced brother, not concern about safety.

Watching him muster strength, Vanessa wanted to hug him or hold him. Both were out of the question. A hand on his forearm offered the only support she dared express.

To her surprise, he covered her hand with his and gave her an answering squeeze. Opening the door, he said, "Thanks, Snow. This won't take long."

Mr. Falstone, as plush and dour as his establishment, ushered them through a display of cremation urns and caskets. Without a blink, Nick selected one before the funeral director could begin his spiel. Peering at them over his reading glasses, Falstone then suggested an elaborate memorial ceremony, including a choir, orations and responsive readings.

In spite of Nick's unusual upbringing—and because of it—family and family honor ranked above almost everything else. He would put his disgraced family member in the ground. He would do it with respect and reserve and hard-won control. To others he'd appear calm and dispassionate. But anger and resentment would churn inside him for a long time.

Vanessa cringed inwardly at the pain Falstone's over-the-top ideas must be causing. With a sideways glance at Nick's hard mask, she stepped in and shook her head.

Falstone's jowls sagged when she said with Danielle-cool disdain, "Your simplest ceremony will do. No choir."

They agreed on a date and escaped. Nick had been right about brevity. The entire process had taken twenty minutes.

Only when they reentered the car did Vanessa register that during the entire meeting in the funeral home Nick had kept possession of her hand.

Snow announced, "Street's quiet. Those guys were religious types handing out tracts to the neighborhood."

She could only stare at her hand, now cold and empty.

Nick hit the basement gym as soon as they returned to the Chevy Chase house. He worked out with weights and the punching bag, then ran five miles on the treadmill. Pent-up frustration sweated out, he showered and dressed for dinner. With Janine here, he and Vanessa would dine together for the first time.

After the other night, she might still be wary of him, but he wanted her even more. He shouldn't, but he refused to examine the desire any further.

Janine would leave soon. He and Vanessa would be alone.

He approached the dining room to find her and the house-keeper chattering in French. So ATSA'd chosen Vanessa for this skill as well as her glorious hair and people talents.

Janine's daughter Lise slouched in the kitchen doorway. The bored look on her dusky face was an expression only a teenager could affect. She probably didn't speak her mother's native tongue and didn't know what they were saying.

Nick's French was rusty, but he understood enough to know the Haitian woman was telling his "fiancée" about the troubles on her native island. After violent unrest had killed her husband, she and her then infant daughter had come to the United States as political refugees.

Vanessa made sympathetic comments as Janine described her homeland's lack of jobs and her dirt-floored hut with no electricity.

*"Et votre fille?"* Vanessa was asking about Janine's daughter's plans.

*"Ici c'est meilleur. L'éducation lui donne l'espoir."*

Here it was better, she said. Education gave the girl hope. Nick had never seen Janine so animated. Emotion tinged her cocoa-brown face. The linen napkin she clutched rose and fell with the Caribbean lilt of her musical voice.

With him she was always reserved and deferential. He'd praised her cuisine and her efficiency and tried to converse with her, but she'd never shared anything of herself.

The *real* Danielle would've addressed her only as a servant and elicited no more than a nod. Maybe a damn curtsey. Vanessa, with her warmth, had opened up the woman in moments.

He strode into the dining room and wrapped an arm around Vanessa's shoulders. "Ah, *mes belles,* about time you met."

In the doorway, Lise rolled her eyes. Impatience jerked her shoulders and cocked her hip.

Expression once again shuttered, the housekeeper folded the napkin and arranged it at one of the two set places on the cherry-wood banquet table. "Good evening, Monsieur Nick. The dinner, it will be ready in a few moments."

Eyes downcast, she dashed into the kitchen.

"She's still skittish of me. And the daughter doesn't trust me. Fallout from Alexei's high-handedness. At least I eliminated the silly maid's uniform he'd insisted on."

"Trust takes time," Vanessa said, angling her head to look up at him.

Tucked under the curve of his arm, she was temptingly close. Nick brushed a kiss across her soft lips. Even that light touch kindled a flame. "Miss me?"

"Every minute." Cheeks pink, she slid from his embrace and fluffed her hair.

He preferred her thick mane up in the tumble of brandy-colored curls that offered access to her creamy neck. Stepping behind her, he absorbed her spring-rain scent.

"Thank you, Nick. You're so attentive tonight," Vanessa said, as he held her chair, to the right of his at the head.

"Aren't I always?"

She merely smiled at him as she spread her napkin on her lap. Dressed for a casual evening, she wore a pair of slim black pants and a sleeveless white turtleneck sweater that invited him to caress the toned flesh of her upper arm.

Why not? Wasn't she his fiancée?

Yielding to temptation, he also kissed her bare shoulder as he pushed in her chair. Then he forced himself to move away from the enticement of her sensual curves.

He'd no sooner taken his place than Janine and a pouting Lise covered the white linen with platters emitting mouth-watering Caribbean aromas.

"Let me serve you, darling. Janine's grilled salmon with mango chutney deserves a presentation," Vanessa said after the other women had vanished into the kitchen. She lifted his plate and slid a serving of fish on it. "We've been too busy for me to act the proper hostess for you."

He stared at her. Sarcasm and aloofness were so unlike Vanessa, but too much like Danielle. And she'd hit on the head the other woman's role in his life. Too perceptive.

She lowered the serving fork and touched the abstract silver pin clipped to her collar. "Thanks, Snow. Out."

She pressed the pin and turned to Nick. "Janine and her daughter have left. Their security tail reports they're headed for the Metro stop."

Nick stared at the pin. The microphone. ATSA had been listening to every word. Until now.

ATSA was gone. The housekeepers were gone.

They were alone.

Pleased, he plied the corkscrew to the wine.

Did she always keep the mike off when they were alone? Had ATSA heard his damn confession as well as his aborted seduction?

Even if they had not, the honesty and empathy in her clear green eyes weren't real. None of this was real.

Except for the uncanny way holding her eased the dull ache of grief and anger in his chest.

Except for the threat created by Alexei's rip-off of the New Dawn Warriors.

Except for his attraction to her sweet sensuality.

After dinner, Vanessa followed Nick into the sunroom at the back of the house. Geared for relaxation, the room had a wall of windows facing the terrace, a breakfast nook at the end near the kitchen and a marble fireplace at the other.

A wicker sofa and love seat created a comfortable semicircle at the fireplace. The cushions coordinated with the Oriental rug's beige and green pattern. Lacquered cabinets in the wall hid a state-of-the-art entertainment center and a wall safe.

For a change, the night was cool. She watched as Nick knelt to crumple newspaper and lay kindling in the stone hearth. The movements flexed his powerful shoulder muscles.

Beneath the pushed-up sleeves of his soft navy pullover, dark hairs glistened on his tanned forearms. Only the white bandage on his thumb hinted at any vulnerability.

He was the most striking man she'd ever seen, with danger and brooding intensity lurking beneath a dark and self-assured surface. And a more than world-class butt.

Dragging her gaze away, Vanessa settled on the sofa.

*Detachment,* she reminded herself. She needed to get him talking again. She hadn't made much headway in uncovering details about Somalia. But there were other critical factors. About ten million of them. She couldn't charge directly into that topic, however.

"Janine said your brother never wanted her to cook her Haitian dishes."

He kept his back to her as he struck a long match to the crisscrossed kindling and logs. "He preferred European cuisine, mostly French. Janine's a versatile cook."

"Saturdays and Sundays, she cooks at a French restaurant on Connecticut Avenue. She's determined to get Lise through junior college."

He sat back on his heels. The firelight flickered shadows on his beard-stubbled jaw. For an instant she saw the Special Forces warrior hunkered by a campfire.

His dark brows scissored together as he gazed at her. "How do you do that?"

"Do what?"

"Get people to bare their souls to you like that? You wormed more out of Janine in a few minutes than I have in a month. No wonder Snow called you the Confessor." He shook his head and rose to his feet in a fluid motion.

She felt heat zing to her cheeks. "I wish he hadn't told you that. That nickname makes me sound like the head of a convent or something."

"Honey, I sure as hell don't think of you as a nun."

The sexy resonance of his voice started an erotic ache deep

inside her. She clutched a throw pillow in front of her, as if any physical barrier could block her reaction to him. She must pretend to herself it could, at least.

He was smiling as he joined her on the sofa. "You do have a knack for getting people to warm up to you."

Before she could change the topic, the telephone rang.

Vanessa sat up, alert, and clicked on her microphone. "Snow? You on that?"

"Affirmative," said the voice in her ear.

Nick strode to the phone extension in the living room. "It could be anyone. Falstone. Celia Chin." But he didn't sound optimistic.

Biting her lip, Vanessa watched him lift the receiver.

"Hello." His voice sounded strong and confident, but she guessed his nerves were wound as taut as hers.

Through her earpiece, she could hear the entire conversation. The first words verified that the caller was neither the funeral director nor the import shop manager.

"By now you know that we are *close* to you," said the accented voice. "Are you prepared to reimburse what your brother stole from us?"

"I told you before. I know nothing about your money. If my brother had it, he spent it."

"Ah, no matter to us how you repay the debt. What a shame if harm were to befall the lovely Miss LeBec. An accident or…some mishap. You cannot protect her completely."

Nick gripped the receiver, his jaw firm and his eyes blazing with fury. "I don't bargain with crooks. Your threats won't work. If you come near my fiancée, you'll have to deal with me."

With that, the caller disconnected.

"Snow?" Vanessa said.

"Hell. I should've kept him on the line longer." Nick rubbed the back of his neck as he dumped the receiver in its cradle. "But that supercilious tone burned me. I wanted to stuff the damn phone down his slimy throat."

After a moment, Vanessa clicked the mike off and crossed to the liquor cabinet. "No problem. A trace takes less time than starting that fire in the other room. The bad news is the caller used a cell phone."

"So he could've called from anywhere. And the phone's probably stolen or a throwaway without the subscriber's real name and address."

She grinned. "You sure you're not a cop or something?"

"I read." He scowled at her as if she'd maligned his mother's parentage. "Now what are you doing to this valuable antique cabinet?"

Vanessa stepped back from pushing carved leaves at random. "I thought a sip or two of that lovely Benedictine might be just the thing right now. I hardly had time to taste mine last time."

"I like the way you think." The heated gaze gliding over her body showed appreciation for more than her mind.

Tingles fired on her skin as though he'd touched her. He still wanted her.

Correction—he wanted a woman.

If she could hold him off during a little conversation over liqueur, she could avoid him until the museum reception on Friday. Togetherness only in public she could handle.

Nick pressed the requisite series of decorative ivory leaves, and the cabinet's double doors swung open.

She peered at the intricate inlay pattern. More leaves inside. The cabinet seemed to be deeper than the inside space would indicate. Her pulse danced in anticipation. "This is a puzzle chest, right?"

He nodded, withdrawing the liqueur. "Chinese. Eighteenth-century, I think Alexei said. It's on the inventory. Why?"

"What happens if I press one of the leaves *inside* the cabinet?"

Nick set the bottle beside the glasses on top. "Probably nothing. There are a number of false leaves. What do you think you'll find?"

She shrugged. "Dust? Or maybe—"

"Ten million dollars?"

"Would Alexei hide cash like that?"

"Cash? Doubtful. If he didn't spend the money, it's in a Swiss account or some other safe place." He folded his arms. "Maybe we'll find his bank book. Go ahead."

She knelt on the carpet. The floor lamp cast magical shadows on the leaf design's relief. Reaching around the bottles and decanters, she pushed one leaf and then another.

Nothing.

"Look, Nick. In the back. Isn't that the exact pattern for the open-sesame sequence?" She lifted out two bottles and set them on the floor.

He knelt beside her, his bent thigh against hers, his dark head close. "Where?"

She inhaled his heat and sage-and-cedar scent. A vision of their entwined limbs there on the luxurious carpet rose to her mind's eye.

Blinking it away, she traced the shapes with her index finger. "Try the same sequence."

His bandaged thumb jutted out like an awkward beacon, but he reached in and keyed the series of leaves.

A click resounded against the dark wood. A barely visible seam that followed the design's contours widened.

*"An opening!"* Vanessa whispered. Her heart raced.

"Damn, Sherlock, let's see what's inside."

# Chapter 6

Nick removed the remaining bottles. "You do the honors. This search was your idea."

He watched as Vanessa pulled open the small doors. Her questing fingers closed on a thick packet.

She withdrew a letter-size manila envelope.

He gave a long, low whistle. "If this has something to do with the ten million, shouldn't you bring in Snow or Byrne?"

"I'll report in later," she said, as she carried their prize to the cocktail table. "ATSA doesn't consider having the ten million bucks in hand a priority. Otherwise, a team would've been prying up every board and digging up the yard."

Nick joined her on the sofa with two filled glasses. "I see. Whether the money's found or not has no bearing on capturing Husam Al-Din as long as he thinks I can pay him. I suppose I should be grateful they're not destroying the property's resale value."

She handed him the packet. "He was your brother. You should open it."

Damn, what new lows of deceit and greed would he find?

Catching a curious look from Vanessa, he lifted the flap's metal tabs. He extracted a loose sheaf of papers.

The hand-numbered pages were out of order, some upside down and backwards. "Looks like he dropped them, then had to stash them in a hurry."

Vanessa scooted closer to Nick. The touch of her small hand on his arm drained a measure of tension from him. "What are they? Can you tell?"

"It's an inventory, computer-printed." He began to read. "'Sumerian white marble mask, $2,000 to C.K. Cypress-wood altar, Chinese, from Anhui province, 1750, $300,000 to D.B. Black Babylonian boundary stone, $4,000 to A.R.'"

Looking over his shoulder, she gasped in astonishment. "It's the New Dawn sales."

In precise columns, the page gave each item's description and origin, a date for some, a sale price and the initials of the buyer. She was right. Not seeing the proof of Alexei's black-market dealings had kept that crime less real. Nebulous.

Until now. A band of fury cinched his chest.

"Look on the right," Vanessa said. "The last columns."

One column gave the same price in the listings, but the other had a lower number.

"Double bookkeeping. So my son-of-a-bitch half brother did skim off New Dawn profits."

"Why would he keep such exact records of stealing?"

Nick huffed a laugh. "You saw the shop books. Every detail down to the most minute. Alexei was meticulous. These secret records of his dirty deals are true to form. Even arrogant." He thrust the papers at her. "Here. Looking at it turns my blood to lava."

He slugged down his drink and rose to cross the room. Behind him, he heard her leaf through the sheets. "Ottoman vases and jewelry, Assyrian plaques, Central Asian masks and statues. Pages and pages."

She paused, gave a long whistle. "Ye gods. He sold more than artifacts. There are paintings by well-known artists. Van Gogh, Hokusai, Picasso, more big names. I remember reading about a private gallery heist a few years ago in Vienna."

He unclenched his fists and shoved his hands in his pockets. "Doesn't surprise me. Fanatics like the New Dawn Warriors who'd murder hundreds with bombs wouldn't quibble about stolen artwork. Apparently neither did Alexei."

"Sale prices range from hundreds to several million. Ten million skimmed dollars might be about right."

Nick didn't reply, but his mind turned over the other implications of finding that damn list. He glared at the elaborate tapestry on the wall before him. At any moment it should start to smoke.

"There," she said after a few minutes of fluttering papers. "But this isn't everything. He had at least one more sheet. There's no total. The last line reads, 'converted and secured in…' The printout stops there without the final page. As you said, in a hurry to hide it."

He returned to stand over the low table. Shoulders knotted, he fought to contain his emotion. He accepted the bundle and scanned the last page. "No Swiss account. Alexei intended to return before leaving the country."

"To get the money. Of course."

He knew his avaricious half brother's scheming mind. "What if he converted the cash to something smaller? Something he could hide easily."

"Where could it be?"

Feeling soiled by the packet, he dropped it on the table. "My brother was nothing if not predictable. If he hid this in the house, he also hid his goods here."

"In the house?"

He nodded. "And it's still here."

"He could've bought something small like stamps or one unique piece of art. You can check into recent big sales. The legitimate ones anyway." She shrugged as if she saw little hope of finding any clues. Almost as an afterthought, she said, "Will you look for it?"

He sighed, troubles riding his shoulders. "I'll have to. Now that I believe it's here I can't leave it to disappear or to be found by whoever buys the house."

"If you find the money—or whatever he hid—what will you do with it?"

"The sale of this—" he indicated the house with a sweep of his arm "—and everything that was his, including the ten-million-dollar trophy, will go into a charity fund. I want no part of his damned tainted money."

She started reinserting the transaction records into the envelope, but she looked up. "Whatever you find may not be yours to keep anyway. ATSA won't care, but U.S. Customs might. And the IRS definitely will."

His eyes narrowed as the implication hit him. "Customs won't fine me for what my brother did, and the IRS doesn't matter if the money goes into a charity fund. Alexei's tainted money will help atone for the lives he ruined."

He sat beside her and enfolded her soft hands in his. Her luminous green eyes invited him to trust her. For this request, he had little choice. "Vanessa, will you help me search the house for the money?"

Vanessa shimmied the opalescent white satin down her body. Smoothing it over her hips, she examined the look in the pier glass. Danielle had selected the dress for her from her own closet, saying she adored it but the style needed a wearer with cleavage. More cleavage than was fashionable.

Despite the woman's spiteful comment, Vanessa had to admit the garment suited her. And her one feminine asset, fashionable or not. She grinned.

The cocktail dress, by a new designer named Alba, was perfection—sleeveless, with a plunging neckline in a faux wrap bodice, and a softly draped skirt with delicate cutwork around the calf-length scalloped hem. She had strappy sandals and a necklace with a single pearl to set it off. Janine had helped her pin up her hair so the curls didn't tumble at random, but cascaded in an elegant flow.

Elegant.

Ye gods. Her?

She gave an unladylike snort and sat at the dressing table to finish her makeup. They were to leave for the museum reception in a few minutes.

They'd spent all of Thursday and most of today in the library looking for something that might be worth ten million dollars. They'd checked through every book for hidden packages, tapped and wiggled every shelf and examined every painting and antique doodad.

They'd chatted comfortably during the dusty search. He'd related stories about growing up in different ports and his early attempts at business—selling sandwiches on the New York and London docks. She'd told him about her family, about growing up in Queens with her parents, sister and two brothers. The togetherness was easy, too easy, the kind of personal connecting that sucked her into caring about people.

In this situation, it was riskier than usual—for her.

But they'd barely made a dent in their search. So Nick had arranged for three of the Markos Imports staff to come on Monday to appraise and match furniture and art objects with Alexei's meticulous legitimate inventory. The house's contents would be eliminated from their hunt and ready for auction.

Helping him search for Alexei's stashed fortune meant spending days and nights together. Close together. Just the intimacy she'd sworn to avoid. But she'd reminded herself ATSA wanted her to keep an eye on him.

Last night she'd accessed his laptop and read his e-mails.

She'd found only legitimate business correspondence. Guilt at spying on him and her sense of duty sliced at her with opposing sharp blades.

As an ATSA officer, she was obligated to be skeptical. He was already rich and influential by any standards. Did he need the ten million? He wanted the ordeal finished. Desperately. Would he return the money to New Dawn and scotch ATSA's trap?

And yet Nick's avowal to fund a charity with his brother's money had validated her sense of him as an honest man caught in a juggernaut.

Honest and more honorable than most. Fair and kind. And in his rare, lighter moments, witty and funny. Besides being attracted to him, she liked him too much for her own good, and for that of the mission. Dammit.

And tonight she'd be presented to Washington society as his fiancée. As Danielle LeBec.

Another trouble with undercover roles was separating her inner self from the role. Pretending to be cool and glamorous she could manage easily if it weren't for Nick.

And her attraction to him.

He made this her biggest challenge.

Tonight Nick would be attentive and affectionate and too sexy for words. But not for her. For show. For "Danielle."

*Remember that.*

Vanessa stood, satisfied with the final touch of mascara and pink lip gloss.

*Okay, kid, you're ready to fake it.*

The listening device in her pearl earring seemed hidden by curls at her ears. She clipped the mike to her demi-bra. Snagging her tiny evening purse, she headed out the door.

Halfway down the stairs, she heard a wolf whistle.

Standing in the foyer, Nick winked at her with masculine appreciation. If she'd thought him sexy and rugged in a casual sweater with the sleeves pushed up or imposing and commanding in a business suit, in a tuxedo this man was devastating.

How could mush that used to be legs carry her the rest of the way downstairs?

The jet-black formal suit had been custom tailored for him, she was sure of it. Nothing off the rack could fit those broad shoulders so perfectly, so…*so*. Against his olive complexion, the white shirt was blinding. An onyx stud pinned the formal crossed collar. Smaller onyx studs ran down the shirt front and gleamed at the cuffs.

*He* gleamed.

His white smile and his blue, blue eyes held her in thrall—until she blinked, realizing that somehow she'd arrived at the foot of the stairs.

"No tie," she said inanely, focusing on anything but how gorgeous he was. And how tongue-tied she was. "I've never seen a tux without a tie."

"I don't wear ties. Don't own one." He took her hand and guided her to pirouette.

She felt the approval of his gaze deep inside her. She swallowed. "You don't?"

"I didn't want to forget the blue-collar start of what became N.D.M. International. I didn't want to put myself above my employees. And now it's become a point of pride."

Nearly dizzy from his nearness and her slow turn, she stopped before him. "Commendable attitude. Even in sweats, no one would mistake you for the intern or the shipping clerk."

Nick would stand head and shoulders above anyone who might work for him. No matter what he wore, his inner presence proclaimed him the one in charge.

He tipped his head in thanks. His inky hair, still wet, shone like a midnight sea. "And tonight, honey, no one would mistake you for the cute pal or plain sister. Cinderella ready for the ball, with no ashes from the hearth."

"Or dust from the bookshelves. Thanks, but I feel more like

E.T. costumed for Halloween or a little kid playing dress-up. Not sexy or glamorous at all." Someone was tying macrame knots inside her. She pressed a hand to her stomach.

"You *are* sexy and glamorous, Vanessa." Moving so close she could feel his breath, he curled his warm hands on her shoulders, slicked a roughened palm down her arm. "Where do you get such strange ideas?"

His heated touch made her shiver. "Guys made friends with me or asked me out just to get close to my sister or to her equally beautiful friend Candice. I can't tell you how many times I was used that way."

"Those bums were clueless. Their loss. Glamour's overrated." He reached in his pocket. "But this'll give you an attitude adjustment. Turn around."

"Why?"

"You'll see."

She felt him fiddle with the catch on her pearl necklace. Electric awareness darted over her skin at every brush of his fingers. What was happening? Maybe she was under a spell, a Cinderella spell. She started to giggle.

Until the pearl necklace was whisked away.

And a pendant on a fine gold chain took its place, falling to the neckline's V. Cool as ice against her skin, the gemstone winked at her. An elusive blue fire seemed to flicker within.

"It's a fluorescent diamond," he said. "Rare. *Glamorous.*"

As big as the Capitol Building. Three carats, or more. A marquis-cut, she thought it was called. Her heart raced.

"But…but I can't wear this," she protested, facing him. "What if, what if something happens to it?" Unconsciously her hand pressed the gem to her breastbone as though to imprint it there permanently.

"Nothing will happen to it. And it's insured." His gaze hot and heavy-lidded, he lowered his head.

Ye gods, he was going to kiss her. *Engaged, he's engaged.*

*Suspicion. Detachment...* But oh, how she longed to taste those sensual, sculpted lips again.

She had only a millisecond to breathe in his woodsy scent before his mouth seared her like a lightning bolt, all molten heat and glittering danger. He kissed her with possessive power, making the blood thunder in her head and her insides start to melt.

Ending the kiss, he trailed a finger from her collarbone down the high curve of her breast to the diamond pendant.

Light splintering off the stone's facets fractured her thoughts. She swallowed.

Mouth quirked in satisfaction, he tucked her hand in the crook of his arm. "Nothing is more glamorous than a diamond. When you start to feel like E.T., think of the rare stone in that privileged spot between your breasts. Wear it for me."

When Snow deposited them at the Washington Cultural Museum, a throng of the formally dressed elite crowded the building's entrance.

Nick let Vanessa precede him up the wide marble steps. He tried not to stare at the way her hips swayed beneath the shimmering white skirt. The dress was simple, the perfect showcase for the jewel inside—the woman, not the diamond.

At a landing, Vanessa paused and turned to him. Her hand darted to the pendant.

He smiled. Was she already feeling the pressure to be glamorous—something she believed she wasn't? Touching the inner swell of her breasts, smooth and supple as a petal, and tasting her nectar-sweet mouth was glamour enough for him.

But instead of clasping the blue-hearted stone, she snaked a finger inside her bodice. "We're here. Going inside."

The microphone. Relief flowed into him that she'd had it off earlier. But it was on now.

And they were on.

His smile settled into a grim line.

Nick took Vanessa's arm, and they filed to the door.

Uniformed guards checked his pockets and Vanessa's purse. They entered the high-ceilinged great hall. Enormous banners proclaiming the museum's major exhibits adorned the walls. A string quartet beside the buffet and bar battled with the cacophony of voices.

"I've never been here at night," Vanessa said, peering up at the glass-beaded chandeliers. "The museum is stunning."

In that slithery dress that hugged every luscious curve, *she* was stunning. And forgetful. Enjoying the freedom to touch her, he guided her with a hand at the warm small of her back. "I thought you'd never visited Washington before, *Danielle.*"

She pouted her lips, very Danielle-like. "But darling, surely I told you *Adorn* sent me here two years ago for a shoot at the Smithsonian. A fabulous piece comparing original fashions with retro ones."

He tipped his head. "My apology."

Not forgetful. Danielle had prepped her well. He hoped ATSA had prepped her even better.

Snow had informed them that ATSA security outnumbered official museum security. At least a dozen were scattered throughout the reception as guests and staff. Video cameras would monitor and record every movement, every face.

Vanessa should be safe, but most of the people in tuxedos and cocktail dresses were strangers to him. New Dawn attackers could lurk in alcoves and shadowed corners and in the mock-ups of tombs and tribal dwellings.

The idea turned his gut to ice.

At the outset, ATSA's idea of setting Vanessa up as bait had seemed like a good idea, but no more. He wouldn't let her out of his sight. He'd stifle the sizzle she ignited in his blood. Maybe his discarded military instincts would kick in, and he'd spot trouble in advance.

A thin-faced man scowled past them as he leaned against a marble column. Nondescript, fit but not too tall, the type not to be suspected or noticed. The man shifted on his feet. He was sweating. A bulge in his tux jacket raised Nick's hackles.

The guards had missed this one.

Nick looked around for a likely ATSA operative.

"Sweetie, the line took forever. I'm sorry." A brunette rushed up to the nervous man. She carried two glasses.

He slipped a clutch purse from beneath his jacket and traded it for his drink. Guzzling the whiskey or bourbon, he nearly drained the glass. No terrorist. Only a harried alcoholic embarrassed to hold his wife's purse.

Vanessa hooked her arm in Nick's. "I saw him, too. Relax."

He rubbed his neck. Maybe he was overanxious. Had he lost the battle-proofing his SF training had instilled in him?

He noticed that her razzle-dazzle appearance wasn't her only change for the evening. The cool alertness in her eyes reminded him she was an experienced government operative. She surveyed, scanned, scrutinized the room. A look he knew.

That of a soldier on patrol.

He recognized as an ATSA operative the waiter who approached with a tray of champagne cocktails. They were to accept drinks only from his tray.

Nick appropriated two glasses. He managed not to curl his nose in distaste. "Scotch next time if you can manage it." Although watered wine wouldn't dull his edge.

He handed Vanessa a glass. "Time to mingle. I see Dwight Wickham back there by the statue of the two-headed god. He's being two-headed about buying Markos Imports. Maybe your lovely smile will convince him. Ready to dazzle?"

"I'll do my best." Bobbling her diamond pendant at him, she enveloped him in her warm smile.

Wickham had to be dazzled. He sure as hell was.

Polite chitchat, a little politics and some horse-trading zigzagged them around the room for the next hour. He garnered more prospects for buying the shop, nibbles but no bites. Men ogled the woman on his arm, but none attacked her.

What would New Dawn try?

What were they waiting for?

He worked his jaw as Vanessa herded him into the adjacent gallery to view the Yamari exhibit.

The tiny kingdom of Yamar had spawned the isolationist, extremist New Dawn Warriors. The former king and his son, both Western-educated, and the new regime embraced an open policy. But that didn't mean the government didn't contain New Dawn moles, even among the Yamari diplomats on hand tonight.

Nick would keep Vanessa by his side. They turned to the right to make a circuit of the displays. Two swarthy men followed them as they looked at the first exhibit. When Nick spotted three of their regular ATSA surveillance team closing in, relief blunted a spike of nerves.

"I read about this exhibition in the *Post*," she said, peering at a stone bust labeled "Goddess of Victory." "Two thousand B.C.E. Ye gods. Yamari culture is as old as Mesopotamia. Odd that none of Alexei's transactions listed Yamari antiquities."

"Maybe old Husam's ethics don't let him trash his own country." Like hell. He probably sold those off first.

The next display was a miniature of an excavated village, with the temple where the goddess statue had been found. Nick only glanced at the description plaque. Concentrating on it would distract him from shielding Vanessa.

She read the next plaque and oohed and aahed over gold beads in a marble jewelry box. Then he noted her head tilted to keep an eye on their shadows. There was that soldier look again. He reminded himself she knew what she was doing.

But he wouldn't relax.

"Can it be coincidence the museum decided to showcase the homeland of Husam Al-Din at the same time we're trying to capture him?" He didn't believe in coincidences.

"I think the current interest in Yamar stems from the recent political changes there. The king's abdication in favor of an elected government intrigues Americans."

Nick had understood their mission, but the magnitude of capturing the fanatical leader hit harder now.

"Husam Al-Din must want to squash the fledgling democracy. That's why he's hot for so much money. His attack on Veterans Day must strike at the heart of democracy."

"All the threads are woven together. No coincidences." Her eyes were solemn as she took his arm again. "Other ATSA units are working on identifying probable terror targets. Al-Din is our mission. We have to trap him."

"We will."

Her incandescent eyes glowed with fervor and dedication. She was no pampered, shallow princess like the jet-set partyers he knew. Including Danielle.

Vanessa could play his fiancée's—ex-fiancée's part convincingly, yet they were nothing alike.

It was the difference between fire and ice.

From her fiery mane to her loyal and passionate heart, she was flame. He burned to touch her again, intimately, in every way a man could touch a woman.

Willing away the lust that shot through him, he lifted her hand to his lips.

The light kiss would have to do.

By the time they'd finished the Yamari gallery, Nick had glared a warning at every man who eyed Vanessa or who wouldn't meet his gaze. Tension burrowed a headache into his temple.

"There's a man beckoning to you at the exit," Vanessa said. "Who is he?"

Nick braced himself. "A wily fox. Honey, hold tight to your purse."

# Chapter 7

"Ah, Markos," said Abdul Nadim, ebony eyes twinkling with humor in his leathery face, "here are some people you should meet if you want to forge new connections for Markos Imports."

Two Middle Eastern men and a woman stood to one side, waiting with guarded interest, unlike the enthusiastic Nadim.

Nick shook hands with the ebullient Arab-American. The barrel-chested entrepreneur was up to something. "I'm honored to meet your friends, Nadim, but you know I plan to sell the business, not expand it."

The other man wagged his head from side to side. "We shall see. We shall see."

Introductions followed rank.

Prince Amir Ben Rashid Qasim was the eldest son of the former King Fadil. Tall and fit-looking, he wore a Western-style tuxedo, as did Nadim. His penetrating eyes gazed down his hawk nose at Vanessa with avid interest.

Nick shook hands, but kept his other arm at Vanessa's waist. So the prince thought he was a damn ladies' man. Not with her he wasn't. Anger spurted heat beneath Nick's collar.

The second man was the Yamari ambassador to the United States. Fiftyish and compact in a gold-trimmed abaya over his black business suit, Lufti Khalil looked the part of the distinguished, respected diplomat. He'd been runner-up to the newly elected president of Yamar.

Nick greeted the ambassador, then turned to the prince. "Your country fills the news lately, your highness. How's the government transition going?"

A wide smile brightened the young prince's somber features. "The transition is gaining speed like a train leaving the station. My father is happy in retirement," he said in clipped British-educated tones.

The prince must've looked forward to his turn to rule. Nick smiled to take the edge off a question that could be considered rude. "And you? Are you adjusting?"

"I am pleased. Being my country's economic envoy gives me the opportunity to bring more prosperity to my people. And the opportunity to meet such lovely ladies as Ms. LeBec." He bowed his head slightly and flashed Vanessa a toothy smile.

"You flatter me, your highness," she replied warmly.

The jerk's come-on was older than the Great Pyramid and about as pointed. But the telltale apricot blush on her cheekbones told Nick the hokey line had had its intended effect.

His headache pounded. M-16 rounds ricocheted around his skull. He refocused as Nadim introduced the bright-eyed, older woman in a modest tunic and trousers. She was Khalil's wife, Dr. Kamilah Sharifah, a pediatrician.

"I am so honored to meet you, Dr. Sharifah," Vanessa said. "A friend has told me of your important work in your country with the poor and with orphans."

The Yamari woman inclined her head modestly. "You are too kind, Ms. LeBec. But I do not work alone. The more people who know of the plight of our poor—we have so many refugees—the more assistance we receive. Perhaps your magazine would like an interview."

Vanessa smiled. "*Adorn* is a fashion magazine, but I'll see what we can work out. Thank you for your generous offer."

"As intelligent and diplomatic as she is beautiful," Prince Amir said, his dark eyes skimming Vanessa's curves. "My compliments, Mr. Markos."

Nick didn't trust the smug bastard, but he stretched his lips into a tight smile.

The prince bowed slightly to Vanessa. "You must join me for dinner one evening. I would be pleased to offer Yamari hospitality."

Vanessa began to reply, but Nick cut her off, pulling her closer to his side. "You are too kind, your highness. *We*'ll have to check our calendars."

Sucking in his cheeks at the reprimand, Prince Amir nodded. Ambassador Khalil cleared his throat as the prince turned to speak to one of the Yamari aides standing by.

Nick took the opportunity to slip away, but not before Nadim had coerced him into a business lunch with Khalil and the prince.

"The snake," Nick muttered as he hustled Vanessa back to the great hall. "He thought he could slither right in."

Vanessa cocked her head at him, the movement bouncing the curls on top of her head. A few strands had come loose, and his fingers itched to caress their springy softness. "Do you mean Mr. Nadim? I thought he was trying to help. An infusion of new imports would boost the shop's sales until you can sell."

"Not Nadim. He merely wants a piece of the profits."

"The prince? He was just being gracious."

She wasn't that oblivious, was she? "Gracious, my ass. Prince Smarmy was coming on to you."

She shook her head. "Meaningless. With Amir's reputation, flirting is expected. With any woman he meets."

Forgoing the Scotch, he accepted the club soda Vanessa lifted from the ATSA waiter's tray. Away from the Yamari delegation, he began to cool down. The M-16 bursts dulled to a low throb. What the hell was wrong with him? Letting the prince's ogling needle him. Wanting to punch the man.

Nick was acting as if Amir had hit on his *real* fiancée. Must be the headache.

When he noticed Vanessa studying him, he kissed her lightly. "Forgive me. Chalk up my reaction to method acting."

"Nicolas Markos, good evening." A stunning blonde in black sequins stepped from a laughing group to greet them.

He'd tried to prepare himself for this encounter, but seeing her skewered him with shame.

Here was the woman Alexei had tried to murder twice.

Vanessa placed her hand on Nick's forearm.

He covered it with his. How did she always know?

"Ms. Rossiter," he said.

"It's Ms. Stratton now. I was married in September. But call me Laura."

The scoop neckline of her dress in no way concealed the still livid knife scars on her neck. She held her head high as though proud to display badges of courage. Which they were.

"Congratulations." He dragged his gaze from her scars.

The two women knew each other, but in case New Dawn was watching, he introduced them. "Danielle, Laura's one of the curators of the Washington Cultural Museum. She organized the Yamari exhibit."

"The exhibit's wonderful. Fascinating. You're to be commended," Vanessa said.

She and Laura shook hands, holding on in a barely hidden emotional connection. They chatted about the exhibit.

Nick had met Laura once before, at Alexei's hearing. Seeing her again brought back the entire nightmare scenario.

A year ago, Alexei had acted as middleman, selling art and antiquities to fatten New Dawn's coffers. He'd consulted

Laura for authentication. When a purported Persian mummy turned out to be phony, Alexei strangled the unfortunate dealer. And Laura happened to witness the murder.

Alexei's henchman had beaten and stabbed her, then locked her in the trunk of a junkyard car to die. Through sheer force of will she escaped, from the trunk and then from the hospital.

After many months, Alexei'd cornered her in Maine, where the Anti-Terrorism Security Agency had helped trap him, but only after more attempts on Laura's life. Undercover to protect the woman, Vanessa had befriended her.

A tall, dark-haired man appeared behind Laura and slid his arm around her waist.

Laura's expression brightened as if the sun had just come from behind a cloud. She smiled up at him.

The love in her eyes told Nick the man was Laura's new husband. An ATSA officer, he'd coached her to greet Vanessa tonight as Danielle. She must also know about the extra ATSA security arrangements. And the reason for them.

"My husband, Cole Stratton," she said. "Danielle LeBec and her fiancé Nick Markos."

"A pleasure, Ms. LeBec," Stratton said over Vanessa's proffered hand.

"Congratulations on your recent marriage, Mr. Stratton. You make a striking couple." Humor and affection lit her eyes.

"Yes, congratulations, Stratton. You're a lucky man," Nick said, holding out his hand.

"Markos." Stratton's steely gaze speared suspicion at Alexei's brother. He released Nick's hand just short of turning the grip into a duel. "Thanks. Believe me, I know."

Vanessa watched the two men sharpen their weapons. Cole's anger was palpable. Allowing this couple at the reception put his lady in danger again. Nick glared back, intent and defiant, shielded by the dented armor of his embattled honor. Their hands would've gone to their swords if they'd had any.

A smile lifting her lips, Laura fanned herself with her

beaded purse. "My makeup's melting from all the testosterone around here. Danielle, would you like to freshen up, too?"

The museum curator had no smudged mascara or lipstick. Every golden hair lay smoothly in her French twist. Whether linen or silk, nothing she wore ever dared to have a wrinkle or a stain. She was the quintessential upper-crust, sleek blonde, whose classy beauty intimidated lesser mortals.

And yet Laura seemed unaware of her effect on people. She was brave and kind, and Vanessa liked her.

She grinned. Tonight she didn't feel rumpled and unkempt beside the other woman. Tonight they were equals. After all, she had the blue-hearted diamond lending her its allure. "While we're gone, maybe these two will learn to play nice."

Nick kept possession of her arm. He shook his head. "Going off by yourself isn't a good idea."

She peeled off his fingers. "I'll be fine. The rest room's right there. Along with two people I know." She indicated the marked door and the formally clad ATSA couple lounging nearby.

From his forbidding expression, Nick clearly didn't like it, but the women sashayed away.

Before they could enter the ladies' room, Vanessa stopped. More than life-sized on his four-foot pedestal, the leering two-headed marble deity loomed over them as if to eavesdrop. Him, she'd allow.

"Unlikely, but the rest room could be bugged. Let's talk here first." She nudged her friend closer to the wall.

A matron in a red-sequined dress limped by in stiletto heels that barely contained her fleshy feet. A cloud of perfume trailed in her wake. A small group stopped to chat a few feet away. Layers of voices and clinking crystal and the occasional inspired violin note cloaked conversation.

"I must apologize for my husband's macho attitude," Laura said, gripping Vanessa's hand.

"After what he went through protecting you in Maine, I'm

sure he can't wait to end this entire mission." A contract killer had mystified and endangered them all.

"Exactly. And seeing Alexei Markos's brother here doesn't help. Cole considers Nick a threat."

"Guilty until proven innocent. Laura, Nick isn't like his brother. He's appalled by everything Alexei did. He's on our side."

Once she'd uttered the words, she knew she believed it. Nick wouldn't betray ATSA's goals. He had the same goals.

"I see he has a defender. His caveman protective manner reminds me of Cole. They could be brothers with their black hair and blue eyes." She chuckled. "And you look at him the same way I look at Cole. You're falling for him, aren't you?"

A glance back found the two men facing each other with ramrod backs and defiant stares. But they were talking.

Vanessa sputtered, "I, uh, oh no, it's just part of our engagement act."

A few inches taller, Laura tilted her head like a stern teacher correcting a recalcitrant student.

Vanessa sighed. "The hazard of going undercover with an attractive man. I'll get over it. Besides, he's in love with the real Danielle." It was Danielle he was engaged to. She had to remember that.

"You're the one he has his hands on. I get the impression he'd do more than that if you weren't in public. He's attracted, and he cares about you. You must see that."

She hadn't let herself think of his heated remarks as jealousy, but maybe… "Nick did seem to overreact when Prince Amir complimented me."

Laura waved a dismissive hand at the understatement. "So the playboy prince's flirting hit the jealousy bull's-eye. Nick's not thinking of any other woman but you. The real you."

The notion that he desired her curled around her chest. Impossible. She might be glamorous tonight, but tomorrow Cinderella would be herself—the buddy, the ordinary sister.

She had a hard enough time reining in her emotional involvement as it was without impossible dreams.

Vanessa shook her head. "It's better if he thinks of Danielle. Nothing can happen. I won't risk the mission. Especially not for a fling that can go nowhere."

Laura clucked her tongue. "Good-looking, principled, rich, sexy. You shouldn't let him get away."

"You don't understand, but I can't explain." Vanessa slipped her arm through her friend's. "Let's go to the ladies' room before the men send out a search team. I haven't seen you since your wedding. How's your adorable little girl? Tell me everything."

After the women left, Nick schooled his emotions to withstand Stratton's hostile scrutiny. The man's pale blue eyes seemed to bore through blood and bone. His predatory demeanor and a pair of chalk-white scars belied the civility of his tailored tuxedo and polished black shoes.

Stratton stared in silence.

Nick stared back.

Stratton's eyes narrowed. He blinked. "You military?"

Nick gave a sharp nod. "Special Forces. Third SFOD group out of Fort Bragg. You?"

Now that the staring contest had ended, he spared a glance at the back of the room. Vanessa and Laura were just entering the rest room. The female ATSA operative followed. Damn straight.

*"Semper fi."* The former marine stood at ease, sliding his hand into a trouser pocket. "What was your AO?"

His Area of Operations. By his appearance, Stratton was a few years younger. What would he know about those earlier SF days? But he saw no reason to conceal facts. "Kuwait as regular army. Special Forces in Somalia."

Stratton scrubbed his chin. In his eerie gaze, respect replaced suspicion. "Somalia. A meat grinder. You're lucky to be in one piece."

Sometimes Nick wasn't so sure. "Yeah, well, some others got chewed up." And he hated this dicey situation forcing him in the zone, dredging up memories to be replayed in digital color and sound in his dreams. "Where were you deployed?"

"Bosnia. Another U.N. Task Force op."

"A more successful one." Hairs prickled Nick's nape again. Having Vanessa out of his sight was shredding his nerve endings. "What's taking those women so damn long?"

What might've been humor twitched up one corner of Stratton's mouth. "Making you nuts, is she? She can take care of herself. Take my word for it."

Both men turned.

The rest-room door opened, spilling brightness into the softly lit reception area. Vanessa and Laura headed toward them, weaving past knots of guests.

A smile on her lips, Laura lifted a hand to wave to her husband.

Beside her, Vanessa scanned the crowd.

As they approached the marble statue, Nick saw a shadowy figure slip between it and the wall.

The god dipped his two heads. The statue was falling.

Toward the two women.

*"Look out!"* Nick shoved past Stratton on a run.

Vanessa glanced up. She yanked Laura backward. Both women stumbled on their high heels and went down.

The statue crashed in front of them. One head snapped off at the neck. It rolled before coming to rest in front of Nick's feet. Marble eyes stared in sightless surprise.

Nick's gaze shot to the empty pedestal. *Gone!* No one lurked behind it. His heart setting a new Grand Prix record, he detoured to get to Vanessa.

A nearby group scattered amid startled shrieks. Stemware shattered on the floor. Conversation hushed as if switched off. The string trio scraped to a squeaky halt.

"That thing just fell over," a voice shrilled into the pregnant silence.

"It could've killed someone."

"I walked in front of it only a minute ago."

Nick scooped up Vanessa as Stratton was helping his wife to her feet.

Museum personnel encircled the broken marble and dispersed the crowd that had gathered. Violins and voices once again vied for attention.

When the statue had toppled toward Vanessa, Nick's heart had leapt to his throat and the ricocheting in his skull had cranked up. Only now were his pulse and the ache ebbing.

He patted her shoulders, her back. He ached to pull her close, but held her loosely in his arms, in case she was bruised. "Honey, are you hurt?"

She drew a deep breath and sent him a reassuring smile. "I'm fine. Someone pushed the damned thing over. I caught only a glimpse. Did you see him?"

Nick shook his head. He'd seen only a form. Whoever it was must've blended immediately with the crowd.

The cameras would have the entire scene on tape.

"What do you mean, the cameras didn't pick it up?" Vanessa swung away from the computer monitor. Her eyes burned from replay after replay of the doomed god biting the dust.

The two night-duty officers glanced up at the outburst, then returned to their monitors. Long after midnight, the glowing screens were the only lights in the command post. The other operatives slept peacefully elsewhere in the house.

"You got it," the ATSA control officer said with annoying good cheer. "Our guy knew the angles. Behind the statue was a dead spot for the cameras."

With perpetual two-day stubble and a diamond stud in his left earlobe, Simon Byrne looked more like the undercover DEA agent he used to be than the control officer for this mission. But the nonconformist also possessed a blade-sharp intellect and a staunch heart. He shoved back a shock of brown hair.

Byrne and the surveillance unit had confiscated all the tapes from the Washington Cultural Museum. The techs were working to match frames of people with the guest list. But the two tapes the CO had brought over to show Vanessa offered no clue as to the identity of her attacker.

"One camera above the statue aimed to the left. Another caught the posh noshers to the right and in front of it. None of them was aimed at the statue."

"Damn." Vanessa slumped in the swivel chair. "I know there were New Dawn Warriors at that party. One of them pushed that statue, and we could've had him."

"Roger," Byrne agreed with a grin. "All our leads have fizzled like wet firecrackers. Their cars have been stolen or had stolen plates. The SUV was rented with fake ID."

She waved an arm in the direction of the mansion next door. "Since we found the cut boards in the fence, no one's been back. We need a break."

"Time's short. Little over a week until November."

"Any progress on Husam Al-Din's plot for Veterans Day?"

"Slow. Another unit's checking out all the ceremonies planned. The finish line looms." Simon didn't look worried. Vanessa knew he thrived under a deadline.

"Pressure's on in more ways than one. I see news stories every day about New Dawn. Congress wants to investigate. The press is hounding the president's security advisor." If he wasn't worried, she sure was.

"Hey, relax. We're doing all we can. Stratton's working with the CIA to uncover New Dawn's big goal."

"I know, Simon, but Husam Al-Din has acquired a big international following. And he has more money than I can even imagine. The danger has increased exponentially."

"Yeah, but Al-Din *is* New Dawn. Other extremist groups are loose and splintered. Not New Dawn. Al-Din runs the show from the top. We get him and the whole house of cards collapses."

"I hope you're right. Maybe I should stop reading the *Post*." Concentrating on her job made more sense. On being the bait so New Dawn made a mistake and led ATSA to their leader.

Leaning forward to view the Humpty-Dumpty fall again, he made kissing sounds. "Man, that was some fancy bash. You clean up good. Even falling on your ass you look hot, kid."

*Kid.* She winced inwardly. He might've as well said *pal.* It was long past midnight, and she'd removed her glass slippers. "Thanks, Simon. I'm glad to be off heels as skinny and high as stilts though." She wiggled her toes in her sneakers.

He picked up his paper coffee cup and glanced hopefully inside. With a shrug, he tossed it across the room into the wastebasket. "Two points."

"Nah. Free throw. One point." Vanessa pushed to her feet. "I'm calling it a night."

Byrne accompanied her to the door that would lead across to the Markos house. "I see you're still wearing his rock."

At Byrne's critical tone, she glanced down at the paste engagement ring on her hand. No. He meant the real rock hanging around her neck. "I didn't feel safe taking it off until I can return it. Do you have a problem with that?"

"Not as long as you don't." His cocky irreverence slid into stern disapproval. Byrne folded his arms. "You two looked cozy as hell in the videos, a regular pair of lovebirds. You'll need a new code name. *Fiancée* instead of *Confessor.*"

Vanessa's stomach knotted. "Just part of the act."

"Make sure you remember that. He may be richer than my aunt Minnie's cheesecake, but most of his money's tied up in his and his brother's businesses. Who knows what other connections he has? I don't trust him. Watch your step, especially if you find that ten mil."

Heat climbed her neck. "You do your job. I'll do mine."

She had to force herself not to slam the door behind her.

But was she doing her job? Or had she already lost detachment by getting too involved with the assignment? She had to keep reminding herself of the threats they faced and that she shouldn't trust Nick.

Deep breaths of air perfumed by sere leaves and a tree-lined view of the star-spangled sky should've soothed her. But she felt no better.

But she could act objective and professional. Dammit, she still had the detachment to do her job. In spite of how her heart twisted at having to continue with deceptions and subterfuge.

Her stock in trade.

Before she went upstairs, she slipped into the study and booted up Nick's laptop to look for nonexistent treachery.

# *Chapter 8*

Nick didn't see Vanessa the next morning until it was time for them to leave for luncheon with one of the potential buyers of Markos Imports. Over the next couple of weeks, they had more luncheons and parties, including embassy receptions. He'd enjoy them only because she'd accompany him.

She'd been spectacular last night, carrying out her role as Danielle and bewitching him as herself. But the woman was a puzzle. Self-doubt, warmth and sexy curves packaged with clandestine skills and smarts. Today she was a walking temptation in a knit dress and jacket that matched her eyes.

He shouldn't, but he had to know more about her. Much more.

Or was that just self-defense, a way to distract himself from their nerve-racking masquerade? From the stress of being thrust into chaos, as they had been last night? From the potential hyper-reality sensations of combat? From situations he'd avoided thinking about for so long?

If more chaos arose, so be it. He'd endure what he had to to help capture Husam Al-Din and recapture his honor.

Logic told him protecting Vanessa wasn't his job. ATSA covered their backs. But the thought of anything happening to this remarkable woman had him gnashing his teeth. Tension hummed in every muscle as they left the house's protection.

They were sitting ducks. No helmet. No flak vest. No M-16. The sense that he might need them knotted his shoulders.

As soon as he saw the bruise-colored shadows beneath her eyes, he stifled questions about what the surveillance tapes had shown. She covered a yawn as he handed her into the car.

He hadn't slept much himself.

ATSA had refused his help viewing the tapes. They didn't trust him beyond his official role. And they shouldn't. But damn it, bile crept up his throat every time he pictured that massive marble figure tilting toward Vanessa and Laura.

He dug into his impressions of last night's attack and came up empty.

Grant Snow guided the powerful automobile through light traffic. Although the restaurant wasn't far from the Washington Cultural Museum, the ATSA driver chose a different route from the previous evening.

"Anyone back there?" Vanessa asked.

"Only our official tail," Snow replied.

A half hour later, they entered the American Grille at L'Enfant Plaza Hotel. The contemporary Asian decor of Chinese-red banquettes and bonsai trees suited the topic of the coming negotiations.

In the white-linen-and-crystal setting, Vanessa slid into her role as Nick's loving fiancée and hostess. Seated between him and Dwight Wickham, she made the reluctant buyer comfortable.

After the waiter had delivered menus, the sharp-featured businessman, his long graying hair held at his nape with a velvet ribbon, eyed her critically. "My dear Danielle, should you be here? Were you injured in that…incident last night?"

Nick and Vanessa exchanged glances.

"I'm fine, Dwight," she answered. "The statue missed me. Did you see it fall?"

He shook his head as he perused the menu. "Just caught a glimpse as the thing toppled over. Damned scary. You'd think the museum would take more care at securing those pieces."

Nick opened his menu, but scarcely focused on the seafood specialties. "The whole thing went, pedestal and all. Maybe someone leaned on it too hard. Did you happen to see anyone?"

Wickham's alert gray eyes held a shade of suspicion before he shrugged. "Sadly, no. There was such a crush."

"Pity," Vanessa said. "The museum will want to know the cause of such an accident."

Lowering his menu, Nick said to Wickham, "Have you had a chance to look over the financial records I sent you?"

As if he hadn't spoken, the man turned to Vanessa. "My dear, you've been living abroad, so don't miss this chance to enjoy the Grille's Maryland crab cakes. You'll forget all about *boeuf bourguignon* and other French fare."

"Crab cakes it is." Vanessa winked at Nick.

He flapped open his menu. Ginger-grilled shark. Might as well since he was swimming with sharks.

It would be a long luncheon.

When they exited beneath L'Enfant Plaza's portico after two, Vanessa saw the stress tying Nick in knots. Her face hurt from smiling, and the cheesecake sat heavily on the crab.

A deal with Wickham for the shop eluded Nick. The crafty bargainer had hedged by saying he needed more time to look over the records. He'd be in touch.

Maybe what they both needed was a little fresh air.

Mackerel clouds in the mostly blue sky portended rain, and

the autumn air was balmy. There should be plenty of tourists around them as buffers.

"Feel like stretching your legs?"

Nick's mouth curved in pure delight, the first sign today of anything but grim determination. "You read my mind."

Warmed and a little mesmerized, she forced her gaze away from his killer grin and the way his dove-gray suit conformed to his hard body. The natural way he wore the band-collar shirt made men in ties look fussy.

She tapped on the driver window of the Mercedes. "Grant, we're going to take a walk along the Mall. You can pick us up at the Capitol in an hour."

Slipping her arm into Nick's, she savored the sage and cedar that stamped him. As they strolled up 9th Street toward the Mall, she heard Snow sputtering expletives into his radio.

"He or Simon'll tear a strip off my hide later, but we'll be safe enough. We have our guardian angels—the other car and two guys scrambling to catch up to us on foot."

"Three guys." He jerked a nod toward the other side of the street.

"I stand corrected." She gave his solid forearm a pat. "You still have your Special Forces instincts."

He scowled and clammed up, so she let the issue go. For now. She'd hit a wall in researching Nick's misadventure in Somalia, but she wouldn't give up.

At Jefferson Drive, Vanessa glanced left toward the Washington Monument at the far end of the Mall. Too far, so she suggested they turn right toward the Capitol Building.

Government staffers with briefcases shared the sidewalk with senior citizens in matching windbreakers and young families with baby strollers. The vendor on the next corner was tying balloon animals for laughing children.

She said, "I love this Mall. It's so friendly and open, a living demonstration of this country."

"Little Ms. Optimist, aren't you?"

.    "I can't help it. Guess I'm giddy from this heady chance at freedom." She covered a yawn.

"Not giddy. Tired. Late-night sleuthing?"

"For all the good it did." She explained about the camera dead spot behind the statue.

Disappointment pulled his brows together. "Damn. All those tapes, and nothing. It can't be coincidence. The attacker must've scoped out the camera angles."

"That's my conclusion, too. He visited the museum more than once in preparation. Matching the video clips with the guest list will take time."

"They planned ahead." As if mulling that thought, he ran his tongue around his teeth. "Knew we'd attend the reception. The guest list was no secret, but not public knowledge."

"Who did you tell about the reception?"

"Janine knew, of course. Emil Alfieris and Celia Chin at the import shop." He threw up a hand. "Hell. Any number of people knew. I made sure to mention it to business contacts during the last week."

"No wonder Abdul Nadim wasn't surprised to see you."

"Neither were the other three possible buyers. Too bad Wickham didn't see something—or someone."

"Give me a list, and we'll check out connections to New Dawn." She flipped her hair off her shoulder and smiled. "Pretty smooth way you questioned him."

"Call me Agent Smart." His tone darkened the light words.

A block farther, at the Hirshhorn Museum, they followed the steps down to the sculpture garden. Their path took them in and out of the shade of the looming modern figures that surrounded the massive circular building.

Vanessa peered up at a gently rotating, bright blue Calder mobile. "I love how those things move. Mom always has a couple of small mobiles and some wind chimes. Seeing this one reminds me of home."

"Your parents have room for this one in their yard?"

She laughed. "Only if we demolish the Palmeiris' house."

That he was enjoying a little humor with her lit a glow in her chest, but a tiny voice inside her head doused the nascent flame. It warned her not to lose her professional edge, not to become involved. Her throat tightened with anxiety.

She couldn't let immersion in her role jeopardize the mission. Stopping New Dawn was too important.

Important to Nick, too.

He was squinting into the sun as he puzzled out a tubular shape labeled Dome.

How long since she'd scanned around them? Had she missed anything? No. Their ATSA tails were still with them. No one else around them but lovers and vacationing families.

She sighed in relief and put a hand to her throat.

Her eyes popped wide, and she straightened. "Oh, I almost forgot." She pulled the gold chain from beneath her sweater, unfastened the clasp and extended the pendant to him. "Thanks for letting me wear this last night. I did feel glamorous. Until I landed on my butt." She gave a nervous laugh.

He hesitated, but took the necklace. "You were indeed glamorous. And courageous. Your fast reaction saved both Laura and you from serious injury."

Heat rose to her cheeks. "Thanks. I was just doing—"

"Your job. Yes, I know." He took her hand and headed to another part of the garden. "You're an enigma to me. How can a beautiful and sophisticated woman like you doubt your own appeal? Just because some clueless guy once—"

"Not just one guy. Not just once." Damn her redhead's complexion that broadcast her every reaction. "But thanks for the compliment."

"Are you sure you weren't overly sensitive?"

A small boy ran by, holding aloft a toy airplane that he'd probably just bought at the Air and Space Museum. He made buzzing and whirring noises. Like the whirring in her stomach.

"You really want to know?" She laughed self-consciously.

"I'm hoping I can acquit my sex."

Her gaze lofted to his. "Not all of your sex are as concerned with honor as you. But okay, my embarrassing secrets are yours."

She could almost see his chest swell. Sharing a secret meant a measure of trust. Maybe he'd trust her with his.

They continued to amble around the garden, stopping to read the placards for the most interesting pieces.

"It started in junior high. Boys I'd been friends with all through elementary school would drop by to shoot a few hoops. Before we could finish a game of horse, I was benched and they were wowing Diana with jump shots."

"Rough. Especially for the big sister." His big fingers played with curls at her temple, sending shivers across her scalp. "A tomboy should have an advantage. Knowing about guys. How they think."

She shrugged. If only she did know how guys thought. "Maybe. Most tomboys don't have a drop-dead-gorgeous sister."

His expression turned wistful. "Our situations were different, but I felt shunted aside, too, in favor of Alexei."

She could picture the serious boy, hurt by indifference, working harder to get his father's attention. The gentleness of his touch and the sadness in his eyes filled her with longing. "Alexei the charmer and Nicolas the serious one."

"Exactly." He tucked her hair behind her ear and took her hand. They ambled on to the next exhibit. "But we were talking about you. Teenaged boys can be thoughtless and single-minded. At puberty their brains slide below their belts."

She gave him the sweet smile and wide-eyed Kewpie-doll expression learned from Diana's model friends. "Is that a nice way of saying their heads are up their asses?"

Nick blinked, as if he couldn't believe his ears. His mouth twitched. His eyes crinkled. Then he laughed, a great belly laugh, and slung one arm around her shoulders. "Honey, I think that says it all."

They sat on a bench beneath one of the building's large pillars and watched the fountain geyser up like Old Faithful. Held in the shelter of his embrace, she felt protected and cherished. She could stay like that forever.

But all she had was this moment. A bittersweet ache coiled through her.

She wasn't his real fiancée. *Remember that, you ninny.* But here in public, where he was supposed to act as if she were, reality was hard to hold on to.

Way past losing detachment, she was in danger of falling in love with an impossible man. She meant to respond to his laugh with a flippant remark, but she was fresh out.

Nick ruffled her hair and kissed her temple. "Teenaged boys are their own species. Fast forward to men. Tell me they have more sense."

She sighed, reluctant to lose the intimacy of the moment. "You tell me. How about Richard? We dated for three weeks in college until I introduced him to Diana. Then I was history."

His brows came together in that thoughtful pleat she was coming to know. "And how did Diana handle this?"

She tried to ignore the twinge of jealousy his question aroused. "Diana's not the problem. My sister and I understand each other. She always saw through those not-too-subtle ploys and cut those guys off at the knees. She had her own problems with guys treating her like a doll." Vanessa wouldn't mention that Diana always had ten other guys waiting in the wings.

"Just because you have a cover-girl sister doesn't make you the perpetual best buddy. Some of us appreciate cute and freckles that look good enough to taste."

"Thanks, Nick. That's very sweet."

She could give him a list, but she'd said enough. The guys she worked with treated her like a pal. She encouraged it since that was better than the harassment some female operatives experienced.

Someday a man like Nick would fall in love with her for herself, not as a means to her gorgeous sister and not as her undercover persona. But not Nick. Never Nick. Merely thinking the words produced a sharp spasm in her heart.

His heated gaze cruised all her assets and curled her toes. He pulled her to her feet, and they continued walking.

She didn't know quite why she'd confessed all her insecurities, but blithering on kept her from hauling him close for a mind-bending kiss—what she really wanted to do. Every nerve ending she possessed sparked with awareness.

*No, no and no,* she berated herself. He was engaged, and she shouldn't trust him that way even if she didn't believe he'd betray ATSA's setup. *Detachment, detachment.*

Nick pointed toward a tarpaulin-covered shape in the plaza. They'd completed the circuit of the garden surrounding the massive circular museum and were returning toward Jefferson Drive. "A new addition to the collection."

Grateful for the change of topic, she hurried toward the indistinct lump. "Ah, this must be the pedestal for the sculpture donated by the new Yamari government."

"Yamar again. They're everywhere." That pinch between his raven brows was back.

"Laura mentioned this sculpture last night. A Yamari artist created it to commemorate Washington's assistance with their transition to democracy. There's an unveiling ceremony soon, I think."

"Bully for them. I wish they'd unveil Husam Al-Din instead." His scowl darker than the shadows beneath the Hirshhorn's pillars, he shot his cuff and looked at his watch. "I've seen enough. Snow'll be waiting for us."

Vanessa tucked her arm in his as they crossed 7th Street. "Now don't go all stormy on me again. We were having fun. You can't deny it. If I'm Ms. Optimist, you're Mr. Grim."

"If only this were a fairy tale." He lifted her hand and kissed her fingertips. His breath across her hand ribboned warmth inside her. "You've lifted my spirits with your kindness and that sexy dress, and I'm grateful. But—"

The screech of tires not far behind them alerted Vanessa. She stopped, turned.

Nick spun on his heels. He tucked Vanessa behind him.

A green sedan pulled to the corner, the window open.

*"Down. Now."* Vanessa yanked hard on his sleeve.

Together they dove to the ground. Nick rolled over to shield her with his body.

Three loud pops shattered the tranquil afternoon.

The sedan pulled away.

Another squeal of tires and the ATSA car roared up in pursuit of the attackers.

Vanessa lay flat, half on the sidewalk and half on the adjacent grass, sheltered by Nick's big body. Had he been hit protecting her? Fear clutched her heart. She pressed a hand to his chest. His heart raced as fast as hers. "You all right?"

"Fine. You?" His voice sounded mechanical, automatic. Special Forces soldier mode.

She pushed against him to free herself. She needed to see what was going on. An immovable cage held her fast.

"Wait," he commanded.

Pounding feet raced to surround Nick and Vanessa—their ATSA protection.

A little late.

Nick sprang to his feet and helped her up.

A scattered circle of pedestrians gaped at them.

"False alarm, folks," said one of the officers, shooing them away. "Just a backfire. Everything's all right."

Farther down the street, the sedan ducked down a side street. The ATSA car sped along in pursuit.

"Did you get their license?" Vanessa demanded. She clicked on her microphone.

"HQ's running it now," said one operative.

Snow pulled up beside them in the Mercedes. "Get in," he said grimly.

She nodded. Time to face the music. But where was Nick?

He stood apart, his back to the others, shoulders rigid. He appeared to be staring at the Capitol Building, but she'd bet his gaze focused inward.

"Nick, we have to go."

Without looking at her, he marched to the car. Sweat dripped down his temples. His hand shook as he reached for the door handle.

On Monday morning, Vanessa went over the day's schedule with Janine. Baking aromas filled the kitchen, brightening an otherwise gray day.

A bell rang, and Janine whisked to the oven to remove two browned loaves. "Banana bread," she announced as she slid the pans onto wire racks.

At the breakfast bar, Lise and her boyfriend Ray bent over Lise's college textbooks. Notebooks and scribbled-on sheets fanned across the counter. Ray kept his academic abilities under wraps, but Janine had told Vanessa that he helped the girl with math.

"You can go about your usual routine. We shouldn't be in your way," Vanessa said. "Are you all set with lunch?"

Janine picked up a file card. "Grilled chicken breasts in lime marinade served on mesclun greens and with fresh-baked French bread. Kiwi-peach tarts for dessert."

Just after breakfast, and her mouth was watering. "Just like an upscale menu. You should have your own restaurant."

The housekeeper's mouth curved into a dazzling smile, and a rosy tinge highlighted her cocoa-brown cheeks. *"Oh, mademoiselle, c'est mon rêve."*

"What is your dream?" said a deep voice behind Vanessa. Her pulse skipped, and she turned on her heels. Nick had come soundlessly up behind them from the sunroom. How could such a big man move so silently?

"Oh, it is nothing, Monsieur Nick," Janine said, flustered. "Would you like some coffee?"

He shook his head. His damp hair gleamed like black ice, but his Mediterranean-blue eyes held warmth. The corners of his eyes crinkled. "It's good to have a dream. A goal."

Good. He wasn't letting the wary housekeeper push him away this time. "Janine's dream is to own a restaurant." Vanessa turned to the woman. "Caribbean cuisine?"

Nick slipped an arm around Vanessa and pulled her against him. He was all heat and hardness and woodsy scent. Oh, how she wished this casual affection were for real. She linked her hands at her waist before she yielded to an impulse to touch his freshly shaven cheek.

"Caribbean, yes. Island cooking."

A disdainful snort came from the breakfast bar.

The housekeeper's gaze darted to her daughter and Ray.

Scowling, Lise scooped books and papers into her backpack. Ray jammed folded papers in the pocket of his worn camouflage jacket.

"I got a class," Lise barked, as the two shot down the stairs that led to the garage.

"Lise doesn't approve of your dream?" Vanessa asked.

The other woman lifted her shoulders and tilted her head in a classic Gallic shrug. She began to slice the banana bread. "She does not believe it is possible."

Nick filched a slice of the warm and fragrant bread. "You have two necessary ingredients, talent and hard work. You'll get there." He bit into the slice and murmured his delight.

Janine flashed him the first genuine smile Vanessa thought she'd ever granted him. "Thank you, Monsieur Nick."

A rush of pleasure swept through Vanessa's blood, warming and softening. In spite of the turmoil and anger inside, his kindness and sense of fair play shone through.

Saturday he'd protected her with his body.

With his life.

He hadn't been injured, physically. She knew the carnage was emotional, and her heart bled for him. The shooting incident had thrown him unwillingly into combat mode and revived his nightmare. The adrenaline rush had left him sweating and shaking. When she'd tried to thank him for protecting her, he wouldn't discuss it. Today he seemed to have shoved the demons back in their cages.

She slipped an arm around his slim waist and nudged him toward the door. "I'd better get this man out of the kitchen before he eats up all the food."

"Thanks, Janine." He snagged another slice. "I plan to work the import staff hard. They'll need sustenance."

Vanessa slipped from beneath his arm as soon as they had passed through the sunroom. Being near him danced electric attraction on her nerves. Those careless embraces were to convince everyone of her identity as his fiancée.

She needed no convincing. Quite the opposite.

They continued in silence to the library, where Nick had organized clipboards with copies of Alexei's inventory and appraisal list. The import staff, experienced with art and antiques, would compare the listed values to the rooms' contents. Whether or not they found some new priceless treasure, the inventory would be updated, ready for auction.

Nick leaned against the mahogany desk. "Could Janine or those two kids know where the ten-million-dollar jackpot is?"

Vanessa flipped through one of the clipboard lists. She narrowed her eyes. "The kids might know where things could be hidden in this house. Janine has no idea, doesn't want to know. She just shakes her head about your brother and how obsessed he was with wealth."

Nick levered away from the desk and lifted the clipboard from her. He tossed it back on the desk and took her hand in both of his.

"Thanks for helping with this whole thing. I'm glad it's you here with me."

Her gaze tangled with his. The anxiety and affection in those deep blue pools dissolved her effort at distance. The seductive stroking of his thumb on her palm stirred an ache deep within her. Her heart slammed against her ribs. She shouldn't ask, but the words came out anyway.

"And...not Danielle?"

# Chapter 9

Nick rolled his eyes. "Danielle wouldn't have the patience or the generosity."

How odd. What was his relationship with his fiancée? Theirs was a strange sort of engagement, with him coming on to a substitute. Curiosity elbowed aside detachment.

She pursed her lips, ready to delve. Bad idea for lots of reasons, but she couldn't seem to stop. "I haven't heard you say more than a few words about Danielle in the two weeks we've been together. And those words have mostly been critical. You don't talk—or act—like a man in love."

His eyes narrowed. "You have the mike on?"

Her free hand flew to the high-tech pin on her sweater. She didn't blame him for wanting to keep his love life private. Anxiety tightened her stomach at what intimate secrets he might reveal to her. Did she really want to know?

"Mike's off, but I'll turn it on when the import staff arrive. Even though they've been vetted, the CO's antsy about their running free in the house."

He lifted one shoulder, and his gaze slid away. But he didn't release her hand. "Love doesn't enter into my relationship with Danielle. We have an...arrangement."

"An arrangement. What do you mean?"

"Our marriage will be mutually beneficial. She gets security, prestige."

"Sounds more like a merger than a marriage. What's your benefit from this contract?"

"A hostess." He eyed Vanessa. "Regular sex."

Glaring back at him, she yanked her hand away. "Arm candy. What else?"

His throaty exhalation was a good imitation of Lise's snort. "Mamas will stop throwing their socialite daughters at me. Women will stop seeing me only as rich husband material."

He folded his arms, pulling the crew neck of his white sweater down so her gaze was drawn to the crisp, dark hairs curling at the base of his strong neck.

She dragged her gaze back up to his smoldering eyes. "Sounds like Danielle."

"At least she's honest about it. No fake lovesick sighs or declarations of love."

Like the guys who used to hit on her to wangle an introduction to Diana. The painful similarity hit Vanessa square on the chest.

She hadn't given up. But he had.

She considered changing the subject. Her probe had surpassed professional need to know. She cared about him. The new insights ought to deter her. Instead empathy propelled her onward. A loveless marriage would be a grave mistake for a man who felt so deeply.

Her chin went up. "And what about a family, children?"

"No children." He clamped his mouth into a grim line.

Her heart twisted at the pain and longing that flickered in his eyes before pride concealed it. "But home and family are what marriage is all about. Kids to play ball with, to read bedtime stories to, to teach to ride a bike. A family to love. You don't want that?"

He strode around the desk and organized the already organized clipboards. A muscle jumped in his jaw. "I won't cheat a family by not being there for them."

Ah, he didn't want to be an absentee father like his. He didn't trust in love from others, and he didn't trust himself not to fail those he loved.

She leaned forward, her palms on the desk. "Nick," she said softly, "you're not your father."

She felt his heated glare burning a hole through her.

"You don't know anything about it," he said in a raspy, disgusted voice. "You see me here full-time. But this domesticity is temporary. I travel from New York to London to Hong Kong. My business is important. I don't have time for home and family."

"Bull-oney! You're lying to yourself. You're the poster boy for family loyalty. You've hidden Alexei's crimes and the circumstances of his death from your father, the father you love in spite of his absence from your life."

"How could I tell him? He's a sick old man."

"You've left your business to try to redeem your family's honor and make up for the transgressions of a half brother you despise. Think about it."

"I had no choice."

"Oh, you had a choice. You could've let ATSA handle everything. You could've stayed in New York. You could've shipped Alexei's ashes to New York or Athens for burial. You could've flown off to join your *real* fiancée. No choice? There are always choices."

He leaned on his palms and brought his face so close to hers she felt his heat and the angry puff of his breath. "May I remind you that it is *my* life? And I damned well *choose* to build my company."

"For whom? Why? What do you have to prove?"

In response, chimes tolled an Oriental-sounding melody. The doorbell.

"They're here," Nick said, lifting the stack of clipboards. He marched out the library door as though at the point of a spear.

"Saved by the bell," she muttered.

Vanessa held the clipboard while Emil Alfieris foraged through the Internet for information on the marquetry table beside the spindle bed. She had to find the hidden ten million, to take it out of the equation. Then ATSA wouldn't hound her so about keeping Nick with the program. They'd have one less reason not to trust him.

For her peace of mind, what she needed was more reasons not to trust the man. More reasons to hold the line. The line she'd leapt across this morning like a broad jumper. And landed with both feet in his love life!

She shook her head and returned to her task. So far the inventory wasn't making her hopeful of finding Alexei's stash. This bedroom at the end of the hall seemed to hold all the antiquey clutter he couldn't find other places for. Every bend of an elbow threatened some delicate object.

None of them priceless.

Dammit, she'd threatened something priceless earlier. The tenuous rapport she had with Nick.

She should've kept her mouth shut. If he wanted a marriage of convenience with Ms. Iceberg LeBec, that was his decision. No, even if her probing skewered tender spots, she wasn't sorry. Not if it made him think more deeply about what he was getting into. Her concern was for him, for his happiness.

His marrying Danielle made no difference to her personally. If she believed that, she wouldn't have thistles rolling around in her belly pricking her. She wouldn't feel this hot tightness in her throat.

No involvement, remember? She was supposed to be proving to herself she could remain detached and neutral, but she was failing miserably.

"Ah, here it is." Alfieris clicked madly on his laptop. His bow tie bobbed with his Adam's apple as he spoke. "It's a reproduction. Too bad. This listing has it at $400."

She ran her finger down the list. "The inventory says $350. Should I change it?"

"I'd leave it. You probably won't get more than that at auction anyway."

She glanced down the list. "We're already halfway through. You're good at this, Emil. Quite the expert."

The dapper little man beamed at her. "Thanks. Someday I'd like to have my own antique shop."

"I suppose a would-be dealer must already be a collector," she said.

"I have a few pieces. Nothing like Alexei." He lowered his gaze to a tall cobalt-blue-and-white urn. "Nothing like this. Alexei has it listed as eighteenth-century Ming-style, but that's wrong." He turned the urn upside down. "This four-character mark is by the early fourteenth-century Imperial artist Hongwu. Perfect condition. Typical dragon and phoenix design."

"You must have to be careful. Choose wisely, I mean."

"Right. I don't want to waste money." He set down the urn and tapped on the keyboard. "Wish I had some of that pricey stock Alexei sold for those terrorists. Chinese cabinets and Assyrian plaques and bronze statues. I'd be all set."

"And how about that urn?" Maybe the Ming was their El Dorado. She held her breath.

Alfieris emitted an appreciative whistle. "Whoa, this is the most valuable piece we've found today."

"How much?"

"Looks like at least fifty grand. Here, I'll write down the description." He slid the clipboard from her hand.

Vanessa slumped. A week ago if anyone had told her she'd

be disappointed at a find worth fifty thousand dollars, she'd have called them nuts.

"What's next?" she asked.

A complete ass. That's what he'd been, allowing her to suck him into that useless argument. Why should he have to defend his life to her? She didn't understand. She couldn't.

Nick tramped from room to room observing the import staff as they examined and measured every piece of furniture and art, estimating and comparing with the research on their laptops. But his thoughts barely grazed the household inventory, or even the reason for it.

No, damn it, his addled brain ping-ponged between the shooting attack and today's stupid confrontation with Vanessa the Confessor.

*What do you have to prove?* Ridiculous question.

He had nothing to prove to anyone. He ran N.D.M. for himself, for the challenge, for the commitment and control. He was responsible for hundreds of employees, for a network of buyers and distributors. Achieving success and immersing himself in work were matters of pride, of honor. He shouldn't have to tell Vanessa that. Or anyone.

What he did have to do was tell Vanessa about his engagement. To tell the truth—at least to himself—if Danielle hadn't ended it, he would've pulled the plug before any exchange of vows. Not that Vanessa was right about the kind of marriage he wanted.

He should've told her the truth at the outset. Damned awkward at this point. He cared about her. A lot. Just seeing her every morning lightened the load, made the day go a little easier. He had to find the right words, the right time.

Deception was her stock in trade. Maybe his lie of omission wouldn't matter to her.

Like hell.

* * *

In the living room, Celia Chin glanced up from the blue vase she held. "So far, Mr. Markos, the inventory appears to match what I'm finding."

"Excellent. Keep up the good work." He slid from the room before she launched into her acquisitions-and-contacts litany.

Vanessa was upstairs, helping Emil Alfieris, probably opening him up like a clam. Her way of making people comfortable enough to blurt out their secrets combined with subtle questioning skills fascinated him. *She* fascinated him.

But Nick would keep away. Let her work as coolly as if she hadn't been shot at two days ago.

Besides the fact that no one was hurt, the only good thing about the shooting incident was that his combat instincts were still intact. He'd dived into protection mode and covered Vanessa. Not that she'd wanted shielding. Professional that she was, she'd struggled to get a better look at the shooter and the vehicle.

No, ol' GI Joe had kept her pinned so she couldn't see. But damn it, he'd protected her, want it or not. She hadn't been shot. No one had been hurt.

Not like in Somalia.

But escaping unscathed had been luck, not any foresight on his part. Or ATSA's, for that matter. Going for a walk on their own had delivered her right into New Dawn's sights. Stupid? Sure as hell.

But wasn't setting her up exactly what ATSA had in mind by putting her undercover?

His chest hurt from the ache in his heart, from wanting this whole sordid mess over and done with. Not finding Alexei's blood money twisted knots in his gut. Vanessa's being in danger yanked them tighter.

He'd rather have her safe than all the honor in the world.

The terrorists had tried to kill her this time. Snow'd reported that the green sedan with its stolen license plate had vanished into traffic. The two bullets dug out of the grass had landed too damned close to where they'd gone down.

Had Husam Al-Din given up on the kidnapping scenario? Had he changed plans because he suspected a trap?

Vanessa's life and safety meant far more than any cost to Nick. He could handle a case of the shakes if New Dawn tried again. He'd do his best to defend her, but ATSA needed to stick closer. They'd be stupid to trust him to spot ambushes.

That thought tied another kink in the knots.

A good workout was what she needed, Vanessa decided that evening. Nobody should be in the gym at eleven. She'd have the place to herself. A run on the treadmill, some weights, and exhaustion would be her lullaby.

The entire mission was not going well. The finished inventory had uncovered no treasures, no ten-million-dollar objet d'art. ATSA had found no links between any of Nick's business contacts and the New Dawn Warriors.

She'd found more on Somalia, but needed facts before she broached that topic with him again. Since their "discussion," the tension between them, thick and gummy as a model's hair spray, recast their engagement charade as engagement farce.

Dressed in leggings and an old tank top—hers, not one chosen by Danielle—she jogged into the downstairs gym.

And stopped dead.

Nick stood at the far end of the room. He wore black gym shorts and sneakers. That was all. No shirt. He was doing curls with free weights—what looked like a thirty-pounder in each hand. Gleaming with sweat, his impressive biceps heaved, his neck tendons bulged and his shoulder sinews bunched. No gloves. Now she knew where the calluses came from.

Her pulse stuttered, and heat licked up her spine. Run on a treadmill? She could barely catch her breath at the sight of him. Concentrate? She'd trip over her own feet.

Vanessa started to back out the way she'd come.

"Don't go." Nick deposited the barbells on their rack.

She took a tentative step into the room. Maybe he was finished. He'd leave, and she'd be able to breathe after all. "Um, you don't mind?"

"I'm not Alexei," he said, his dark brows diving into a scowl.

"I'm sorry. I didn't mean—"

"I apologize. Of course you didn't. It's me. I was just making myself angry all over again. I fume about his lavish lifestyle, yet I make free use of his extravagances." He spread his arms to indicate the gym. "*You* might as well."

"No need to martyr yourself because you disapprove." She strolled over to the treadmill and stretched back her left leg, then her right to ready the muscles.

"I'll work my anger out with the bag." He jammed red leather boxing gloves on his hands and yanked the laces tight with his teeth.

Vanessa pushed buttons on the treadmill and began a slow jog. "Pretend it's Husam Al-Din."

With his first swing at the leather bag, he barked a laugh, the first she'd heard from him since Monday. He hit slowly at first, then worked into a rhythm of left-right, left-right that set a demanding pace for her run.

She increased her speed. Looking away, she tried to focus on the wall ahead and on her balance. No luck. Her gaze kept veering back to the man pummeling the terrorist's stand-in. Fit male bodies were no novelty to her, for goodness' sake. She had two jock brothers, after all. And she'd done physical training with the best, both in the FBI and in ATSA.

Who was she kidding? This was Nick. He was more than a fit male body. Powerful, protective and tormented, he had more layers than the padded gloves he wore. Desire and fascination, not curiosity, glued her attention to the slide of sinew on bone, to the taut grid of abs dusted with ebony hairs, to the arrogant nose and fierce, uncompromising line of his jaw.

Her foot caught on the rubber tread.

*Oof!*

She dropped on her side like a felled tree. The impact blew her breath out in a whoosh. In the next instant, the conveyor belt dumped her on the floor in a heap.

"My God, *latrea mou,* are you hurt?" Nick knelt beside her, a worried expression darkening his face.

She couldn't answer. A steel belt cinched her chest, squeezing her lungs flat. No sharp pains stabbed her, just an overall ache that radiated through her body. Breath by halting breath, her lungs reinflated.

"I…I'm okay." She closed her eyes and concentrated on inhaling.

"Don't move yet. Let's make sure." Soft pats traveled up her legs and back and down her arms. "Nothing broken, I think. Can you sit up?"

"I think so." Opening her eyes, she twisted upright. Then she laughed. "I've heard of handling someone with kid gloves, but I don't think they meant this style."

Humor glinting in the blue depths of his eyes, he held out his boxing gloves for her to unlace. "Would you have let me inspect your…attributes without them?"

In that moment the earlier strain between them morphed into a different tension. His stare held enough sizzle to melt her running shoes. Her heart gave a kangaroo kick. Flustered, she fumbled with the gloves until finally the laces gave.

"I think I can get up now. I'm all right." Everything worked, but her shoulder protested.

He dropped the gloves and held her hand. "Give it another minute. Just to be sure." When she started to object, he said, "Humor me," and sat back on his heels.

They were close enough that she could've reached out to trace the salt trails down his chest. His heat and hardness and male sweat might have repelled, but instead they mesmerized.

What was it about this man that sent her hormones into

cartwheels? Her body thrummed with awareness as she sat beside him on the hard floor. She couldn't just sit here staring at him. Talk. That was it. Talk about…

"Yes?" He bent closer and peered at her. "You started to say something?"

Ye gods, she was an idiot with men. It was a wonder they even wanted to be her pal. "The tapes. Um, the analysts finished with the videotapes."

"Ah, and what evildoers lurked on them?" The merest hint of sarcasm colored his words.

His deep voice resonated within her. She suppressed a shiver. "As I think you already suspect, none. The faces on the tapes match the guest and employee list."

"Even all the Yamaris? No New Dawn moles?"

"All accounted for and identified." Remembering something else, she pursed her lips. "That reminds me. Grant Snow tells me you took a phone call from Prince Amir. *For me.*" She cocked an eyebrow and waited.

He released her hand. "The bastard changed his tune when I answered. Probably wanted to arrange a private rendezvous."

She smiled at the fury in his tone, the fire in his eyes. "What *did* he arrange?"

"Asked me to be sure to bring you to our luncheon tomorrow. Said he had a gift for you from his country." He picked up one of the leather gloves and slung it across the room. "How dare the bastard come on to my fiancée like that!"

Was he beginning to believe their act? Foolish hope fluttered her heart. "Nick, your show of jealousy is flattering. You don't need to bellow like a wounded buffalo. May I remind you that your fiancée is in London?"

He sighed like a deflating dirigible. "Ah, but she isn't."

# Chapter 10

Vanessa straightened. She winced and rubbed her shoulder where she'd landed on it. "What do you mean?"

"My fiancée isn't in London. She isn't anywhere. I don't have a fiancée." His head drooped like a chastised puppy. "I should've told you this in the beginning, but I thought it might affect the op."

"Tell me what?" Although her instincts already knew.

"Danielle broke up with me after the attempted kidnapping. Said she wanted no man who trafficked with thieves and murderers. She was afraid of scandal more than the terrorists. At any rate, I'm no longer engaged."

Vanessa stared at him with suspicion. "Not engaged. Why didn't Danielle tell me?"

He clasped her hands in his. "I convinced her that silence was safer. But if I know her, she's keeping her options open until she sees how this plays out."

Building anger sharpened Vanessa's tongue. "Is that what you were doing? Keeping your options open?"

"With ATSA? Or with you?"

Once again a man had deceived her, had used her. His pretense couldn't compare to men reaching Diana through her, but she didn't want to examine that. She needed to hold on to her ire, clutch it to her as a shield. Getting involved with her assignment had once again come back to bite her.

Righteous indignation burned her cheeks. She firmed her mouth. "Take your pick."

He shook his head. "I was afraid the trap might not work if the truth leaked out. I didn't plan on being attracted to you. I think you feel the same. Awkward, but there it is. I'm sorry for the mixed messages. I should've told you long ago."

"And that whole thing about a sterile marriage—that was a lie too?" She struggled to her knees.

He clamped his big hands on her shoulders to prevent her from rising farther. "No. Everything I said was true. But arguing about it prodded me to analyze my goals and motives."

"Bully for me." She shoved at his chest. He released her and sat back as she scrambled to her feet. "I don't believe you. You've lied to me from the beginning. You lied to ATSA."

Her heart throbbed with anger at his deception. She'd been right not to trust him. If he lied to her about the broken engagement, couldn't he be lying about his reasons for cooperating with ATSA? Or about his feelings for her? She knew him well enough by now to know the answer to the first. And she was afraid to examine the second. Not daring to look at him, she stomped to the doorway.

But his voice, or her ambivalence, stopped her there.

"The attraction between us, coming to care for you—it was unexpected. I confess to using the engagement as a defense tactic." The magnetic power of his liquid velvet words curled around the muscles of her chest.

"Camouflage, not defense." But hadn't she done the same thing? She wielded her duty to spy on him as a defense against her feelings. The tactic didn't work for either of them. Her only defense for the moment was keeping her back to him.

"You were right about the arrangement being more of a merger than a marriage. I can see now it wouldn't have worked out." He paused, and his voice lowered to a husky rumble when he continued. "For lots of reasons."

*Am I one of those reasons?*

She clamped her lips so the words wouldn't slip from her brain to her mouth. He wasn't engaged. He'd lied, hadn't he?

But… *Ye gods, he's not engaged.*

Danielle was history. He was free.

Anger floated away and disintegrated like soap bubbles on a summer breeze. In spite of her reservations, her heart skipped happy dance steps.

But… *Oh, no, he's not engaged.*

He was free. One less barrier to keeping her detached. Uninvolved. Who was she kidding? Only herself. She might as well admit that she'd left *uninvolved* in the distant dust.

She turned around to face him.

He rose on his knees. The sincerity in his blue eyes held her. "I didn't lie about my attraction to you. I think you know that. Come here, Vanessa."

As if drawn by an invisible force, she found herself kneeling on the mat with him.

Surrounding her with his heat and scent, he pulled her close. His thumbs traced circles on the bare skin of her shoulders, and heat spiraled from the pit of her stomach to seep through her body.

The moment spun out on a fine strand of sensuality.

The need for her fisted into Nick, delivered a punch to the groin. The scent of her sweet, wild energy floated to him with her shampoo and female musk. The raspberry-colored leggings defined her toned yet lush body. The tank top stretched over her full breasts. When she'd appeared in the doorway, he'd nearly dropped the barbells on his feet.

She was different from the society women he knew—dedicated, competent and caring. But trusting her beyond sex and the moment was impossible. Deception was her profession.

At the moment he didn't care. He had her in his arms.

Her fall had knocked the French braid askew. Tendrils corkscrewed wildly around her delicate face. He tugged the rest loose and buried his hands in the silken mass.

She was warm and passionate. That was real. She wanted him as much as he wanted her. He saw it in her vibrant green eyes, in the tilt of her head, in the softness of her lips.

He lowered his head and took her mouth. Her sweetness flowed into him, deep and drugging and addictive. The feather touch of her fingertips on his chest hardened him to steel. His hand found one breast, cupped its lush weight, teased the nipple into attention.

She melted against him, and he palmed her shirt and bra out of the way. He took her turgid nipple in his mouth to absorb more of her essence. When she sighed, he began to sink to the floor with her in his arms.

She stiffened. "Wait, Nick. Oh, stop."

Light-headed with desire, he forced himself to pull away. "What is it? What's wrong?"

Adjusting her earpiece, she scooted into a sitting position. "Two men have just broken through the back fence."

She leapt to her feet and dashed out the door.

Nick reeled from the about-face. What was she doing? He had to stop her before she ran out into danger in her raspberry tights. Still groggy, he staggered to his feet.

He caught up with her in the darkened sunroom.

She stood at the terrace door, her fingers wrapped around the handle.

"Don't," he said, crossing the room to join her. "Your cover could be compromised. It's a good bet they're armed."

Vanessa turned from staring out the glass-paneled door. She folded her arms. The movement tightened the sexy tank top across her breasts and made it harder for him to emerge from his sensual fog.

Harder, yes. The nylon shorts hid nothing. Thank you for a dark room.

"Give me some credit, Nick," she said, yanking her hair back and binding it with an elastic doodad.

Reality slapped him a stinging blow. He'd jumped to a wrong conclusion. Plus he'd insulted her professionalism. "You weren't going out there. You were just watching." He could kick himself. At least his body was subsiding.

"Right." Her smile deadened the sting of his blunder.

"I apologize for my brain short-out, but not for wanting to protect you." ATSA'd placed her in his care. That was that.

"Protecting me is ATSA's job. Look outside."

He noticed for the first time that brilliant spotlights turned night into day. The glare illuminated grass, trees, shrubs and at least a dozen people. Men and women in black jumpsuits encircled two figures prone on the stone terrace.

"They caught the intruders."

She grinned. "Just as planned. Now maybe we'll get somewhere with finding their leader."

"Don't count on it. Convincing them to talk could be harder than bargaining with my Hong Kong supplier. Husam Al-Din still wants the ten million. You're still in danger."

Outside, ATSA personnel hauled the two captives to their feet. Shackled hand and foot, they were marched around the house and away. Moments later, the house and grounds once again lay in darkness. No moon penetrated the cloud cover.

But the light of understanding penetrated Vanessa's brain. She watched the slight leap of a muscle in Nick's neck, the rigid angle of his jaw. His protective drive grew from roots deep in his soul, the same roots as his sense of honor.

That perception and Nick's revelation about the engagement clarified nothing, only confused her. The burgeoning feelings in her heart tossed and plunged in an emotional storm. She'd be foolish to think his freedom made any difference.

Being sidetracked with sex might interfere with ATSA's operation. Part of her job was to be suspicious of him, to check his computer files, to make sure he stayed with the program. She wanted to trust him. She did trust him.

But he wasn't for her. She had no luck with men, and this man had sure disaster—a shipwreck of her heart—stamped on his forehead. He was rich and powerful and sexy. She wasn't the type of woman he wanted. Not really.

She was just…handy.

If she remembered that, maybe she could pull back. She'd lost the battle to remain neutral and uninvolved, but she could draw a new line. She could help him shake some of his demons. He could get on with his life. And so could she.

She turned to him, but clasped her hands behind her back. Touching him might sink her good intentions. He'd kissed her into oblivion, and they'd almost had sex on the gym floor. Ye gods, she still tingled. He'd donned a T-shirt. Good. She could talk to him without the added distraction of his sculpted chest. Maybe.

"I'm hitting the shower. We won't know any more about those guys tonight." He started to walk away.

"Nick, you can't be responsible for everything. You're no more responsible for my safety than you were for what happened in Somalia." Which he still hadn't spelled out for her.

Halfway across the room, he stopped and pivoted. Light from the hallway silhouetted him. She noted the stiff set of his shoulders, the tight stance, the deceptively casual curl of his hands alongside his sinewy thighs.

She'd touched more than one nerve. Swallowing her trepidation, she waited. She couldn't see his face, but knew his brows had pulled together over a formidable glare.

"What do you mean? Do you know something I don't?"

"Not yet. I've been…researching. On the computer. The sparse data about that mission is suspicious."

"Suspicious. How?" In precise, military strides, he returned to face her. Tension rolled off him like sweat.

She forced herself to look into those intense, frosty eyes. "The four men who died are listed as killed in combat, with no details. Reports filed by your commander and his exec are just as sketchy as the paragraph in your file."

"Cover-up," he said in a flat tone. "No surprise. The mission was classified. That doesn't absolve me. I know what happened. What I did and failed to do."

She shook her head. "After the wipeout in Mogadishu, other classified ops were leaked. Never this one. Why would command protect a green assistant operations sergeant?"

Approaching footsteps brought Nick's head around. He hunched over in a combative stance.

Grant Snow appeared in the doorway. He flicked on the overhead lights.

Nick straightened slowly, his face a bland mask.

"What're you two doing here in the dark? Show's long over." Holding up a sheaf of papers, Snow crossed to them.

"Let me guess," Vanessa said. "Our burglars have warbled like the proverbial stool pigeons. ATSA has Husam Al-Din in custody. The op's over."

The tightness in her throat cut her glib chatter. If the gig ended, so would her sojourn with this man she shouldn't care for.

"Dream on, kid," Snow replied. "But we did find some interesting evidence on the New Dawn agents." He spread out his three papers on the nearest table.

Each of the sheets of ordinary white copy paper contained pen-and-ink diagrams labeled in English block capitals. Under each word were characters in another alphabet.

"The house," Nick said, bending over the table. "The bastards had plans of the house. Where'd these come from?"

"I was hoping you could tell me, Mr. M." He peered at Nick expectantly. "Were they stolen from the house?"

"I've never seen them before. These drawings are crude, not to scale. Someone who's been inside drew them."

"Possibly from memory." With a forefinger, Snow tapped the page showing the second floor. "Our translator tells me these Yamari words are translations of the English ones. 'Master bedroom, Bath, D's room.'"

"*D* for Danielle. Ye gods, they know where I sleep." Vanessa peered at the drawing. "Everyone was supposed to think I'm, um, sleeping with Nick. How did they plan to get to me?"

Snow shrugged. "Maybe wait in your room until morning and snatch you then. We'll try to find out."

"How well were the burglars prepared?" Nick asked.

"They had it all. Ace tools. Detectors for picking locks and other electronics for freezing security. Berettas with silencers and a syringe full of something yet to be analyzed." Snow refolded the papers and pocketed them. "If we hadn't nabbed them, who knows how far they might've gotten."

A syringe. They'd planned to drug her. Vanessa felt the blood drain from her head. Until now, she'd felt safe in the house.

Nick edged a step closer to her as if to defend her from the would-be kidnappers. Unnecessary, but his instinctive move eased her nerves from jumping-bean force.

"The house plans have to be recent," Nick ruminated. "Only a few people besides ATSA officers have had access during the last few weeks."

Vanessa nodded, thinking of Monday's inventory. "The import staff crawled all over the house like ants. Janine and Lise are here three times a week, but they wouldn't..."

"And Ray," Nick said. "Don't forget Ray. When I entered the kitchen the other morning, he slipped some papers in his pocket. Could've been these sketches."

\* \* \*

After Snow left, Vanessa and Nick trudged upstairs.

"If you dig up any more on Somalia, I want to know." Nick's even tone belied the intense emotion she knew lurked below the surface.

"Okay. You thinking about what I said?"

"Yeah." He uttered the word with the finality of a slammed door.

Time to move along. Too much probing at any one time scraped old wounds raw and bleeding.

"We may have a lead in a few days on who provided the map." Yawning, she stopped at the bathroom door. "ATSA will check bank accounts, tap phones and increase surveillance. Whoever it is may slip up, or New Dawn may contact them."

Stiffness from her fall was creeping into her joints. She needed sleep. And ibuprofen. She rolled her sore shoulder.

"Al-Din'll know soon—if he doesn't already—that his burglar-kidnappers failed, that they're in custody. He'll know my protection isn't just paid bodyguards. What he might do next is anyone's guess." He leaned against the doorjamb.

His apparent calm didn't deceive her. She recognized the wary stillness and cold, predatory gaze. Special Forces mode.

Protecting her meant he was breaking his own rule about avoiding combat situations. ATSA wouldn't allow him in the loop. She had to convince him to back off. For his own good.

And she had to back off from him. For her own good.

"You have a point, but the CO planned for this. Word's already out that Chevy Chase's finest have arrested two men for breaking and entering at this address. When they're suspected of being illegal aliens, they'll disappear into federal custody and off the radar screen."

She yawned again, covering her mouth with one hand. "Now if you'll excuse me, I need a shower and some sleep."

"I'll be on guard here while you shower." He didn't move from his position.

"On guard? That's not necessary now. The excitement's over for tonight."

"Take your shower."

"But Nick—"

"I saw your face when Snow listed their little bag of tricks. You were scared, professional or not. You had every right to be. I'll be here."

She slumped. He was right. She was still scared. And too tired to fight about it. "Thanks, Nick. I won't be long."

Hot needles of water drilling into her back leached the stiffness from her muscles, but couldn't wash away what her brain conjured up.

One minute, in the swirl of water, she saw two dark forms looming over her bed. She shivered with fear.

The next, she pictured Nick, divested of his shirt and shorts, joining her in the shower. Shampooing her hair revived the sensation of his fingers spearing through it and cradling her head. Lathering up made her nipples tingle at the reminder of his mouth on her. Her heartbeat sped and pulses throbbed.

At this rate, if she slept at all, she'd have X-rated dreams instead of nightmares.

She rinsed and dried off quickly. She wrapped one of the guest terry-cloth robes around her and sleeked her damp hair back from her face. When she left the bathroom, sure enough, Nick was standing guard.

The tang of male sweat triggered the image of moisture gleaming on his burnished-olive muscles as he beat the punching bag into submission.

"Don't you need a shower, too, Rocky?"

"I'll clean up as soon as you're settled. Get whatever you need for the night. You're sleeping in my bed."

At first she didn't think she'd heard him right. But he waited, patient and still. Inflexible. Resolute.

The nerve of the man! Anger boiled up her neck into her

cheeks. "Now listen, Mister Caveman. Just because we shared a hot kiss—"

"Honey, I'd call what we shared more than a kiss." The corner of his lips twitched, and the look in his eyes went from confident to cocky.

"—doesn't mean I'll hop in your bed at your command." She yanked the robe collar more tightly about her neck and turned toward her room. She didn't have a whole lot of experience, but she was no doormat.

"I know that."

"What?"

"I wasn't inviting you to *share* my bed. Although I'd be lying if I said I didn't want you naked with me on those decadent silk sheets." His languid gaze cruised her body as if penetrating the thick robe.

Sparks danced along her nerves. The back of her throat dried. She tried to swallow. "What, then?"

The hot look dialed down to cool and assessing. "Vanessa, you'll be safer in the master suite. You can have the bed. The security monitor will be right beside you. And don't worry— I'll sleep on the floor."

And how long would that arrangement last? He already had her off balance. *It's not you he wants, Vanessa. It's the illusion, the role.* The man turned her on without even trying. Her efforts about clearing up Somalia slipped her further into his life. But she would draw the line at sex. If she were to survive undercover, she had to.

Facing facts strengthened her resolve, but didn't douse the flame he'd ignited.

"I'll be all right in this room," she said. "The fence is fixed and the bad guys are gone."

"And you'll sleep like a baby? You won't lie awake listening to every creak and groan in this old house? Hearing footsteps? Or tools on the locks?"

"Well…"

"You don't know they were alone. You don't know that was the only map. ATSA protection isn't with you 24/7. I am. Or I will be from now on."

Every feminine instinct she possessed to the contrary, a few minutes later she found herself ensconced in the king-sized bed in her faded old nightgown. Maybe the long sleeves and high neck would quell his libido. And hers. Maybe she could fall asleep before he got out of the shower.

The water was running. She pictured it coursing over his shoulders, over slabs and ridges of muscle and through crisp hairs curling around his flat nipples. Down his belly to—

Flopping over on her stomach, Vanessa pulled the pillow over her head. She shut her eyes.

The shower stopped. She heard thuds as he stepped from the tiled stall. Now he was drying off. Stretching the big, fluffy towel behind him, working it back and forth to dry his shoulders, his back, his taut butt.

At that image, a pulse throbbed between her legs, and heat spread through her body. She squeezed her thighs together.

*Don't think about him.*

But if she didn't think about him, her thoughts meandered to her precarious position as target. Nick was right. Alone in that other room, she wouldn't have been able to relax.

Not that she was relaxed now.

And she couldn't stop thinking about him. Everything about this Greek tycoon was contrary to what she expected. Yes, he had his arrogant moments. He liked to be in charge, but she felt protected and cared for, not patronized. He perceived her fear and insisted on watching over her, yet he respected her abilities.

In shock, she lifted up on her elbows so suddenly she knocked the pillow on the floor. She'd done what she'd sworn not to do.

She loved him.

No denying it. She was in love with a rich man who preferred society women or models like Diana. In love with a man who didn't believe in love. In love with a man her job forced her to spy on and distrust. Impossible.

She retrieved the pillow and sank down with it over her head. Her heart pounded like native drums. The steel belt again banded her chest, and she hitched up the pillow for more air. But she didn't dare come out from under.

Even in the dark, he'd see her heart in her eyes.

From beneath the pillow, she heard the bathroom door open. Bare feet padded to the sitting area. He dragged the cushions from the settee onto the floor. The bed gave as he snatched a pillow.

A blanket flapped. A body settled. Sighed deeply.

Only a few feet away.

Then silence except for Nick's even breathing.

And her drumming heart.

# Chapter 11

The next afternoon, Nick took Vanessa's arm as they left the Canal Bistro. They paused on the deck while they waited for their companions.

Vanessa gave a three-sixty-degree perusal of the area, ostensibly admiring the dramatic view. That and the Mediterranean cuisine made the restaurant Georgetown's newest rage.

"All clear. Snow, we're ready," she whispered into her lapel-pin mike, then turned toward the river.

Nick leaned an elbow on the railing as he scanned the few diners occupying the deck with them. Not that he distrusted Vanessa's judgment, but an extra pair of eyes couldn't hurt. Upscale shoppers with Georgetown Park shopping bags and upcoming professionals with laptop cases, all with cellular phones no bigger than a credit card.

No one suspicious. No one paying them any attention.

"Look, Nick." Vanessa pointed to the right across the

C & O Canal. "There's the Key Bridge to Virginia. I love that old bridge, but the Potomac looks better on a sunny day."

Nick relaxed and slung an arm around her shoulders. "I have the view I prefer right here."

She grinned and poked him in the ribs.

He was close enough to enjoy how good she smelled—a subtle fresh scent and female flesh. Close enough to enjoy her female curves pressed against him. And close enough to admire her creamy cheeks and the dusting of freckles across her nose.

In three-inch heels, she still seemed small beside him, delicate. She was anything but. Bad guys with God-knows-what drugs had frightened her, but she'd have toughed out the night if he hadn't insisted on moving her into his bed.

He could've had her last night. She wanted him as much as he wanted her. His damned sense of honor'd stopped him from taking advantage of her anxious state. Another night of togetherness would pump the torture level to the red zone.

Her night had been as wakeful as his. He just hadn't wrestled the sheets as much—a by-product of SF training. The only sign of fatigue was the droop to her eyelids. Sexy, damn it. Except for the plunging neckline of the silk blouse beneath, the conservative navy pantsuit concealed most of the softness he'd held against him last night.

Discretion meant not waving a red flag at Prince Amir. Or at himself, for that matter. He'd take the trade-off.

Vanessa angled her head at him. "What is it, Nick?"

"What could be wrong besides the cloudy weather? I've just stuffed myself with lamb Niçoise and Caesar salad. I have my arm around a beautiful woman. The usual New Dawn tails took the day off. Happy Halloween."

Doubt crinkled her forehead. "I wonder if New Dawn is holding back because ATSA nabbed their burglars last night."

"They seem to change tactics every other day. At the moment I don't care. I welcome the breathing space."

"And the end of this business lunch?"

"Like clear skies after a flood." Sometimes she read his mind. Unaccountably pleased, he tightened his arm around her.

The anticipation of this blasted meeting had ground his gears since the museum reception. He had to admit the meal had rolled along smoothly. Abdul Nadim played jovial host, oiling the conversational pistons with questions and good cheer.

Ambassador Khalil, waiting to see the route of trade negotiations, kept his comments neutral. "Yamar will benefit from trade with U.S. partners," was his only input.

Prince Amir signaled interest in Nadim's ideas for sales in modern crafts as well as antiquities. While remaining as neutral as the ambassador, Nick offered ideas from his experience in the international restaurant supply business.

Business was business, Nadim had said more than once. The man was a damned persistent huckster. Nick's insistence that Markos Imports was for sale had yet to deter him.

Nadim and the others strolled out to join them.

"Do not worry, my friend," the entrepreneur said, patting his ample belly. "Our discussions are like that bountiful meal. Each delicious course will reveal itself in good time and be digested and resolved."

"I have no cause to worry, Abdul," Nick replied. "Thank you for the lunch and the stimulating conversation."

Prince Amir lounged against the railing nearby. Designer sunglasses allowed him to ogle Vanessa freely. Forgivable under the circumstances, Nick decided. The deposed prince, although attentive to "Danielle," remained courteous and respectful.

Nick's uncompromising manner on the phone had apparently stifled further trespass.

With one small exception.

Vanessa cradled her gift in her hands. About the size of a thick paperback novel, the olive-wood box was inlaid with a floral design in antique ivory and lapis lazuli. Though it was a personal gift, Nick couldn't fault the prince for such a stunning example of his country's craftsmanship.

"Thank you for the lovely present, Your Highness," Vanessa said, smiling. "I'll keep my best treasures in it."

"You are most welcome, my dear," Amir crooned in his unctuous manner. "But the most beautiful jewel is the one holding it."

Anger steamed the neckband of Nick's shirt. He'd thought the same sentiment about the diamond pendant, but hadn't had the wit to express it.

Amir made a small bow. "This jewelry box is two hundred and fifty years old, but artisans in Yamar make equally beautiful ones today."

"I foresee a perfect arrangement." Nadim gazed into an invisible crystal ball in his cupped hands. "The modern crafts in one of my businesses. The antique boxes in Markos Imports."

"It's a conspiracy," Nick said with a laugh. "Old friend, you never quit."

Vanessa shook hands with Nadim and the others, but sent a teasing look to Nick. "Business is business."

Even the dour ambassador laughed at her adoption of Nadim's favorite saying.

When Nick saw Grant Snow pulling up in the Mercedes, he managed to make their farewells.

"Sit rep," Vanessa said, requesting a situation report, as they entered the back seat.

"We've acquired an admirer," the officer said. "The green sedan again. New license plate. Also stolen. St. Gabriel has put two vehicles on them." Nick recognized another nickname for Gabe Harris, who usually coordinated their escorts.

Snow signaled and waited for a break in the traffic lane.

"Maybe ATSA can snag a couple more New Dawn warriors," Vanessa said. "Someone who will blab."

He pulled onto M Street. "We'll all have trouble in this traffic. Thick as grass on a putting green."

Antique and decorative arts shops lined the wide street.

Shoppers and tourists crowded the sidewalks. Modern buildings stood shoulder to shoulder with quaint old brick structures.

Snow stopped for a red light at the next corner. "Keep an eye on them. I have this alternate route planned out." He handed Vanessa his notes.

"You going to try to outrun them?" Vanessa asked, scanning the list of streets.

"Enough to let our guys cut them off. Here we go," he said as the light turned green. The powerful German car zipped across the intersection, leaving the sedan lagging behind. Snow hung a sharp left onto the next street.

Nick looked back. As the sedan followed up the narrow one-way, two Ford Explorers boxed it in. "Got 'em!"

"Home, Jeeves," Vanessa said. "Well done."

"Thanks, ma'am." He tipped a nonexistent chauffeur's cap. "My day'd be complete if I could get in nine holes later."

"How's New Dawn doing it?" Nick asked. The import staff knew of his meeting, but not the location. No one but ATSA personnel knew. Vanessa wore a GPS button, but it was on a secure frequency. "This car bugged? GPS or something else?"

Snow stopped at an intersection. "No way. I swept her this morning before we left the house, and she hasn't been out of my sight since."

The narrow, potholed street backed onto shops and restaurants. It curved uphill as they proceeded. On the left a jumble of trash cans and larger metal containers beside rear doors. On the right a line of parked cars.

Both could hide an ambush.

Vanessa's index finger tapped her lips, a gesture that spoke of her apprehension. He knew it bugged her that she couldn't carry a weapon.

Unease prickling his scalp, Nick started to suggest they find a more populated street.

Ahead a car door opened. A bearded man wearing a baseball cap pulled low stepped out into the street.

Adrenaline buzzed into Nick's system. He tensed for tricks not treats. He sensed Vanessa doing the same.

The man leveled a semiautomatic pistol at the windshield.

"Get down!" Snow yelled to his passengers. He stomped the accelerator and yanked the steering wheel to the left.

Bullets shattered the passenger-side windows.

The Mercedes slammed into a row of trash cans, scattering them into the street like tenpins. Bags of garbage split open and disgorged their contents across the brick pavement.

"A trap!" Vanessa smacked a hand against the console. "They used our trap to funnel us into their damn trap. We're cut off from our escort cars."

She spoke into her miniature microphone. "Harris, come in. We're under attack." Tersely she explained.

"Keep going. Get us around this container," Nick yelled.

"Backup's on the way," Vanessa said. Training and experience focused her as adrenaline revved her heart.

The car rolled to a stop against the heavy steel container. Snow slumped against the steering wheel.

"He's been hit!" She reached over the seat. "Nick, help me drag him into the other seat. I'll drive."

Pushing between the front seats, Nick muscled the other man, about the same size as he, across the console and into the passenger side. Pebbles of window glass littered the leather seat, but it couldn't be helped.

Snow clutched the side of his neck at the right shoulder. Blood trickled between his fingers and stained his shirt. He was silent in his pain, but Vanessa groaned at the sight. They had to stem the flow of blood long enough to get medical help. She snatched Snow's jacket from the driver's seat and pressed it to his wound. "Hold that tight."

She could see no sign of their attacker, but heard an engine fire up. Beyond the container, trash cans clattered as someone rolled them out of the way. "We have to move fast." She started to climb into the front.

"I'll drive," Nick said, shaking his head. "It's my car."

"You don't know the streets. I do." She wriggled between the seats and into the driver's seat. "Trust me."

"M-Markos," the injured driver mumbled, "take…my gun."

Vanessa watched as Nick hesitated. She knew how he felt about just this sort of ambush situation.

"I haven't fired a gun in years," he said, anguish and uncertainty in his eyes.

"Nick, there's no time. I need you." Fear, regret and recriminations could wait. "Shoot back only if you have to."

Like clicking a camera lens, he shuttered his expression. His face hard granite and his eyes blue ice, he palmed the Sig-Sauer P-226 with an assurance born of experience.

Grant Snow slumped lower. Vanessa thought he passed out. At least the bleeding seemed to have slowed.

"Get us out of here," Nick shouted.

She rotated the key in the ignition. The engine roared to life. Automatic. Not as much control as with manual. She slammed the gear shift into Reverse and backed up.

Pulse pounding in her ears, Vanessa swung the Mercedes around the left side of the metal barrier, between it and the building. The fender left sparks and silver paint as it scraped by the masonry. As the car roared away from the doorway, she had the fleeting impression of a man in a chef's hat waving a long wooden spoon and yelling.

They made it to the corner before their pursuer could pull his sedan from its parallel space.

"Three men," Nick said. "Can't tell how many weapons."

Vanessa stomped the accelerator to the floor. The Mercedes's tires shrieked as it sought traction against the bricks. The car fishtailed. She steered into the spin and controlled it. She zoomed ahead.

The attackers sped up behind them. Parked cars and trucks were the only other vehicles on this quiet back street.

*Thunk! Thunk! Thunk!*

Bullets penetrated the car's rear.

Fear scrambled Vanessa's heartbeat. She'd never forgive herself if this operation resulted in harm to Nick. She shoved the emotion away. "Nick, are you all right?"

"A-OK, honey. Just drive." His voice was tight, but sure. "I'll buy you some space."

He lowered the rear side window and fired several rounds at the other car. "They're backing off. Step on it."

A delivery van labeled with a cartoon fish had pulled out behind her. That would help.

"They're passing the van. Can you evade?" Nick fired another shot that caromed off the street.

The tan sedan hung back. So did the van.

"Roger that. Hold on!" Every muscle and nerve in her body twitching at the reins, Vanessa hung a right at the next corner, a left after that. Tires squealed, and pedestrians on the sidewalks jumped and pointed.

In the rearview mirror, she saw no tan sedan. Two other cars pulled behind them, inadvertently running interference.

Four blocks ahead the street ended in a T intersection. The cross street was a one-way left. An idea flashed in her head. If she could get there far enough ahead of them...

The buildings at the end loomed closer. She approached the stop sign. A huge delivery truck came from the right. As it entered the intersection, the driver gaped at the fast-approaching silver Mercedes. He braked and stalled his engine.

The delivery truck, as big and solid as a steel building, blocked their exit.

Excitement and anxiety spun through Vanessa. If she miscalculated, they would be a humongous bug splat.

Only a newspaper-vending machine on the sidewalk. No pedestrians, she registered. All the winters she and Jason had spun around on that frozen lake and the E&E driving learned at Quantico would pay off. She could make it.

She tapped on the brakes and whipped the wheel to the

right. The car skidded before the four-wheel drive caught purchase. It grazed the vending machine. The device wobbled, but stayed in place. The car bounded across the sidewalk.

On the cross street, Vanessa powered the Mercedes the wrong way on the one-way street.

Horns blared and brakes shrieked as vehicles swerved to avoid the crazy lady. At the next corner, she hung a sharp left and zipped up a residential, tree-lined street. She didn't know or care which direction it went.

"We're out of sight now," she said, gulping air as she slowed. "They won't know which way we headed."

"Impressive," Nick said. "You ever do any stunt driving?"

She laughed, albeit a little nervously. "I'll tell you all about it sometime. First we need to get Snow to a doctor."

She punched her mike. "We're clear, Harris. Direct me to the nearest hospital. And where's our damn backup?"

Vanessa and Nick delivered the wounded Grant Snow to the Georgetown University Medical Center emergency room. They paced the waiting room until they got word that he'd regained consciousness after surgery. His condition was pronounced serious but not critical. The bullet had damaged muscle, tearing through his neck within a millimeter of an artery. He'd lost a lot of blood, but would recover.

Three ATSA operatives arrived to stand guard. Once stabilized, Snow would transfer to Walter Reed Army Medical Center to recuperate.

Under escort by two ATSA cars, Nick drove his abused silver Mercedes to Chevy Chase. By the time they pulled into the garage, darkness had fallen on the dreary day.

When they exited the car, Vanessa clicked her tongue at the scrapes and dings. "Sorry about your baby, Nick."

"She'll heal." He scratched his head. "Don't know exactly how I'll explain this to my insurance company."

"Don't. ATSA will cover you."

"Like they did this afternoon?" His blood still simmered. ATSA hadn't detected a trap. Backup had arrived too late to do anything but escort them to the emergency room.

"The CO'll knock some heads together over that one. The traffic on M Street held them up. We had cars waiting on three different routes. Nobody anticipated the bad guys'd have the same strategy. They haven't hacked into my tracking device or bugged the car. Low-tech surveillance, but thorough."

An ATSA officer opened the door. After assuring them the house was clear, he vanished. Janine had left hours ago.

Nick led the way to the kitchen. "I'll make some coffee."

"Good idea," Vanessa said. She lifted a note from the countertop. "Janine left a main course and salad in the fridge." She paused, her hand on the refrigerator door. "I'd expect a restaurant supply magnate to be a chef, but Janine creates all the meals."

"That sounds like a challenge. Honey, I know my way around every kitchen from a greasy spoon to five-star dining. I'll cook for you one evening. My specialty." A nice candle-lit dinner would be a good break for them both.

"It's a date." She opened the door and ducked inside as if to conceal the apricot-colored blush tinting her cheeks. "Yum, looks like shrimp scampi. Ready for nuking."

He retrieved coffee beans from the cupboard. Noticing his hands were steady, he exhaled slowly in relief. He'd held up through the attack, had even put a few slugs in the sedan's grill. Afterward the shakes had hit, racking him like a pneumonia sufferer. He'd surfaced before the drive home.

He measured out the beans into the grinder and pushed the button. The coffee's rich fragrance soothed his senses.

"You all right?" Vanessa set the salad bowl on the breakfast bar, then took the two steps to stand beside him.

"I'm fine. No problem." He didn't want her hovering, babying him. Or did he? Ground coffee and water went into the drip machine. He starting the brewing and set out mugs.

"Snow nearly died. You both could've been killed." She looked up at him, the concern in her candid green eyes turning to anguish. "You did an ace job, but you shouldn't have had to pinch-hit for ATSA today."

So could she have died, but she wouldn't appreciate his reminding her of that possibility. He swallowed the spasm of fear for her.

He schooled his expression and voice not to give away his emotions. "Someone had to step up to the plate."

She smiled. "The rust on your Special Forces skills didn't show. From where I sat, I saw a confident sortie."

She was partially right. Their success at escaping the ambushers had given him another measure of confidence. But… "False confidence. Put me in combat, and I'm in the zone. Training and instincts kick in. But only as an infantry grunt." No one should trust him to set up an operation.

Before she could object, he added, "You were the real heroine this afternoon, Ms. NASCAR. Your battery must need recharging." He handed her a mug of coffee.

"Thanks. I was in the zone, too." Falling silent, she sipped her coffee at the breakfast bar. She'd pulled her hair on top her head with one of her doodads.

The microwave beeped. He checked the temperature of the shrimp dish and carried it across the kitchen. Vanessa'd already put out plates and cutlery. They served themselves and ate in silence side by side.

He smiled. With her, even the silence was companionable, comfortable. Damn. Besides all the turmoil surrounding them, Nick had a new problem to contend with. Vanessa.

The woman, not the government officer. This thing between them was more than casual. More than sexual attraction. Although he hadn't been this obsessed with sex since he was a hormonal teenager.

Every day she slid more under his skin. He found himself

thinking about her at odd moments, picturing her face or recalling her sexy laugh or the way she knew to offer comfort and understanding with a touch on his arm.

Whether her empathy was part of the undercover role, he didn't know. Maybe it didn't matter. After his aborted engagement, Nick didn't want anything serious. Or even long term. Vanessa was right about his family issues, family honor, but wrong about what it meant for his life. He worked fourteen hours a day in his business because he had to. A family of his own was out of the question.

But not a brief liaison. After this operation ended, she'd leave and so would he. They'd never see each other again. He ignored the tightness in his chest at that thought.

A blazing affair that scorched those silk sheets was what he needed. What she needed, if he read her signals right. Their having sex couldn't be any more of a distraction than the frustration of not having sex. She'd see that, too. Her professional barrier crumbled more each time they kissed.

Looking up from the temptation of her elegant neck, Nick observed her frown. He knew what was bothering her. "So if they didn't track you and didn't follow us to Georgetown, how did New Dawn know where we were?"

"If I could answer that," she said through a bite of cucumber, "we'd have a prime lead to Husam Al-Din."

"Our lunch companions all have ties to Yamar."

"Prince Amir is reported to have led Yamari troops when New Dawn guerrillas tried to disrupt the presidential election. Do you suspect Nadim or Ambassador Khalil?" Vanessa rolled her shoulders. Her muscles were probably stiffening after her strenuous stint at the wheel.

"Nadim? Not a chance. He's the ultimate Western capitalist. But Khalil is an enigma. Remember, he lost the election. He could've been president."

"You're thinking he might have changed allegiance?" When he nodded, she said, "It's worth looking into."

The telephone jangled. Nick's pulse jumped. He knew who it was before he picked up. "Markos here."

"Arrange for a transfer of funds," said the accented and still-unidentified voice, "and your woman will be in no more danger. Nor will you. I will be in touch again soon." A click terminated the call.

Nick regarded Vanessa expectantly.

After listening intently to her earpiece, she shook her head. "Cell phone again. Different number."

Good thing they hadn't found the ten million yet, he mused. He'd be tempted to give it to New Dawn just to end the threat. "Al-Din won't quit. You'll sleep in my bed again tonight. And every night until this is over."

Her gaze flitted away. "We'll see." She rubbed her shoulder, the one she'd fallen on the previous night.

He turned and kneaded her shoulders. "Your muscles are tight as sailors' knots. Later I'll give you a good rubdown."

The thought of massaging her soft flesh tightened his body. Tonight. It was time.

She stiffened, then slipped off the stool and ducked away. "Debriefing's starting in a few minutes. Don't wait up for me."

She hustled out the kitchen exit and toward the house next door.

His mouth twisted in a wry expression. Removing her barriers might take a little more doing than he'd thought.

# *Chapter 12*

By Sunday evening Vanessa was as tightly wound as the space robot Troy'd had at twelve. He'd tinkered with it and powered it up to the point of critical mass. Metal and plastic limbs and stalk eyes and internal winky-dinks had cannoned all over the living room. If her nerves didn't give soon, she'd explode like that juiced-up robot.

The high-priced artwork on Alexei's sale list had indeed come from the Vienna robbery and two other gallery thefts, but the black-market sales were so far untraceable.

ATSA'd made no gains in tracking down Husam Al-Din. His captured goons would say only that New Dawn would prevail. The two burglars had entered the U.S. on student visas, and the other two, picked up in the initial stage of the Georgetown car chase, had no papers. All were dead ends, yielding no clues to their esteemed leader. The other ATSA unit had a list of possible targets for the Veterans Day attack, but nothing firm.

November second. Veterans Day was only nine days away. D-Day, and they had no idea where New Dawn would strike.

She and Nick hadn't located the ten-million-dollar dingus. And she'd made little headway in peeling off the layers of the military's cover-up of Nick's Somalia mission.

But none of those frustrations were responsible for her ragged nerves.

Nick took all the blame.

Nicolas Markos. And her tangled emotions.

She sipped her wine. The French champagne—from the house cellar—looked like liquid gold and tasted like heaven. But the intoxication fizzing in her blood came from the man in the kitchen. He was cooking for her tonight, something delicious-smelling called Greek beef. He'd settled her on the sunroom sofa with the wine and a tray of appetizers.

*Settled* wasn't exactly the word. She hadn't settled since their sweaty session on the gym floor.

When she'd returned late Friday from the debriefing, she'd discovered that he'd waited up after all. He'd rubbed her shoulders with fragrant lotion until all her muscles and bones had liquefied. Then he'd tucked her in bed—his bed—kissed her sweetly and left her for his pallet on the floor. The only reason she'd closed her eyes at all was her lack of sleep the previous night.

After yet another night in the same room, the tension had risen to a fever pitch. It was as if a magnetic field arced between and around the two of them.

She felt off balance, as sensitive as a hair trigger. His every action seduced her.

Common sense and her professional duty told her to beware, but her foolish heart ignored the warning. She knew Nick would never betray ATSA's plan, so what was the harm if they yielded to chemistry?

A relationship with Nick could be only sexual. She wasn't the woman for him. She wasn't sophisticated and beautiful like Danielle—well, that was a bad example—or Diana. What would a world-traveling executive see in a plain government officer other than the undercover role she played?

And he had all that baggage of lost honor to work through. Darkness lurked at his core like a coiled force. Yet his mood had gradually lightened during the past few weeks. Maybe he felt empowered by taking part in ATSA's plans. The slight change had nothing to do with her, for sure.

He wanted the persona she projected in her rich-girl clothes. At least he wasn't using her to get to Diana or some society babe. A brief encounter was all she could expect. When this operation ended, the affair would end.

That knowledge lodged a hot ball in her throat. Her heart would break whether or not they made love.

He didn't love her, but he wanted her. That was clear.

He constantly touched her—her hair, her cheek, her mouth. As they walked, he kept his hand on the small of her back. He spoke softly into her ear, privately, just for her. That deep, sexy voice made an inventory list sound like a hot proposition. Every look, every touch weakened her knees and her resistance. Away from the house, her protector, he hovered, his rangy body tensed for danger, his expression flinty, his eyes alert as a hunting hawk's.

The man was a walking aphrodisiac.

He crossed the room to her now with the champagne bottle. Her pulse jumped like a cheerleader at homecoming. In black trousers that clung to his sinewy thighs and a silk T-shirt the color of fine red wine, he nearly had her drooling.

He eased down to the cushion beside her, close enough to wrap her in his familiar scent. He turned toward her, his left knee bent and touching her thigh. Not in protection mode at the moment, he appeared focused solely on her. His Aegean-blue gaze cruised her face and down her body with blatant male heat. "Wrap your mouth around one of these."

Before she could compliment him on the variety of bounty, he popped a stuffed grape leaf in her mouth. Blinking, she bit off half. Chewed slowly. Fought for equilibrium.

The man was hand-feeding her.

The dinner was cooked. And so was she.

"Well?"

She swallowed, cleared her throat. "Delicious."

"More?" He offered a ripe olive as large as a plum.

"Whoa, buster," she said, holding her champagne flute in front of her. "We have the whole evening."

The olive went back on the tray.

The corners of his mouth kicked up in a smug smile. He stretched his left arm behind her and rested it on the sofa back. The powerful male animal surveying his prey. He curved his right hand casually over her knee, an invitation to closeness, to intimacy.

The blue flames in his eyes glowed with banked desire. "You're right. Why rush things? Slow and easy works for me."

Was his seduction deliberate? Oh, yeah. A rheostat dimmed the lighting. Logs crackled gently in the fireplace. Champagne. Succulent appetizers.

Seduction.

Turnabout was fair play. If she could slip into her undercover woman-of-the-world role, she'd steam up the room.

He was making her melt. She would make him sweat.

She plucked the olive from the tray and put it to her lips. The ripe fruit dripped with a savory marinade. She licked at it, sucked gently before biting into it.

Nick's mouth was hanging open, so she fed him an olive. Startled, he nearly swallowed the thing whole.

"Mmm, these olives are *so-o-o* good." She ran her tongue slowly around her lips and purred.

He swallowed, cleared his throat. He adjusted his position as if his trousers were too tight. "They…they come from my family's olive grove."

"I thought your dad was a ship's captain." She looked up at him from beneath lowered lashes.

The fire and Nick's nearness had warmed the room. *Here goes nothing. Or everything.* Slowly she peeled off the cardigan of her rust-colored twinset. She smoothed the sleeveless V-neck at the waist of her matching slacks. Tugging the knit tightened it over her breasts to show more than a hint of cleavage. A woman was entitled to use her main asset.

His hand on her knee was sweating. It twitched. His eyes looked unfocused.

"Um, right." Nick picked up his flute and swigged half the champagne in it. "When he retired, he and Sophie bought an olive grove from her family in Greece. That's where they live. Pop's an olive farmer now, when he's well enough."

She refilled his glass and hers, leaned closer so her right breast pressed against his side. "Did he teach you to cook Greek food?"

"No, that was Sophie. I was already interested in the restaurant business, but she started me cooking."

"You like her. That marriage has worked out then?"

He nodded. "Third time's a charm, I guess. She takes good care of Pop."

She cuddled closer, tilted her head the way she'd seen Diana do, so he'd recognize the desire in her eyes. "In a good relationship, a man and a woman take…care of each other." She left it to his imagination what kind of care she meant.

He slid his arm to curve around her shoulders. Lifting her hand to his lips, he said in a husky voice, "We've known each other only a short time, but you've taken better care of me than anyone I remember. Thank you."

His warm breath and his lips, slick with olive marinade, sent tingles up her arm. Her breath stuck in her throat. "Me? What did I do?" A squeaky voice didn't sound sexy, but she didn't have control over her vocal cords.

His gaze was languorous and sultry. "You've been my rock. You've taught me to smile again."

Before he could ramble on and she became too embarrassed, she had to stop him. "I was just doing my job, Nick."

He sat very still, just looking at her, his sexy, muscular body ready to pounce. His heat and woodsy scent wove their spell.

The mood between them shifted again. At first it had been light, then suddenly serious. Now the air thickened and throbbed with a heavy sensual beat. A beat she felt with every nerve ending and in a pulse between her legs.

He released the hand he held and lifted the flute from her other. "Your job doesn't include defusing my anger at my half brother's crimes. Your job doesn't include urging me to examine myself. Your job doesn't include this."

As his mouth found hers, he pulled her close. Heat flashed through her. Her entire body tightened. She fisted her hands in his shirt. His right hand burrowed beneath her sweater to caress her spine, her ribs. Her skin tingled at the rasp of his callused fingers. They teased one nipple through her silk bra.

A long flutter of pleasure and need flowed through her. It surged into a wave of yearning for this strong, sexy man whose pride and honor drove him.

He pulled her on top of him as he stretched out on the cushions. A rush of heat and electric awareness licked every point up and down her body where they touched. Her breasts felt full and flushed.

"I can't get enough of you. I'm hungry for more than this…appetizer." His voice was low, a velvet growl against her mouth. His fingers slid up her nape to massage her scalp. His thigh nudged her legs apart, and his rock-hard arousal throbbed between them. He was so beautiful, yet so indelibly male, with every sinew straining and bulging.

Tingling pleasure radiated from his caresses, and she clenched her thighs against his hardness in a vain attempt to assuage the ache he'd triggered.

Her foggy brain struggled to maintain a bantering tone. Keep it light, keep it safe. "Nick, your Greek beef, is it ready?"

His response was a muffled groan. "The Greek beef? Dinner'll keep. What—"

"Not dinner." She cupped her fingers around the heated length tenting his fly. "I was talking about this Greek beef."

Rasping words in what she thought was Greek, he twisted on the sofa to bring her beneath him. His heavy body pressed her into the cushions. His burgeoning arousal pulsed against her mound. "Are you sure?"

His potency and male heat and bottomless kisses filled her, invaded her very soul. Sex with him would be a shattering experience. He would make love as he did everything—with intense focus and expertise. Her nerves skittered.

Ready or not, her need for him bordered on desperation.

In reply, she unclipped the miniature microphone from her sweater and the receiver from her ear. She reached out to drop them on the cocktail table beside the appetizer tray.

"There might not be enough heat left in the fireplace to keep you warm," he said as he tugged up her sweater.

"Then you'll have to do it." She fumbled with his belt buckle.

His big hand covered hers to stop her. "Slow down. Nice and easy, remember, *latrea mou?*" He skimmed her sweater up over her head, her bra with it. "I want to see you. I love your skin, like fresh cream with dots of butter. I could lap you up like a cat."

*Latrea* what? She remembered he'd called her that once before, during their hot encounter in the gym—another intimate situation. The notion that his falling into Greek meant he forgot himself buoyed her confidence in her appeal. "What did you call me? *Latrea* something?" Heat swept through her from the wet heat of his tongue on her nipples. Good thing she was lying down. Her legs could never hold her.

"*Latrea mou.* It means sweetheart or honey." He started on her zipper.

She repeated the Greek endearment, savoring how the ending puckered the lips for more kisses. "Wait. I want to see you, too. I want to feel you against me." She yanked at his silk T-shirt.

He laughed as he toed off his shoes and divested himself of his shirt and trousers, leaving on only low-cut silk briefs stretched even skimpier by his straining arousal. "Done with slow and easy?"

"There's a time for everything." She shimmied out of her slacks. Her slides joined his loafers on the thick carpet.

With a murmur of contentment and excitement, he burrowed onto her again, rubbing skin against skin, his crisp chest hairs tickling her sensitive nipples. "So sweet, so sexy, so much woman."

At his whispered words, suddenly her doubts prodded her with icy needles. She didn't want to make love with him as her undercover persona. The falseness of her mask closed over her nose, her mouth, and she struggled to breathe. She couldn't let her sense of self burn to ashes in the fires of passion.

She pushed at the immovable wall of his shoulders. "Nick, say my name."

Eyes glazed and mouth wet with passion, he levered up on his elbows. "What is it? What's the matter?"

"Say my name. The real one." Her breathing raced like her heartbeat, and she fought down tears. "Say it!"

"Vanessa." Then again more softly, "Vanessa." He held her chin between two fingers and gazed into her eyes.

He watched as her eyelids closed. Tears leaked out and trickled into the hair at her temples.

His heart thundered, and his blood was on fire. Never before had he ached so much to possess a woman. She'd flirted and flaunted her assets, sending steamy smoke signals. And then *boom*. "What's this about?"

"I'm nearly naked with you." Her voice was thick with emotion, raw and husky. "Just plain Vanessa. Not the glamorous model Diana. Not the cool sophisticate. Not the seductress I've been channeling. Just Vanessa."

The light of comprehension clicked on in his dazed brain. The old insecurity monster had reared its ugly head. "Ah, you want to be certain I know who I hold in my arms." He beetled his brows in a scowl. "I'm insulted."

She sniffed to banish her tears. "Dammit, I hate crying. Other women look gorgeous even when they cry—" he knew she meant Diana "—but my eyes get puffy and my nose gets as red as Rudolph's."

"Red or not, you're beautiful, not plain." Her glorious hair tumbled around her head like a sunset cloud, curls and tendrils damp against her temples. Mussed, flushed and sultry, she was sure as hell not his buddy. "Your nose *is* a little pink. But so are your cheeks." He lowered his head to kiss one budded rose-colored nipple, then the other. "And so are your breasts. Very sexy."

She drew a deep breath. "Thank you for that. I'm sorry. It's nothing you did. It's me. It's—"

He silenced her with the brush of his lips. "Shh, Vanessa. I'm insulted that given absolute proof—" he ground his hard and aching arousal against her "—you still don't believe in your feminine appeal."

"But you're sure it's *me* you want, not the identity I've assumed these past weeks? Not someone like Diana? Oh, I know that sounds juvenile, but I have to know." Against his chest, he felt the tension knotting her stomach.

Feelings of protection and possession surged through him, constricting his chest. She made him want more than he'd thought possible. And she made him want yet more for her.

When he could breathe again, he said, "I know exactly whose soft curves are driving me nuts. And whose lush breasts are rosy from my attentions. I never got this…close to Diana, but I could never mistake you for her." When she tried to speak, he stopped her with another kiss.

He had to find the right words, so she understood her unique worth. From the first moment they'd met, she'd seen into his soul. She saw the torment and offered comfort. She didn't let him intimidate her in any way. Her warmth and sensitivity were lifting the heavy darkness inside him. With her, he didn't feel so alone, so empty.

But how could he tell her? Insecure, she borrowed sophistication from her undercover role. No poet, he needed to borrow that damned Prince Amir's glib tongue.

"Diana is model-perfect, granted," he said, mental fingers crossed. "With the cool, remote blond beauty expected of a woman named for the goddess of the moon. A *Greek* goddess, of course."

"Yes," she said. "Yes, she is. And…" Her words died. Maybe she'd seen the heat and ferocious need in his eyes.

"You, Vanessa, are the sun." He feathered a finger down the delicate arch of her neck and around the silk of each bountiful breast. "You are red and molten gold and life-giving warmth. You are fire and life. You've stoked hot coals in me since we met. I burn for you."

"Oh, Nick." She cradled his beard-rough jaw in her hands and tugged him to her seeking mouth. His awkward but heartfelt words seemed to be what she needed to hear.

And then his mouth and hands streaked over her body. He found her most sensitive spots and gave them his undivided attention. She writhed beneath him as he stroked and kissed.

He stripped off the white lace triangle that passed for panties to reveal the thatch of cognac curls he'd imagined. His seeking hand cupped this source of her fire and his intoxication. "*Latrea mou,* you burn."

When his fingers found her sensitive nub, she arched beneath him. His body clenched with a fiery need bordering on pain that he longed to shout to the world.

Twisting beneath his body, she dipped inside the silk briefs to grip his aching flesh. He tore the garment away, giving her free access. Hot and hard and heavy, he leaned into the firm grip of her soft hand.

He groaned at the sensation, his eyes clamped shut. He arched up, his weight on his straightened arms. "No more!" he growled. "Vanessa. Now."

When he flicked two fingers inside her, Vanessa's body seemed to thrum with tension. "Yes, Nick. Now!"

He fumbled a foil packet from his trouser pocket. Sheathed, he slipped between her legs. Desire darkened her green eyes and fluttered her lashes. He stroked her again with his thumb, and took one nipple in his mouth, suckling to raise her to fever pitch.

Delirious anticipation thrashing him, he sank into her. She lifted her hips and took him deep. When she tightened convulsively around him, he went absolutely still for a heartbeat, his gaze lasered on her. Sensations rippled through him, sensations that surpassed the physical. Joy and fulfillment and contentment.

"Ah, Vanessa, I knew we'd burn each other up."

Pleasure built as they found a rhythm together. Slow, silky and sinuous, with long, wet kisses, then intense and insistent, with panting urgency. Ecstasy hovered just out of reach. Sharp sensations exploded as he pistoned into her, his body bowing and arching as she shuddered around him and they clung together.

Slowly Vanessa became aware of the cool air on her damp arms and the heavy, sprawled weight on her body. She never wanted him to move. Aftershocks still rippled through her. The absolute power of their lovemaking made her feel that she glowed from the voltage they'd generated.

Nick's face pressed into the curve of her neck and shoulder, and he kissed her there before pushing up. The hint of wariness in his eyes tripped her heartbeat.

She smiled up at him to eliminate any awkwardness. "Whew, that was some powerful Greek beef!"

His rumble of laughter vibrated through her. "I suppose

that'll have to do for 'honey, was it as good for you as it was for me?'" In one fluid motion, he rolled off her and to his feet. He held out a hand for her.

Standing flush against his heated body, she hugged him and pressed a kiss to his sternum. "I think I worked up an appetite. Are you still going to feed me?"

"The other Greek beef is coming right up. I hope it's not too dried out." His eyebrows shot up. A hint of embarrassment colored his cheeks. "Don't touch that line."

Sputtering with laughter, they cleaned up and dressed.

Dinner was not ruined. They sat side by side at the round glass breakfast table in the sunroom and ate cubed beef in a garlic-and-cinnamon-flavored tomato sauce over noodles. By candlelight and over coffee and baklava, they talked companionably.

"Tell me more about Sophie and your father," Vanessa said, curious about his family.

"Not much to tell. They're happy. Perhaps it was the right time in their lives for them when they met, his career at sea nearing an end, children nearly grown—until Mikela came along. Family's always welcome at the villa—hers or us two." His gaze turned contemplative. "No, only me now. Not Alexei. Funny, we never got along, but going there next time will seem strange without him."

"Are you okay about tomorrow?" She placed her hand on his.

Monday was the funeral, a simple memorial service at a private chapel near Rock Creek Park. The ashes in their bronze urn would be flown to Greece for burial. Vanessa'd spent the afternoon helping to coordinate security arrangements.

He turned his hand, linking his fingers with hers. "Fine. It'll bring closure and allow his employees and business colleagues to pay their respects. Perhaps our guy'll show up."

"Husam Al-Din?" She laughed. "Don't hold your breath. But speaking of him, I talked to Grant Snow on the phone this afternoon."

"What a rotten thing to happen," he said, pushing away his half-eaten dessert. Anger darkened his eyes to cobalt and bunched the muscles in his jaw. "There should've been a way to prevent the ambush. To prevent his being shot. I should've seen it coming."

There was his overdeveloped sense of responsibility again. "You? Like you should've seen a different ambush coming? No. In Somalia, you weren't alone. I'm sure of that."

His expression hardened. "It's not the same thing."

Close enough, but she wouldn't argue until she had all the facts. "Maybe. But yesterday's security definitely wasn't your job. ATSA should've anticipated it, had better intel."

With a slow shrug, he seemed to shake away the distancing mood. He brushed a hand along her jawline. "So how's Snow?"

She smiled at the caress. He was still touching her even though he didn't need to convince her of his desire. The notion fed her feminine ego and her all too vulnerable heart.

"Grant's doing all right. His first question to the surgeon was about what the injury would do to his golf swing."

They laughed together, the mood between them once again easy and intimate.

Later they walked upstairs, his arm around her shoulders and hers around his waist.

"Can I convince you to sleep in my bed again tonight?"

The tension radiating from his big body at the notion she might refuse didn't come from his need to protect her. That he wanted her again cheered her heart and heated her blood. She could no more refuse him than she could take him in hand-to-hand combat.

At the door to the master suite, she paused, hands on hips. Tilting her head, she deepened her voice to what she figured was sexy. "I'll sleep in your bed on one condition."

"What's that?" Worry furrowed his brow.

"That bed's way too big for one. You have to join me."

# Chapter 13

Nick crouched beneath a stunted thorn tree beside the muddy stream. Around him in the stygian night, unseen creatures slithered through the arid grassland. He knew of at least ten varieties of poisonous snakes a man could step on.

No stars, no moon relieved the opaque blackness. Acacia smoke and the cloying stench of something rotting hung on the heavy air. The night pulsed with danger. The beat built to a strident throb like kettledrums.

The op was going down.

A figure hunched toward him, low, blending with the grass. *Badger.* A monster made of bunches of grass and leaves over a camouflage uniform. The man stopped short of Nick's position.

Why didn't he just use the radio?

"Yo, soldier. Sit rep," Nick said. The throbbing accelerated, amplified. He strained to hear the soldier's report over the pounding.

The man stood there without speaking, without moving.

A grenade or maybe a flash-bang exploded off to his right. The blast illuminated Nick's position and the man with him. Dangerous. Nick flattened on the packed earth.

Badger just stood there.

Then Nick saw why Badger didn't report in.

His chest was gone. Missing. Blown away. Blood and bones within a hollow shell. His eyes were blank.

Nick could only stare. He couldn't move.

More explosions shattered the night. The pounding rose to a deafening pitch that filled his head.

Another soldier shuffled toward him. *Slick.* He held his head in his only hand. And another man and another, bloody and blackened and blown apart, came to stare sightlessly and silently at him. The four raised bony fingers and pointed their awful accusations at him.

The subtropical night wrapped around Nick's mouth and nose like a hot blanket. He struggled to breathe. Flaming debris rained around him in a crimson wall. Only then did he realize that the frantic throbbing was his heartbeat.

He thrashed and clawed at the binding that smothered him.

"Nick, wake up. You're dreaming. *Nicolas!*"

As the gentle voice parted the haze, he wrenched into a sitting position and peeled away the clammy sheets. He must've thrashed and nearly choked himself with the damn covers.

He gulped in great drafts of air. Swiping at the sweat running into his eyes, he blinked and tried to focus.

"Nick, are you all right?"

Her hand on his arm brought him back to reality. Vanessa. Sweet Vanessa. They'd made love a second time and fallen asleep in each other's arms. As the present penetrated, his icy soul seemed to expand with warmth, and a shimmer of renewed sensation curled through him.

She sat beside him, the sheet tucked under her arms and over the high swell of her breasts. Her rust-gold hair formed a nimbus in the low light of the bedside lamp. An angel come to haul him from the depths of his personal hell.

"Just a dream. I'm okay." He twisted to peer into her shadowed face. "I was fighting the sheets. Did I hurt you?"

She shook her head, tumbling curls around her shoulders. "You were fighting something, but it wasn't the sheets."

He scrubbed his knuckles over his beard-roughened jaw and wished he could scrub away the ugliness that still flashed in his mind.

"Nick, you were fighting what happened in Somalia. It haunts you. Does the nightmare come often?"

"Not in years. A couple of times a week recently."

She didn't comment. She probably knew as well as he did what had brought the horror back. Alexei, protecting her, this op, ATSA—all of it was too similar to a Special Forces op. He'd tried to avoid anything that brought back that part of his past, but the memories and guilt dogged him anyway.

Perhaps telling it to someone as caring and understanding as Vanessa would quell the ache in his chest, would lighten the darkness within him. She knew the basic story, but by spelling out his culpability, he risked losing her.

The irony and irrationality of his fear punched him in the heart. Lose her? He'd never had her. The closeness they shared was temporary. He had nothing to offer. She wouldn't want a man without honor.

Was she really different from other women? The ordinary sister-buddy issue, was that for real? Or was her enjoyment of affluence and her elegant portrayal of Danielle for real? Deception was her profession. He could trust her with his nightmare and his passion, but no more.

He refused to examine the erosion of his limits.

"I want to tell you about it, about the mission in Somalia." As soon as he'd uttered the words, the dark weight in his chest eased.

"The more I know," she said, "the more tools I can use to dig out all the facts."

He shrugged. Facts? He had all the facts he needed to know that responsibility sat squarely on his shoulders. If she wanted to look under rocks, why the hell not? He tossed back the sheets and pushed to his feet.

Cross-legged in the middle of the bed, Vanessa watched as he paced in front of her. Unabashedly naked, a beautifully sculpted warrior, hard-eyed and savage, he girded himself to bare his pain. Strain stretched the skin of his face into a taut mask of tragedy. Her heart fissured at his suffering.

"We received humint—intelligence from locals—of a warlord and a cache of arms in the Karkaar foothills. Other sources bore out the intel, so the exec and the team sergeant had me coordinate the mission. We were to destroy the arms and arrest the guy. He was just a small-time gangster."

"That was your job as assistant operations sergeant?"

"Collecting and analyzing intel, yes. And planning and executing small unit strikes."

"Like that one."

"The village was only a few huts by a stream. Remote. No town or road within miles. After the helo dropped us, we crawled on our bellies through tall grass to within a hundred yards. There were six of us. I was in the rear, on the radio, coordinating deployment. The others fanned out to make the assault. There were supposed to be only the warlord and two men in the target hut."

"But the intel was wrong?" She fought back tears at the agony on his face.

He slumped and came to sit on the bed beside her. With his rough hand, he smoothed back her hair, then clasped her hand. His eyes were stark with pain and longing.

"Wrong or false or compromised, I never found out. We went into an ambush. The arms and explosives there were used against us. As the men deployed to attack, gunfire from rock outcroppings beyond us cut them down. Then the huts exploded. Blew what was left to blood and gore."

"You and one other survived."

"Cruiser was wounded. He lost a foot later. I had a few scratches." She saw the survivor's guilt, a clawed demon, riding on his shoulders. "After the firefight ended, I gathered up the others' dog tags. We made it back to the pickup zone and got lifted out."

"The warlord and his men?"

"Dead. We got 'em." His lip twisted in self-disdain. "Mission accomplished."

"Those men…they were your friends. I can't imagine—"

"Friends, yes. I'd been SF for only a short time, but when you're hunkered down in dangerous country, you become tight damned fast."

She felt he needed to keep talking. "Tell me about them."

He hesitated. Finally he began in a hoarse whisper. "Antowan Donaldson. He was called Badger because once he latched on to something, he never let go. He was our weapons specialist, for all the damned good it did him." He paused as if gathering strength to relive the memories. "Joe Ramirez, known as Slick because of his way with women. And Gerry Saban. He— You sure you want to hear all this?"

"Go on. I want to know about the others." She listened, rubbing his arm with her free hand and wishing she could absorb his pain.

With gentle prompting from her, he recounted personal memories about each man in the squad. Five brave and skilled men, the wounded and the dead, with buddy names like Donut and Cruiser and Shark. Toward the end, his voice was raw, as if each word was jagged shrapnel gouging flesh from his throat.

She squeezed his big hand, damp with cold sweat. "You said the humint had been verified. You had reliable intel. You couldn't have known you were going into an ambush."

Her chest clogged with sorrow, Vanessa reached out to pull him into her arms.

Moisture glittering in his eyes, he wrenched away and stalked across the room. Every muscle in his sweat-sheened body bulged with tension.

He fired out a string of obscenities, clenched his hands into white-knuckled fists. "When we returned to base, the local informants had disappeared. I should've seen through their lies. Checked more sources. Something."

"Maybe the translation from Somali to English was the problem. Or the interpreter."

He shook his head, slowly and with difficulty, as if his skull were too heavy to move. "No interpreter. We spoke in Italian. Odd, but that's one of the local languages."

She remembered that one reason Special Forces had recruited him was his language fluency. There had to be more to the story. "How was their information verified?"

"Flyover surveillance, other reports. The exec gave me the file." He faced her, the low lamplight sketching harsh shadows on the angles and planes of his bold features. "Your investigation doesn't mean squat. In the end, I'm still responsible. Those men died because of my screwup."

Her breath hitched at the grief in his words, at the emptiness of lost honor and pride in his voice. "Nick, your story hasn't changed my mind about a cover-up. I'm convinced there's more you don't know. Missions fail. Mistakes happen. Look at all the roadblocks in *this* op. And ATSA's supposed to be the elite force."

His gaze softened, crinkling the corners of his eyes. "Vanessa, sweet Vanessa. Ms. Optimist. My only defender."

"Did you see anyone after? I mean like a counselor?"

"The army shrink. I know all about PTSD—post-traumatic stress disorder. Counseling might've helped more if you'd been my shrink."

The tension in his body slowly transformed from fury to

something else. He ambled toward the bed. Hunger darkened his eyes and set his shadowed jaw. He stared at her with such intensity that her pulse stuttered.

The potency of his male beauty held her gaze. Naked, his rock-hard strength displayed in taut sinews and defined abs, he made her heart nearly leap from her chest. His phallus, quiescent during his ordeal, now thrust toward her, imposing and imperious. Heat rose in her and licked up her belly.

Nick saw her eyes go wide at the realization of his intent. Afraid she'd refuse him, he hesitated at the bed's edge. "I need you, Vanessa. *Latrea mou.*"

She smiled and opened her arms. "Come to me, Nick."

Tumbling her back onto the cool silk, he covered her with his length. They gathered each other close, fitting softness to hardness, swells to hollows. Her heat surrounded him, seeped into his body, into the dark, aching places, a balm to his unseen wounds.

She clung to him with the same fierce instinct that drummed in his blood. A vise of more than sexual need gripped him, a need greater than he'd ever known, greater than he'd thought possible, to possess this generous and gentle woman who fitted in his arms as though she belonged there.

She was ready, wet and reaching for him. Passion surged in the heavy beat of his heart. He barely had enough control to sheath himself before he sank into her welcoming body.

Pleasure erased boundaries, so he didn't know where he ended and she began. She pulsed around him almost immediately, her climax wringing urgent whimpers from her and ecstatic groans from him. Then all he could do was piston into her and ride the shock wave to a shattering release that exploded from him like spasms of thunder.

The next morning, Vanessa sat beside Nick at his half brother's funeral service. A black-robed woman played the organ. The dolorous chords of Brahms's Requiem echoed against the stone walls of the small chapel. Candles flickered beside an open bible at the altar.

A wreath of flowers draped a bronze coffin. An empty coffin. Alexei Markos's ashes lay in an urn ready for shipment to Greece, but Mr. Falstone had asserted that at a funeral people expected to see the coffin.

Rain dripped from their shared umbrella, leaning against the pew in front of her, to form a small puddle on the slate floor. With each drop she felt her time with Nick slipping away. For now, she just wanted to make it through the service and return to the house safely.

She shuddered, but not from the damp and cold.

Last night's lovemaking and his tormented confession had brought them closer. Gradually the tension and anger had seeped from Nick. He'd been romantic and tender and both gentle and demanding. The mere memory left her breathless and dizzy. He'd held her and loved her as if he'd never let her go. Reminding herself that this rush of elation was only temporary took every ounce of willpower she possessed.

She'd awakened alone. When she found Nick at his desk, he'd said only that he needed to catch up on N.D.M. business before the funeral. Perhaps that was true. Or perhaps he was pulling back from a relationship that could go nowhere. The notion seared her heart like fire, but she refused to dwell on it.

The housekeeper had arrived early and insisted on preparing them a hot breakfast. As usual, she'd clucked her tongue at Nick's lack of a tie, but Vanessa had no complaints about his attire. The charcoal suit and slate-gray turtleneck conveyed perfectly the requisite somber attitude as well as the formidable bearing he wore like armor.

A new driver, an African-American ATSA officer named J. T. McNair, had brought them to the funeral in the scarred Mercedes. Speedy Glass had replaced the windows, but the scrapes and bullet holes would have to wait.

Janine balked, insisting she could take a bus or the Metro,

but Nick ignored her protests and hustled her into the back seat with them. When he winked at her, she responded with a tiny smile and seemed to relax.

Though Nick had begun the day with outer calm, Vanessa'd observed the tension in his jaw as they approached the hearse and other cars parked on the circular drive to the chapel. Between the stress of his tortured memories and that of his half brother's crimes, he found little respite.

He sat beside her now, eyes forward and shoulders rigid. His woodsy scent floated to her with the less pleasant ones of wet wool and hot dust from a seldom-used furnace.

As he had on the day they'd visited the funeral home, he kept a constant grip on her hand. Did that mean he wasn't withdrawing from her? No, she wouldn't go there. But if she could offer him this small lifeline, he could have her hand forever.

At the unintended double entendre, a tremor shot through her. Nick thought he desired the real Vanessa, but desire was fleeting. The tomboy and the tycoon? Her love would find no forever with Nick. All she could expect was one day.

One day at a time. To play her part.

She needed no reminders to be Nick's loving fiancée, but today she struggled to concentrate on who else she was.

*Vanessa Wade, Anti-Terrorism Security Agency officer. Specializing in undercover love and self-delusion.*

Clamping her lips together to keep them from trembling, she turned her head and caught Simon Byrne's eye. The mission control officer nodded almost imperceptibly, then scanned the sparse gathering of mourners in the ten rows of pews.

"More security than mourners. Alexei's legacy," Nick murmured.

"So far all I see are the usual suspects." Vanessa recognized everyone in the chapel. The five employees of Markos Imports, owners of neighboring shops, a couple of D.C. detectives and Alexei's defense attorney. And, of course, Janine, who had come for them, not for her former employer.

Quiet whispers brushed the chapel's stone walls like wind gusting through desiccated leaves. The dour Mr. Falstone stepped to the podium. The susurrus ended.

Nick squeezed her hand as the funeral director began to read a prayer. After a Bible reading and two hymns, the service mercifully concluded.

"Now comes the hard part." Nick stood and turned to face the curious and the concerned.

Employees, business contacts and a few others regarded Nick as if expecting him to voice a tribute to his late brother. Vanessa knew there was no chance in hell of that.

"Dwight Wickham and Abdul Nadim are sitting together." A low rumble of displeasure emitted from Nick's chest. "Look for blood in the water."

"Tsk, tsk. Nadim seems like a teddy bear, not a shark."

"Trust me. Abdul doesn't get regular write-ups in the *Post* financial pages by being cuddly. If those two sharks team up, I'll be lucky to have a bone of profit from any sale of Markos Imports."

They proceeded down the aisle and waited at the open doorway to accept greetings and condolences. Wickham and Nadim hesitated by the doorway. Even in suits and somber ties, the two entrepreneurs had the avaricious air of used-car salesmen.

Maybe Nick was right about sharks, Vanessa speculated.

Nick drew back as he recognized the hawkish features on a face behind the last guests to leave.

"Prince Amir. Another shark. Why the hell is he here?" he hissed. Wariness deepened the cleft in his chin and narrowed his eyes to laser-blue slits.

By now she was accustomed to Nick's illogical dislike of the suave Yamari prince. She whispered back, "To pay his respects, I imagine. Behave."

"I always do, honey. Watch me." A feral smile curved his mouth as the three men approached the doorway.

Most of the others had trudged out into the steady downpour. Janine, clutching her purse to her breast, waited by the last pew. Two ATSA officers dressed in dark suits and darker expressions—undercover as funeral home employees—edged forward, ready to move if the need arose.

Vanessa expected no trouble from these men other than sharp bargaining. ATSA reports said Abdul Nadim and Dwight Wickham were what they appeared to be, successful businessmen. Although the king's abdication had trampled on his son's future ascension to the throne, Amir had no apparent political leanings or ambitions.

Hands were shaken all around as Wickham and Nadim shuffled between polite comments about the ceremony and oblique references to the sale of the business.

"Gentlemen," Nick said, "thank you. On behalf of my family, I appreciate your coming out in the rain today."

Prince Amir bowed over Vanessa's hand. "Appropriate weather for such a sad occasion."

"I wasn't aware you knew my brother." Nick curved a proprietary arm around Vanessa's shoulders. "I appreciate the gesture."

The Yamari prince waved a manicured hand in dismissal. "I knew Alexei but not well. We met a few years ago at an embassy gathering. He subsequently handled the sale of some family pieces. He had wide knowledge of such things."

"Yes," Vanessa hastened to say, "in spite of…his other failings, he was an expert on Eastern antiquities."

Amid farewells, the party stepped out into the rain and mist. Vanessa noted that more ATSA officers covered the grounds. Good. If New Dawn was planning something, instincts told her that now would be the time. But no figurative red flag of danger popped up. Satisfied, she inhaled the raw air, less stifling than the musty confines of the chapel.

Their companions splashed through puddles toward other

cars farther down the drive. A liveried chauffeur at attention held a limousine door for the prince.

Vanessa jerked a nod toward the fawning driver. "McNair could take lessons from him in proper chauffeur protocol."

From the corner of her eye, she saw Janine cover a smile.

Nick snorted his disdain as he took the women's elbows. "I prefer security to sucking up."

The Mercedes was parked in a reserved space behind the hearse about a hundred feet away. Together they traipsed toward it across the wet grass.

"Good thing. You won't get sucking up from McNair," Vanessa observed wryly. "Instead of holding the door, he seems to have dozed off. I see his cap against the headrest."

Silent up to that point, Janine said, "Me, I do like a man in uniform. Something about that cap…" She sighed and lifted her shoulder in a very French shrug.

Cap?

*Ye gods, no!*

Vanessa slipped from Nick's grasp. She grabbed his and Janine's arms. She tugged and gestured to the ATSA officers.

"Quick, get back to the chapel! *Now!*"

A scowl darkened Nick's face, but he let her drag him backward. "What the hell!"

His gaze sharpened as if recognizing the alarm on her face. He curved his arms around the women and began to run.

Behind them, the Mercedes blew apart in a fiery blast of metal and glass.

# Chapter 14

The blast threw them to the ground. Pressure cartwheeled their umbrellas across the muddy lawn. In an eerie echo of Nick's nightmare, sizzling debris, steaming in the rain, poured around them and on them.

Seconds later ATSA officers helped them to their feet.

Nick spat out mud and grass. Heart pounding, he gripped Vanessa's shoulders. He searched her pale face for blood or signs of pain. "Are you all right?"

Mud smeared her wool coat and the knees of her navy slacks. Rust-colored strands of hair plastered the shoulders of her coat, but her eyes were clear. "Fine. Just wet."

He followed her avid gaze to the ATSA control officer— Byrne was his name. Even in a suit, no one looked less like a funeral parlor employee.

Vanessa quivered in Nick's grip like a thoroughbred straining at the gate, but she didn't attempt to break free and join her colleagues. "Danielle" stayed by her lover's side.

"Big blow," Janine said. "But not so bad like the hurricane that blew away my house." The unflappable Haitian housekeeper began brushing at her muddy clothing with a snowy handkerchief.

He'd long ago informed Janine of New Dawn's threats, so he wouldn't have to explain now. She thought the driver was hired protection and knew nothing of ATSA's involvement.

"These enemies of Monsieur Markos, *ils sont méchants.*"

Nick stared at the smoldering ruin of his Mercedes and its grisly passenger. "Wicked. Yes, Janine, very wicked."

If not for Vanessa's sudden alarm, they would've died in the same inferno as the driver. He could've lost her. All that warmth and passion could've been snuffed out in an instant. A steel band vised his chest, and his hands shook.

He'd never cared this much before. He didn't want to hover between such depths of fear and pain and peaks of pleasure and joy. She was a woman meant to have a home and family, a woman with more strings than the London Symphony Orchestra. And he was a man bound to his demons.

He wrapped her in his arms and buried his nose in her hair. Her familiar fragrance blocked out the confusing thoughts and the smells of burning metal, fabric and flesh.

He couldn't yet grasp what he felt, so instead, he said, "I'm sorry about McNair."

She shook her head, her face rubbing against his damp suit. "That's not McNair. It's not J.T. in the car." She lifted her gaze to his.

"You saw something at the last minute. What was it?"

She smiled at the housekeeper, who was gaping at her statement. "Janine, you said something about his cap. We all saw the chauffeur's cap against the headrest. But McNair wasn't wearing a cap."

"*Mon Dieu!* Then where is that man?" Janine exclaimed.

"He can't be far. The…security people will find him." She

stepped back from Nick and stared at her hands. Blood smeared the palms and fingers. "Nick, you're bleeding!"

Up to now he hadn't noticed, but suddenly he felt stinging sensations as if a spray of buckshot had peppered his back. He must've taken the brunt when he'd covered the two women from the blast.

Face pale as parchment, Vanessa turned him around. "Your raincoat's in shreds. Burned and sliced by falling shrapnel. You'll need stitches."

*Shrapnel. Staccato bursts of Kalashnikov rounds. RPGs. The sting of cordite and smoke…and burning flesh.*

The attack in the Karkaar village tattooed his brain. Nick squeezed his eyes shut and fisted his hands to keep them from shaking.

"I be fixin' you a healin' salve, Monsieur Nick," Janine said, clucking her tongue.

Affection and compassion in her luminous eyes, Vanessa lifted his arm around her shoulders, as if her diminutive frame could support him.

He couldn't utter the words that it wasn't today's wounds that coated his face with a cold sweat. If only a salve were the cure. Dredging up strength, he murmured thanks.

Over the fire's roar, he heard the distant scream of sirens and the protest of fire-truck klaxons.

Mr. Falstone stood in the chapel doorway with the organist. Shoulders slumped like his jowls, he didn't look so pompous. He shook his head at the burning frame that had been Falstone and Drumm's newest hearse.

Around them ATSA was slowly bringing order to chaos. Their tiny radios squawking, men and women strode by—crows with black raincoats flapping over their somber feathers.

Behind the barricade the D.C. detectives had set up, the vultures peered and pointed. A man in lime-green bicycle shorts and a helmet craned his neck to see over the somberly clad mourners.

The Somalia flashback receded, and Nick focused on the present situation. Was one of those people a real vulture?

Ice congealed in his gut at the image of Vanessa in that inferno. The bomber had killed whoever had been in the car and might've gotten them, too. "Look at that bunch. Did one of the guests I greeted set up this bombing?"

Vanessa's brow crinkled in perplexity. "Security was tight. And I see no motive. How would Husam Al-Din collect his ten million if you or I were dead? And *who* is in the car?"

Rage boiled his blood. His jaw tightened reflexively. "If I had the damned money, I'd be tempted to give it to the bastard just to end this thing."

He was vaguely aware of her shocked intake of breath, but his brain was working on the problem.

Vanessa had put her life on the line enough. End the threat? Yes, that was what he had to do.

Police, fire trucks and ambulances added to the chaos of who was in charge. No one was injured in the blast but Nick and the mysterious driver. The emergency medics dispensed blankets to keep the others warm until the authorities released them.

Vanessa watched as an EMT cleaned and smeared antiseptic cream on Nick's cuts and burns. Only one cut appeared deep enough for stitches, and Nick persuaded the man to sew him up then and there so he wouldn't have to endure a hospital. She left Janine clucking over him at the ambulance while she went to check on what had happened to J. T. McNair.

After a brief search, Byrne and Harris had found the driver out cold in a clump of shrubbery. Later, Vanessa learned that after he regained consciousness, he said he'd been drugged. A chunky man in a suit and chauffeur's cap had asked him for a light. A quick jab with a needle and he went down.

A search of the burned Mercedes determined that the so-called chauffeur was a suicide bomber. Sticks of dynamite and a detonator strapped around his torso had formed the extra bulk. None of the ATSA personnel knew how he'd gotten to the chapel. And whoever his accomplice was didn't volunteer the information.

Vanessa and Nick returned to the Chevy Chase house in a D.C. black-and-white. Contrary to Janine's protests that she had work to do, Nick commandeered one of his "security" people to drive her home.

When Vanessa returned late that night from debriefing, Nick was waiting for her at the top of the stairs.

Showing no ill effects of the day, he looked just as sexy and dangerous as ever in the worn jeans that clung to his muscular thighs.

His injuries, minor cuts only, were hidden beneath his shirt, a tee as gray as his face had been. She suspected the explosion and seeing his own blood had thrown him back in time, triggered his emotional reaction and shock.

Her gaze wandered from his black hair to his strong features, stamped with arrogance and determination. And yes, pride in the set of his chin. Protecting her was giving him back some of his lost pride and honor. She would help him beat the remaining guilt if she could.

The only softness was in his dark, spiky lashes and the sensuous mouth she knew could kiss her into oblivion.

Knowing the end was inevitable kept her from blurting out her true feelings for him. Their intimacy had grown and deepened. Beyond sex, they'd shared themselves, their hopes and dreams. A naturally dominant male, in bed he took control, but also relinquished it to her. He ensured her pleasure—a mild word for the sparkling wildfires that his lovemaking swept through her—until his own climax destroyed his control.

Leaving him, leaving the connection they shared would

shatter her already cracked heart. She'd feared becoming too immersed in an undercover role and the worst had happened.

She'd fallen in love with a man out of her league. A man who'd hate her if he knew part of her job was to spy on him.

No matter the outcome of their affair, she'd find the truth that would set this proud, honorable man free of guilt.

She longed for nothing more than to lose herself in his arms, for reassurance they were well and whole and together, for the soul-deep wonder she found only in his arms.

But she had a job to do. A job made more dangerous by today's events. And time was running short. There was no time for vulnerability or one-sided love.

After a hot shower, she'd donned her warmest outfit, light wool slacks and a rose-pink cashmere sweater. She still felt chilled to the bone. The bomber had nearly included all three of them in his bid for glory in the afterlife.

What Nick had said worried her more at present. If he found the money, he wouldn't really give any of it to New Dawn. She knew that.

But Simon Byrne didn't.

The ATSA control officer had been standing nearby. He'd heard every heartfelt word. She'd given up searching Nick's papers and laptop, but after today Simon insisted on a nightly report.

She had no choice. Duty came first.

But it made her feel lower than a snake.

She was sure her guilt flashed in neon on her forehead. Nick's expression showed no suspicion, no hint that he knew she'd just come from snooping in the study. So she manufactured a tired smile.

"How's the back?" she asked as she trudged up the stairs. His soreness might give her the excuse to sleep alone.

"No worse than a sunburn. Maybe it's Haitian voodoo, but Janine's salve eased the sting." His too-careful stance said otherwise.

"You'll be sleeping on your belly for a while."

His sly grin and heavy-lidded gaze gave her heart a kick. "And I promised you could be on top tonight."

The sexy rejoinder heated her cheeks and triggered a delicate pulsing between her legs.

He wanted her. Really wanted her. And she tried not to care if he wanted her as herself or as her undercover persona. The way he looked at her with those slumberous dark eyes and the tender way he touched her made her feel beautiful, desirable and, yes, glamorous.

She halted her progress two steps below the top. If she went into his arms, her willpower would melt like an ice cube in a furnace.

The moment and his comment required not drama but levity. And diplomacy. Forming what she thought was a sexy pout, she gazed up at him. "A broken promise. I'm deeply wounded. Maybe this betrayal calls for abstinence."

His look didn't waver in intensity. His hot-eyed gaze cruised her body. "Abstinence would punish us both."

She licked her dry lips. His obvious arousal had her heart thudding. "I don't want to hurt you. Your back."

"We'll apply my company mottos. Innovation and creativity. Come here, Vanessa." It was not a request.

She couldn't very well remain on the stairs all night. Good sense and emotion battling within her, she mounted the last two steps.

When Nick tugged her into his arms, she yielded to his steel embrace and the electric current eddying in her blood. She sighed and rested her head on his solid chest.

"You worked late tonight." His voice rumbled pleasurably in her ear. "Anything?"

"No breakthroughs."

"Husam Al-Din must have incredible charisma and power to convince a man to commit suicide for no reason. It's beyond me. How did he get there? Did he drive one of the funeral guests?"

She shook her head. "Everyone's accounted for. He could've arrived hidden in one of the cars, or he could've sneaked in through the woods. They'll keep checking."

"Do they think the bomb was a warning?"

"It's the only explanation that makes sense. But nothing in this situation makes sense." She ought to escape and sleep in her own room. But not quite yet. Being held felt so good. So right. "I'm sorry about your car."

His chuckle tingled through her. "All taken care of. Now I won't have to find a body shop."

"There's another complication to stir the pot."

He kissed her temple as he pulled her into the master bedroom. "And what's that?"

She shivered with delight when his tongue found the shell of her ear. "The bomber had a button to trigger the explosion, but there was also a remote arrangement. The destruction makes it impossible to tell…" Hypnotized by his velvet voice and his ministrations, she couldn't continue.

"…which way the bomb was triggered," he finished for her. "I see. I've heard of that. In case the bomber gets cold feet. Diabolical." He threaded the scrunchie from her hair and finger-combed the tresses over her shoulders. "So there are several possibilities."

She nodded, lost in the sensuality of his long fingers on her scalp, on her neck. Her knees were dissolving, along with her resolve. "Mmm, possibilities."

"One, either the bomber or the accomplice went for it when they planned to, as a warning. Two, they meant to kill us and triggered the blast when they saw us back away."

She ran her hands up the taut muscles of his back beneath his T-shirt. He smelled of soap and fabric softener and the cedar that seemed to be part of his skin. She'd like to keep something of his so she'd always have his scent.

"Or three, the driver-bomber got cold feet, and the bomb

went off by remote," she said. "Which means the remote holder was there. Was someone we know."

"Nadim or Prince Amir or one of the staff? Damn."

"I've been over and over all this with the team. To no conclusion but one."

"And what's that?"

"If we could find out how they got the house plans, we'd have the link to Husam Al-Din."

"And time is running out." Gingerly, he lifted his T-shirt away from his bandaged back and over his head. He began to unfasten her slacks. "You can do no more tonight, *latrea mou*. You need to get off your feet."

Before she could recall why she should leave him, his hot mouth came down on hers and burned every thought from her brain. Mindless joy swept through her, liquid heat in the onslaught of his raw sexuality.

No, she could do no more. Nor did she have power to walk away from him tonight. Why did she ever think she could?

Bending, he kissed his way up her belly and torso, peeling away her bra and sweater as he went. The fiery demands of his mouth, hands and body ignited flames within her. She dropped onto the bed and pulled him down with her.

Something crinkled and crackled beneath them.

"What's all this? You were working in bed?" she said, laughing and pushing at the papers.

He scooped up the obstructions and tossed them to the floor. "It's the damned New Dawn sales list. I thought I might find items he kept."

"Something worth about ten million dollars?" With an index finger, she smoothed his brow, crimped again with frustration. "Didn't find it, did you?"

He plucked her hand away and kissed her palm. "I fell asleep dreaming of Chinese cabinets and Assyrian plaques and you. I—"

"What? What did you say?" She sat up, trying to dial a vague memory into clear focus.

"I was dreaming of you. Naked, if you must know."

Her system swamped with sensation, she struggled to think. "No, no, the other part."

"What? The Chinese cabinets and Assyrian plaques? You know, from the list."

She smiled, a self-satisfied Cheshire-cat smile. She knew who'd given the map to New Dawn. But nothing more could be done tonight.

About that, anyway.

"What is it, Vanessa?" One ebony brow quirked up. He lay at an angle across the Washington-mall-size bed, his desire for her evident in the prominent bulge in his jeans. One hand propped up his head and the other stroked her bare breast.

She gave herself over to his sensuous caresses and the heated need coursing through her body. "Nothing that won't wait until morning."

Tomorrow she'd confront a traitor and probe the U.S. Army's layers of secrecy.

But tonight was for the two of them.

She helped him skim out of his jeans and briefs. Careful of his injuries, she caressed his taut buttocks and slid her palms up his sides as he rolled on top of her. Sighing, she kissed his flat male nipples and reveled in his rock-hard weight and furnace-like heat.

Her heart swelled with love, and her body tingled with excitement. "Nick, what about creativity?"

"Later. Innovation can wait," he rasped, thrusting home. "Vanessa, I need you."

The next morning, Nick stepped into the garage. A brand-new, sweet midnight-blue Mercedes S600 waited for him. The dealer'd happened to have one in the showroom when he'd called yesterday afternoon.

ATSA promised to cover his loss once the operation ended, but delay in replacing his wheels wasn't an option. They might need the power and security this vehicle offered.

Their driver appeared at the door from the kitchen. He was polishing off one of Janine's apricot muffins. "Morning, Mr. Markos."

"Good morning, McNair. No aftereffects of yesterday's drug to hurt your appetite?"

A wide grin split the man's dark face. "Nothing affects my appetite. Good thing, too. That woman is one fine cook."

Vanessa's heels clicked on the cement as she entered. He turned to admire the curves he knew so intimately hugged by the sexy green knit dress he favored. When her hand reached for his, the tenderness threaded all the way to his heart.

She was sunshine and joy. He'd settled on Danielle, not knowing what could be. Vanessa's warmth and influence had him reexamining his priorities.

And his life.

Pain gnawed in his gut that she would walk out of his life when this was over. A life without her in it looked bleak, as empty as the black hole he'd been carrying around inside for ten years.

He couldn't let that happen. Perhaps success in this mission would restore enough of his lost honor so he'd have a life he felt he could share.

She smiled at her ATSA colleague. "Good morning, J.T. You're lucky to be eating Janine's cooking for free. Someday she's going to have a restaurant."

Unabashed, McNair licked the apricot stickiness from his fingers. "Mmm, I'll be her first customer."

Nick opened the rear car door. "Just don't let your stomach distract you from your job."

Not that he was the man to advise anyone about distractions. Vanessa Wade distracted the hell out of him.

"No, sir. You're safe with me at the wheel." All at once somber, the ATSA driver flapped a small salute. "My nap shut me out of yesterday's fireworks, but I'm not interested in a rerun. No sparks, shells or salvos of any kind today."

Vanessa eased into the car. "Except for the one we're about to set off."

# *Chapter 15*

$A$t Markos Imports Nick met with the two remaining staff, Celia Chin and Emil Alfieris, to go over the last inventory and accounts. In spite of their pleas and Abdul Nadim's finagling, he would sell.

He needed to rid himself of the constant reminder of his half brother's dishonor. Running a business he had no expertise in made no sense. And spreading his business interests too thinly would risk everything he'd built.

The three of them worked at the conference table while Vanessa observed from the ring of comfortable chairs.

The employees barely tolerated him, the executioner, but they loved her. The minute they'd walked in the door, she'd greeted them with personal comments. Celia'd shoved her family photos in Vanessa's face, and Alfieris had smoothed back his overlong black hair and lit up like Times Square on New Year's Eve. She kept them all supplied with coffee while they talked.

Vanessa instinctively knew the right word, the right touch

so people's personal concerns and joys poured out of them like warm syrup. She cared and showed it in ways he'd bet most people didn't perceive or appreciate.

He, on the other hand, was all business. Hell, he was the one paying Alexei's employees' salaries. But it was *her* sympathy and genuineness that kept them doing their jobs with some semblance of conscientiousness.

He had to give the two employees credit for moving around what little stock they had to make the showroom attractive. As the meeting concluded, he told them if he didn't conclude a deal within the next week, the shop inventory would be folded into the house auction.

Celia's mouth thinned with disapproval, but she merely nodded. He figured she'd finally accepted the inevitable. Emil stared at the floor like a man who didn't care.

"I'm sorry a sale hasn't worked out to keep you both on at Markos Imports," Nick said, "but my recommendations should help you obtain new positions soon. We'll stay open the rest of the week. Then you'll have two weeks' severance."

He stood to signal the conclusion of the meeting.

"I should tell you, Mr. Markos," Celia began, "that I have found another position. Bethesda Antiques and Antiquities needed a new manager."

"Congratulations, Celia. That's excellent," Nick said, greatly relieved.

"Thank you for your recommendation." The slender Chinese woman made a small, graceful bow and glided from the room.

"And you, Emil?" Vanessa asked, moseying around the desk.

The bird-like man shrugged as he backed toward the door. A smile tugged at his mouth, but didn't materialize. "I have a few options. Nothing definite."

She linked her arm with one of Emil's and led him back to an armchair. "I was telling Nick how clever you were to recognize the Ming vase."

"Shows some real expertise, Alfieris," Nick said. "My

brother must've relied on you to authenticate and price many items." He settled into a blue brocade chair to watch her finesse the scrawny bastard into folding his cards.

Alfieris fingered his red bow tie and puffed out his scrawny chest. "He was an expert in many areas, but I do have my specialties."

Vanessa perched on the third chair. She smiled sweetly. "Like Chinese art and antiques? Maybe furniture?"

His head and his Adam's apple bobbed in tandem. "I spent a few years in the Orient. Learned a lot firsthand from native experts."

"So naturally, when Alexei needed authentication of some antique Chinese cabinets last year, you were his man."

The assistant manager's pale eyes darted from one to the other of them. Vanessa's expression of open curiosity and Nick's relaxed pose and mask of casual interest appeared to satisfy him. "Well, there were a few."

"Fascinating," she cooed. "With ivory inlay and fancy decorations?"

Her low, sexy voice spiked Nick's blood pressure. He didn't like another man being her focus, even as a pretense. Her hand on Alfieris's forearm as a gesture of eager interest spurted protective instincts within him. His muscles knotted, but he restrained himself.

*Give the man plenty of rope…*

"Yes," the assistant manager finally answered with a smug smile. "There was one in particular. A game box."

"What do you mean?"

"A box about the size of that fax machine on the desk. With ivory and jade inlay in a dragon design. It opened into a dozen small compartments with ivory game pieces, dice and boards. Mahjong, chess and others."

"Wonderful," she gushed. "I remember in the records there were Assyrian plaques and statues of gods and goddesses. Is that another area of your special expertise, Emil?"

Nick couldn't help a smile. The woman was reducing the poor little man to a fawning puppy with her sexy voice and big green eyes, and she believed males considered her a buddy. He'd gladly spend years convincing her otherwise.

Fortunately the other man took Nick's smile as encouragement. The preening peacock puffed out his chest. "I wish. The Assyrian pieces were prime finds. Alexei handled those himself. Him and that woman from the museum." He gave a disdainful sniff. "I personally thought they were worth more than he got for them. Particularly the plaque."

"What was special about the plaque?"

"A most unusual item. Ivory. Of a lion killing a Nubian. Probably one of a kind."

Vanessa folded her hands in her lap and nodded in satisfaction. "I hope Alexei appreciated what a valuable asset he had in you, Emil."

The foolish man had the grace to blush. "I guess."

Nick held his breath as she zeroed in for the kill.

"You should've been well paid for your expertise and your efforts. Did he give you a cut of his commission from New Dawn, or did they pay you separately?"

No proud peacock now, Alfieris looked more like a banty rooster that'd lost a cockfight. He shrank into the chair. His slicked-back hair drooped. His flush leached away. Beads of sweat formed at his temples. "I don't know what you mean."

Vanessa patted his arm again. "No, really. A man of your talents must've been properly compensated." When he didn't reply right away, she recoiled, a shocked expression rounding her soft mouth. She turned to Nick with a crusader's fire in her eyes. "Nicky, sweetheart, we really must do something if Alexei shortchanged dear Emil."

*Nicky?* Nick's brain scrambled to keep up. "Speak up, man. Did my brother cheat you?"

He watched as dollar signs scrolled across the man's pupils. Alfieris's Adam's apple made a slow journey up and down his chicken throat as he swallowed his discretion. Ah, greed. The great motivator.

"I was paid for a few of the extra jobs I did. But not for *all* of them."

Nick waited. Patient silence often lubricated tongues.

"Alexei paid me no extra. The other, the New Dawn man, he paid me a commission. I have no records. You understand."

Nick understood, all right. Like his brother, this worm had trafficked with the terrorists. But unlike Alexei, he was lucky to be alive. So far.

He set down his coffee cup before he crushed it into bits. "Of course."

Vanessa smiled at Alfieris. "And tell me, did New Dawn pay you handsomely for delivering the plans of the Chevy Chase house?"

As her words sank in, his face frosted over like a shallow puddle in a cold snap. "What are you talking about?"

"Those plans were to guide their agents to my bedroom. You're very lucky they weren't successful. The money they paid you could've made you an accomplice to kidnapping or murder."

Fear and guilt slid across his face. "No. I never…"

"Ah, but you did." The even, unemotional delivery belied her accusatory words. "Fifty thousand dollars is a hefty deposit. Clever of you stashing it in a shiny new bank account in Chevy Chase Trust, far from your regular bank."

"Too bad you won't get to use it." Nick leaned forward, his hands loose on his knees, his weight balanced, ready.

Alfieris jerked to his feet, but his knees knocked like two saplings in a windstorm. "You can't threaten me. You're just guessing."

Vanessa made sympathetic clucking sounds. "Emil, if you're going to lead a life of crime, you should be more discreet. The day we inventoried the house, you mentioned the Chinese chest and the Assyrian plaque. I didn't remember until last night that Alexei sold those items on behalf of the terrorists. That list isn't public knowledge. A quick search this morning found your new bank account."

"What is it they say?" Nick said. "Follow the money."

The banty rooster mustered some bravado for another round. "It's just your word. You have no proof I did anything illegal for that money."

"Ah, but you just gave us proof, Emil," Vanessa said. She extracted a tiny recorder from her pocket and held it up like a quiz-show hostess. "You were more helpful than you know."

Alfieris goggled at the recorder. He opened his mouth. Closed it. Opened it again like a landed trout. Clamped it shut as if he saw he was drowning himself with every word.

Nick stood to employ the impact of his greater size. "Some official associates of mine are very interested in this New Dawn representative. Talking to them might make things go easier on you."

Alfieris stuck out his chin and fisted his bony hands at his sides. "I have nothing to say."

Vanessa leaned back in her chair and crossed her legs. "I wonder what would happen if a rumor floated to certain contacts that Alexei wasn't alone in skimming profits from New Dawn. What a shame if you met the same fate as he."

His eyes narrowed at her. "His death was an accident. I read it in the newspaper."

"A knife between the ribs is hardly ever an accident. New Dawn has many tentacles and resources." She examined her manicure before gazing up at him again. Friendly interest and concern vanished, replaced by professional-grade steel.

His face ashen, Alfieris started for the doorway.

In a flash, Vanessa lunged. She delivered a quick chop to his throat.

When he gagged and bent over, Nick yanked his arms behind him.

Alfieris coughed and writhed, but sagged when stymied by Nick's superior strength.

"Ah, there you are, Byrne," Vanessa said. "I thought you'd never get here."

Beyond the ATSA control officer and two others, Nick could see Celia Chin in the hallway. Her eyes were as round as the full hunter's moon.


"The man's a land mine just waiting to blow," Simon Byrne said to Vanessa Thursday afternoon in the command post next door. He leaned back in the upholstered office chair and crossed his booted feet on the computer desk. His usual cocky humor had vanished. "We can't trust him."

Other agents, tech staff and Gabe Harris monitored the security system at other computers. She decided Byrne was lounging nearby just so he could bug her.

Resentment banded Vanessa's chest, but she forced a deep breath before she responded. She paused in running her computer search. She knew Nick better than the ATSA officer. She trusted him. But Simon would think her gut feeling was based on personal emotions and not professional experience.

Emotion had no place in the mission.

She swiveled away from her computer. "Nick Markos won't do anything to jeopardize our plans. Sketchy as they are. He wants his brother's murderers as much as we do."

"Maybe." His feet slammed to the floor. "He wants the danger done, and he has a thing for you. It's the damaged soldier that worries me. You making any headway on Somalia?"

"Some." At least that was an area they agreed on. "I have the names of the men in his A team. People to contact." Maybe the official cover-up hadn't gagged all his former buddies.

Byrne uttered a noncommittal grunt as he stood. "That could take some time. You'd better hope Markos doesn't find that ten mil before we get Husam Al-Din."

She bit back a retort. They'd expected the terrorist leader to make another threatening phone call after the car bombing, and the silence was straining everyone's nerves. Doing her job was her best course of action. Playing her part and spying on Nick.

She was getting damn tired of both. Acting the urbane sophisticate at embassy dinners and penthouse parties and not leveling with Nick had her nerves as scattered as fallen leaves in a breeze.

She printed out the list of names and addresses before logging out. Tomorrow she'd start with the man who'd survived the Karkaar ambush with Nick, Cruiser aka Louis Crusotti.

When Vanessa returned from the surveillance house, she found Nick in the library. His conference call with several of the N.D.M. International managers promised to last most of the afternoon, so she went to the basement gym to work out. Her Pilates routine both relaxed and revived her. Guzzling much-needed liquid from her water bottle, she mopped her forehead with a hand towel. She keyed on the treadmill.

Remembering yesterday's success, she smiled. She and Nick had worked together like longtime partners who knew each other's minds. She knew he'd been prepared to defend her physically, but he'd sat back and watched her work. He'd even played along. Like a pro, in fact. Between them, they'd maneuvered Emil into his corner. If only the little man's information could lead ATSA to New Dawn's leader.

When she finished her shower, from her window she saw Nick standing out on the terrace. The scuffed leather jacket he wore emphasized the width of his shoulders and the taut narrowness of his hips. He'd jammed his hands in the rear pockets of his jeans, and he was staring pensively into the chilly November darkness.

She knew firsthand the tensile firmness of those shoulders and hips, the gentleness of his strong hands. She knew the body beneath the layers. If looking at him clothed was enough to turn her on, good thing she'd finished on the treadmill. Humpty Dumpty might've had another fall.

She slipped on a heavy sweater and traipsed down to the sunroom.

"May I join you, or is this star-gazing for one?" she said as she stepped onto the terrace.

He beckoned to her. "Not many stars. Rain clouds like it here." He scrubbed a hand across his five-o'clock shadow. "I need fresh air after that phone session."

"You don't like being a long-distance boss." No more than he'd be a long-distance dad. The thought blindsided her, and her heart thudded an extra beat. She blinked the notion away. If he were ever a dad, she'd never know about it, would she? "Is N.D.M. chugging uphill or downhill without you?"

He held one hand out level. "On the straightaway. Not downhill, for damn sure. Reports were good. Problem with the Hong Kong supplier's ironed out. New York has the other glitches in hand."

Clouds played peekaboo with the stars and the waxing moon. Now that fall's advance was denuding the yard's surrounding shrubbery, traffic noises drifted to her ears. She caught a whiff of fragrant wood smoke from a fireplace in the posh neighborhood. Designer firewood, she guessed, from the Chevy Chase Market.

Her heartbeat tripped as Nick tucked her beneath one arm. Her mind temporarily snagged on his familiar scent, one she would always associate with autumn leaves and wood smoke. "So delegating responsibility's not all bad."

"Thanks for reminding me I could delegate," he said. "And thank you for your generous words about Alexei. I tend to forget his good qualities."

She tilted her head for his kiss. The electric thrill sang through her body and curled around her heart. He was strong and honorable, and she trusted him. Byrne was off base.

When they finally separated and her brain worked again, she said, "My generous words? What did I say? When?"

"I must be good if my kisses short-circuit that quick brain of yours." He grinned, a lethal curve of sculpted lips that mesmerized her again. "At the funeral, you praised Alexei's expertise to the playboy prince. I meant to mention it then, but events blew it from my mind."

Events like the car bombing. She gave an involuntary shudder.

"You're welcome. I meant it. He was the expert. Emil Alfieris is cocky about his knowledge, but wrong about the Ming vase. According to ATSA's consultant, it is a later copy. Your brother's valuation on it was correct."

He laughed, a hearty rumble that seduced as much as his smile. "I don't mind putting a lower price on the vase. It's worth it. Does our banty rooster know?"

Now it was her turn to grin. "Not yet."

"Has he crowed yet?"

She wagged her head. "Emil clucked a bit, but I think his crowing is done. He did agree to look at pictures to find the New Dawn agent he met. So far he hasn't identified any of their people we know about or anyone in the museum reception pictures."

"Frustrating. They get the breaks, and we get dead ends."

"You must be pleased that neither Lise nor her boyfriend sold us out."

"Relieved. For Janine's sake, more than mine. But we still don't know what Ray's game is."

"Ah, but we do. You know those papers you saw Ray stuff in his backpack?"

He turned to face her. Dark shadows drenched the angles and planes of his strong features. Light from the sunroom glittered in his eyes. The sheer intensity of his heavy-lidded gaze bounced her pulse. "Someone looked in his pack?"

She shrugged. "I can't give away all of ATSA's methods. His papers are a map of this property all right. But of the grounds, not the house."

His brows drew together in a thoughtful caterpillar.

He'd figure it out soon, she knew, but no sense prolonging the mystery. "ATSA has learned that Ray is taking a landscaping course."

"Landscaping." As the idea and its ramifications sank in, he began to nod. His understanding earned her a quick buss on the nose. "So the street tough is a student with a goal. Was he designing improvements to the backyard?"

She wrapped her arms around his waist. "A class assignment. That's why he kept skulking around outside the house. He didn't want anyone to know. I'm not sure why."

"I'll bet his street pals laughed at him. He probably figured we would, too. Does that course of his involve garden walls and stonework?"

"I don't know, but I can find out. What—"

The jangling telephone inside slammed them apart. In two strides Nick entered and grasped the phone.

Vanessa clicked on her mike. "Byrne, do you copy?"

*"Affirmative. Stay with him."*

She closed the atrium door behind her with a quiet click as Nick picked up the receiver.

"How many demonstrations do you need, Mr. Markos, before you see things our way?" said the smooth, accented voice.

"That's enough," Nick hissed into the phone. "I knew you were murdering slime, but now I've seen it for myself."

"Time is growing short," continued the voice as if he hadn't been insulted. "We want our money."

"I'll pay you, damn it," Nick said. "Just tell me when and where."

Vanessa's heart stopped, then stumbled into a frantic pace. Simon Byrne's curse nearly burst her eardrum. "No, Nick, what are you doing?"

He covered the mouthpiece with one hand. "Ending this charade, that's what. No more waiting for a shot or a bomb to explode or thugs to snatch you."

"I am gratified you see things our way," said the voice. "Leave the money in—"

"No. Forget that. I'm not leaving ten million dollars in cash somewhere for your goons to pick up. You, *and only you,* meet me for the exchange, or no deal." His voice serrated with fury and his jaw rigid with uncompromising resolve, he glowered at the phone as though he could see through the lines to the caller's smug face.

Vanessa held her breath while silence indicated the man on the other end pondered the demand. What did Nick mean to do? Would he give them his own money? Or had he found Alexei's stash and not told her? He wouldn't really pay them, would he? Anxiety pinched until her chest ached.

"Very well. Here is what you must do. Put the ten million in a leather laptop case. Take it to the Tomb of the Unknowns at Arlington National Cemetery. Leave your bodyguard at home."

"I can have the money by tomorrow. What time?"

Again a long pause. *Ye gods, what the hell's going on?* She bit her lip in consternation.

"Not tomorrow," said the voice. "Sunday. At four forty-five precisely."

"Why so long?" Nick demanded. "I want this over with."

"One more thing," the terrorist said. "Bring Ms. LeBec with you. As a gesture of good faith."

"No. I won't endanger her any further. I'll come alone."

"Bring the woman or the deal is off." The confident sneer in the voice stung Vanessa's nerves like salt water on sunburn.

Nick sighed in resignation. "How will I know you?"

"That will be no problem. We know you." A soft click terminated the connection.

Nick lowered the receiver into the phone cradle.

"Nick, please, you didn't have to do that. I don't understand." She rushed to him and gripped his arms, more to support herself than to shake sense into him.

He hugged her to him. "It's the only way, honey. Don't you see? I won't put you in more danger because of my brother. When it's over, we can figure out what's real and what isn't between the two of us."

The band around her chest cranked in another notch. Real? *Oh, my love, is anything in our relationship real?* She was afraid that what wasn't real was genuine illusion.

Simon Byrne and Gabe Harris marched into the sunroom. "What the blazing hell are you up to, Markos?"

# Chapter 16

Nick had to convince the ATSA officer his plan would work. He folded his arms and prepared to do battle.

Byrne stood rigid with anger in the middle of the room while the other officer took up a position at the doorway. Was he guarding Nick from danger or preventing him from leaving?

Nick glared at the CO. "You're worried I'll really pay them off. I'm not that stupid."

"Then why bite?"

Nick had worked it out and waited for the New Dawn man to call. "Catching small fish on our hooks has fed you no information. You're no closer to capturing Husam Al-Din now than you were when his agent killed my brother."

At his side, Vanessa dropped her gaze to the floor. He could tell she was pondering his assertions.

A scowl pleated Byrne's forehead. "We're getting closer."

"Not close enough or fast enough. A waiting game is futile. And dangerous. Each time they escalate the violence. We have to force the issue." *Before Vanessa is hurt or killed.* He cared too much to allow her to continue to be the bait. Even if she was willing.

"What makes you think Husam Al-Din will meet you in person? Or that it was him on the phone, for that matter?" said Harris, the other officer.

"If it's not the leader, it has to be a lieutenant in the New Dawn organization. Someone Al-Din would trust with ten million dollars. Someone who can give us what we want to know." Nick waited, breath held, hoping that was enough for the ATSA officer to make the leap.

"Your crazy offer won't work. Might get you killed," Byrne said, pacing the room. "And it's unnecessary."

*"Unnecessary?"* Nick raked his fingers through his hair. "Time is winding down. Five days until November 11. If we get Al-Din now, you can avert their attack and prevent deaths."

The ATSA control officer leaned against the back of the sofa. His assessing gaze drifted from Nick to Vanessa and back. "We can avert the attack anyway."

"What do you mean?" Vanessa stalked toward her colleague. She stopped halfway there, as if weighing her loyalties. Nick crossed mental fingers.

The man lifted one shoulder and tipped his head apologetically. "I just found out this afternoon. Intelligence has scoped out what New Dawn plans for Veterans Day. The president always lays a wreath at the—"

"Tomb of the Unknowns," Nick interjected. "Exactly where the voice directed me to deliver the money. Doesn't that seem too coincidental, too pat?"

Byrne shook his head. "Not from what we know about New Dawn. Relentless but not subtle. They probably see the dual use of that location as symbolic. An ironic joke."

Vanessa spun toward Nick. Her green eyes pleaded with him. "So you see, you don't have to endanger yourself after all. When he calls again, you can say you changed your mind."

God knew Nick would rather skydive without a parachute than be responsible for an op. His instincts and planning had resulted in disaster before.

This time he wouldn't direct the op. Others would. He wouldn't hunker safely in the background either. Pretending to pay off Al-Din or his agent would set him square in the sights of a potential crossfire. And Vanessa had to be by his side.

He might have the shakes. Or another flashback. He might freeze. Fear churned his insides.

But he had to do this. He could do it.

Not only for his honor, but for Vanessa.

His gut warned him the Arlington Cemetery location and time were deliberate and calculated. Byrne was wrong about why. Nick just had to work out the connection. Instead of deterring him, the oddity of the so-called coincidence chiseled his decision in stone.

"I'm going through with the fake payoff," he said. "Will you cover my back or not?"

Nick watched Byrne's eyes. At first they shone as hard as the diamond stud in one ear. Then the corners softened as he glanced toward the ceiling. He was waffling.

Vanessa returned to Nick, linked an arm with his. "Consider the possibilities, Byrne."

"You taking his side now?" But his tone seemed more banter than challenge.

She ignored the question and launched into her spiel. "We could shut this terrorist threat down early with no threat to the president or anybody else. At the very least, we'd have another of the terrorists in custody, a higher-up who may really lead to Husam Al-Din."

"I have the feeling there's another possibility," her colleague said.

"What if you're wrong? What if New Dawn's plans are for some other venue? For instance, the big parade with dozens of dignitaries. What would General Nolan say if he thought we passed up a chance to head them off at the pass?"

Byrne's jaw worked on Vanessa's words as if chewing and digesting them. His expression slid the rest of the way from intransigence to speculation.

Finally he tugged at his studded earlobe. His mouth flirted with a grin. "Wade, I'm damned proud. You've picked up my annoying habit of questioning the agency line. Hell of a thing to be in charge for a change and on the other side."

Nick saw her shoulders relax. "So what do you think?" she said, hope edging her voice.

Byrne folded his arms. "They've chosen the timing carefully. Fifteen minutes before sunset blurs the landscape. Surveillance in such a wide-open spot as Arlington National Cemetery means more personnel than I've been assigned. They've given us three days lead. We'll have to hustle. If I can get the director's authorization, it's a go."

Her cheeks flushed, and she turned to Nick with triumph brightening her eyes.

Before she could speak, he said to Byrne, "I know you don't trust me. I'll wear a mike, do whatever's necessary for springing the trap."

"Tomorrow's Friday. Banks are closed on Saturday," Vanessa pointed out. "Nick, they'll be expecting you to go to the bank for the money."

"Count on it." Byrne levered away from the sofa. "We'll hammer out the details after I talk to the director."

After Byrne and the other officer had left, Vanessa said, "Nick, bringing in Husam Al-Din, ending this operation, isn't your responsibility. You take too much on yourself."

"What do you mean? Someone had to do something. Time's running out."

"First Somalia. Then your brother. Now this. You shoulder responsibility for problems that aren't yours, for more than any man should."

Doubt gripped him. "You think I won't follow through?"

She shook her head wildly, slapping her French braid back and forth. "No, that's not what I meant at all. I trust you. But I worry about you, too."

Nick said, "Thank you for that. I hope I can come through. Your trust means more than anything to me."

The pulse in her throat throbbed, and her eyes darkened. "And your trust means *everything* to me."

To Vanessa's surprise, General Nolan agreed by Friday morning to the fake payoff. The director trusted Nick no more than Byrne did, so the time crunch was the deciding factor.

Veterans Day was Tuesday, only four days away.

Byrne quickly arranged for the bank's cooperation. In the afternoon, accompanied by McNair and Harris as his "security," Nick sauntered into the Chevy Chase Bank with his empty laptop case. A half hour later, the three of them marched out with the case bulging with bundles of newsprint topped with a bundled layer of real hundred-dollar bills.

To any interested observer, the bulge was all cash.

In the afternoon, Vanessa left the rest of the team to craft the net to be spread over the cemetery. They had to knit up any holes their fish might swim through and yet keep the net invisible. Officers had to blend in with tourists and staff while taking positions around the Tomb of the Unknowns.

Timing would be key. The cemetery closed at five o'clock, only fifteen minutes after the rendezvous. Darkness would close in rapidly after that.

Vanessa liked planning operations. Strategy intrigued her—tossing ideas back and forth. Mostly she liked working with the team.

But her job was to be with Nick. When the strategy session ended, she left. As she slipped through the fence to the house, she remembered the scene on the terrace that afternoon.

Nick had hired young Ray Lincoln to finish building the

terrace stone wall. As an apprentice, Ray had no tools for the job, so Nick had financed the purchase. He'd salvaged Ray's pride by arranging to deduct payments from his salary.

As they'd shaken hands to seal the bargain, Ray had said with his chin raised, "Deal. I do good work. You won't be sorry."

Nick wasn't the shark she'd originally expected weeks ago when the director'd ordered her undercover. He dealt always with honor, respect and fairness. And he'd handled Ray with a sensitivity that impressed her.

How could she not love the man? How could she not wish with every fiber of her being for things to be different? For an end to the mandate to spy on him so she wouldn't feel this burden of guilt.

For him to love her back.

She wrapped her arms around herself as if to ease the constant ache in her chest.

Nick trudged into the master suite late Saturday night and kicked off his loafers. He heard the shower running and smiled at how natural having Vanessa there felt.

She no longer bothered with the other bathroom. This one was designed for two. The tiled shower boasted dual heads, a shampoo dispenser and enough room to dance the tango.

He yanked off his shirt and unzipped his trousers.

The pretense of sleeping with him while keeping her belongings in the other bedroom was now reality, the norm. An arrangement he wanted to make permanent. After tomorrow's trap for New Dawn, they could dispense with the damned Danielle charade. The entire mess created by Alexei had taken over his life. Worse, it had reincarnated his old guilt and pain.

On the plus side, the mess had brought him Vanessa.

With her warm cheer and gentleness, she'd poured her sunshine into his heart so the heavy darkness within him had begun to lift. She'd nudged him to reorder his priorities and take a hard look at what passed for his life. He needed that sunshine. He needed her wit and intelligence and kindness. Without her warmth, the old darkness might smother him.

A sound from the shower pulled him from his reverie. She was…singing? A rendition of "Take Me Out to the Ballgame" that redefined off-key. Her laugh and her speaking voice were low and sexy. Her singing grated like chalk on a board.

Grinning, he padded naked into the bathroom and opened the shower door.

A cloud of sultry heat laden with the perfume of her shampoo inundated his senses. She stood with her head back to rinse her hair. The mere sight of her excited him and expanded his soul.

Her closed eyes allowed him to drink in the view unobserved. Her raised arms lifted her full breasts, flushed pink and tempting from the hot water. He ached to lick the cascading water from her budded nipples. Suds oozed down her torso, clinging to the gentle swell of her hips. A fireball of heat roared through his blood and hardened him instantly.

"'Oh, it's one, two—'"

"Do you have a wounded chicken in here?"

She squeaked to a stop on "three strikes" when he stepped inside. Sputtering, she splashed shampoo suds at him. "You weren't supposed to hear me."

Laughing, he stepped into the spray and slicked up against her velvety body. "Then you shouldn't sing so loud. Surveillance probably picked it up on the outdoor mikes."

"Ye gods! The birds must have their heads tucked under their wings in protest." She pushed the soap dispenser and smoothed soapy hands over his chest. Rising on tiptoes, she kissed his chin.

He bent to kiss her beautiful breasts, suckling the pebbled nipples until she gasped. "What other deep, dark secrets are you keeping from me?"

He pushed his arousal between her legs. Shuddering with

pleasure, she squeezed her thighs together, and the pressure of her toned muscles veered the rest of his blood south. He was on fire. If he didn't get inside her soon, he'd explode.

Sighing, she closed her eyes and twisted into the spray. "I've told you my personal secrets. My life is an open book."

He couldn't resist running his tongue along the arch of her graceful neck. "A few bad dates. A voice best kept under deep cover. Not very daring or professional for a hotshot government officer."

A playful smile curved her mouth, and devilment gleamed in her green eyes. One hand closed around his heated length. "How's this for daring? And it's definitely unprofessional."

Raw hunger pulsed through his veins, and he sucked in a ragged breath. "Unprofessional? I've been meaning to talk to you about that. But later. Put your arms around my neck."

Desperation roaring in his ears, he glided his hands slowly over the silken swells of her breasts, down the feminine flare of her hips. She writhed in delight, and as his fingers found the sensitive bud within her moist folds, she shuddered and arched against his hand.

Satisfied she was slick and ready for him, he sheathed himself with the protection he'd stashed on the soap dish. He lifted her against the tiled wall, and she twined her legs around him.

"Now, Nick!" A wild little moan parted her lips. She clutched at his arms as he wedged himself into her tight little body.

He pushed in, slow and deep, groaning at the power of her grip on him. She was so small, he was never sure they'd quite fit, but the fit was perfect. No woman had ever fitted him so well, read him so well, loved him so well.

Arching in his arms, she cradled him in her tight folds. Undulating to match his thrusts, she took him into the heat of her being.

His whole body tingled with pleasure that was almost painful. He gritted his teeth to make it last for her.

Together they found the rhythm that made her ripple against him. Together they fused into one as passion burned away the rest of the world. Together they slid and stroked and surged until heat tore from his body in a wave of ecstasy and she shimmered around him in torrid undulations.

Later when they lay in bed together, Vanessa's body still sang. Her few previous experiences with sex had never brought her such depths and heights. Their illusory affair would end tomorrow or in a few days, but she'd never regret her one-sided love for Nick.

"About tomorrow," she said. She wanted nothing left to chance. "Did Byrne go over all the details with you?"

He lay propped up on one elbow beside her. "As much as he cared to. The man doesn't trust me with the laptop case of fake money. That's locked up next door."

"So you're ready."

"As ready as I can be. I still think there's something about the place and time we're missing. I wish I knew."

The muscles in his face looked tense and hard, a man ready for action. The furrows of worry in his brow meant he'd stay cautious. A safe attitude.

She prayed for his safety.

"Byrne said they chose the time when visitors would be leaving the cemetery and dusk would confuse things," she said. "Our people will blend in the crowd."

"Their people, too."

She moved her lips into what she intended as a cheerful smile, but sadness dragged at the corners. "Tomorrow this entire operation might end."

Nick placed a warm palm against her cheek. "I don't want *us* to end with it."

Her heart hummed with exhilaration, but her conscience poked her with bitter reality. "But, Nick—"

His expression softening with affection, he pressed a long

finger against her lips. "If you're going to bring up the unprofessional issue, forget it. After tomorrow, our being together for real will be no issue."

She scooted to a sitting position. "Nick, we haven't been together *for real.* This is all an illusion. You don't really know me. You know the role I've been playing in designer clothes and at posh restaurants and parties."

He shook his head. "I also know the 'Confessor' who sweet-talked a greedy traitor out of his incriminating secrets. And the tough-minded government officer who faced down an angry superior to argue her case. I know the sexy naked woman who made love with me in the shower. Don't tell me that's not real."

"We have so little in common. I'm a New York cop's daughter, and you're a CEO."

"Who grew up on the docks, no stranger to city cops."

"I'm not your type. Truly, I'm nothing like my sister or Danielle."

"Danielle's defection, if you remember, was more of a deal gone sour than a broken heart. I counted myself lucky. And it's your fault I stopped seeing Diana."

"My fault? I knew it. The paint—"

"Not the paint, honey. You were so damn cute in your painter's hat, your glorious hair piled on top your head, all pink in the cheeks defending your sister, I knew then it wasn't Diana I wanted. It was you. I tried to phone you a few days later, but your mom said you'd left the city."

She stared at him with her mouth slack. She had left the city, as he said, to return to her post in Baltimore. Her mind and her heart groped at his words, and her stomach lurched at the possibility that she'd been wrong all along. But this major shift in belief wouldn't wrap around her mind.

"I know," he continued, "you aren't sure if you can trust me. God knows I don't trust myself. I told myself not to trust you, an undercover operative, experienced in deception. Other women have wanted me for my position, money, influence. Not you. When you defended my actions to Byrne, my doubts fell away."

She ought to say, "I *am* an undercover operative. You *shouldn't* trust me," but the words stuck in her throat. Guilt sat heavily in her stomach, a tight, slick ball of omissions, lies and dissembling.

"I've thrown a lot at you." He clicked off the bedside lamp and tucked her close beside him. "Sleep on it, and we'll work things out together. After tomorrow."

Vanessa lay in the curve of Nick's arms, her back sheltered against his front. The ache of looming loss constricted her chest. She wanted to believe he wouldn't hate her when he learned she'd been spying on him. With all her heart, she wanted to believe he truly cared for her.

Cared, lusted for, even liked, but not the other *L* word.

She wasn't the sophisticated partner a worldly man like Nick needed. The mission had thrown them together.

She'd tried to prove she could stay detached undercover, but instead had fallen into a bottomless trap of involvement. Her loss of objectivity could've risked the mission because of her foolish, soft heart.

Softie or not, she had her orders.

As close as she was to his naked form, she could feel Nick's regular heartbeat and even breathing. He was asleep. For the past few nights, the nightmare hadn't tormented him. She counted on his sleeping as deeply and peacefully tonight.

*I told myself not to trust you.*

Tears burned again, and she swiped them away. He'd been right not to trust her. Tomorrow after the meeting with Husam Al-Din or his agent, she'd confess to him her spying on him.

Then he'd hate her. He'd never want to see her again.

Pain skewered her heart as she slid out of the silk sheets.

# Chapter 17

Nick awoke to find Vanessa gone from his bed. When he didn't hear her in the bathroom or see a light, anxiety prickled the skin on his nape.

Where the hell was she? Leaving in the middle of the night wasn't like her. Perhaps she was thirsty and had gone downstairs for a drink.

Or perhaps the terrorists had set up tomorrow as a decoy and they'd come back to the house for her. Or the money. Or both.

Alarms buzzed in his head and skittered down his spine. He had no pistol, no knife. Only his wits and rusty combat skills.

The security monitor blinked green at him. He pushed buttons. Everything seemed in order. The system was working. No intruders.

What the hell?

He rolled out of bed and into sweatpants and sneakers. He made quick work of checking the other bedrooms and baths.

No Vanessa.

He listened for a moment at the railing. Nothing. Only the normal creaks and shifts of an old house.

Adrenaline surging in his veins, he crept downstairs.

The faint ribbon of light beneath the library door stopped him in his tracks. What would Vanessa be doing in there? Or had the terrorists somehow bypassed surveillance and the security system?

He listened at the door, but heard only the whispery slide of papers. Then a faint hum. His laptop?

Crouched over in combat readiness, he inched the doorknob clockwise and pushed the door open.

Vanessa sat at the mahogany desk in front of his open laptop. The desk lamp's glow shimmered like red honey in the mass of hair falling on her shoulders and in her face. She wore his discarded T-shirt.

And she was leafing through papers from his briefcase.

Pain and fury ripped up from his belly to fill his chest and clutch at his throat.

He stalked forward. "So this is how you show your damn trust in me?"

She shot to her feet. Her green eyes—her traitorous green eyes—filled with guilty panic. Her freckles stood out in stark relief as if painted. "Oh, God, Nick! It's not what it looks like. I…I had to—"

"Had to *spy* on me? ATSA orders, of course. And were you also ordered to ply me with sex? To make sure I went along with their schemes? That sure as hell changes the meaning of *professional*."

Realizing she was no better than Danielle or the other society women cut deep. She didn't want him for himself but for ATSA's security. Her perky, open act had sucked him in, softened him up, had even had him wanting the family and home he'd never expected to have.

He'd given her his trust, and she'd flipped it on him and

stabbed him in the heart with it. The betrayal drummed in his head and clogged his lungs.

"No! Never. How could you say such things? How could you think…?" She laid the papers on the desk. "You have to look at these. I found—"

"You found nothing I want to see. *Nothing but the end.* Put those down and get out." He hardly recognized his voice, flat and cold as winter.

She came around the desk, stumbled and caught her balance on the edge. Anguish and uncertainty glittered in her eyes, but he steeled himself against the show of false emotion.

"I did trust you. I do," she said. "But I had no choice. The director and Byrne were afraid you might actually pay off New Dawn. I was going to tell you everything tomorrow."

Anger twisted his mouth around his reply. "Confess? *Vanessa the Confessor.* That's a laugh. I've saved you the trouble. We have to go to Arlington together tomorrow. Keep away from me until then."

She pressed her hands to her stomach and brushed past him to the door.

Ignoring her trembling mouth and ashen face, he turned aside.


Vanessa trudged up the stairway with the weight of Nick's rejection crushing her nearly double. His painful accusations roiled in her stomach and suffocated her. At the top, she avoided looking in the direction of the master bedroom and stumbled into her old room. She crawled into the four-poster and, shivering, wrapped herself in a cocoon of covers. She'd never be warm again.

He was right that she'd lied to him, that she'd spied on him. And, she supposed, right to believe all of that meant she didn't trust him. He was wrong about the sex. But he wouldn't have believed her if she'd professed her love for him.

Her eyes ached from the tears flowing into her pillow. Oh, God, she'd hurt him so. He'd begun to heal and find his pride and honor again, but she'd torn open his wounds and left him bleeding. It seemed neither his brother's crimes nor his fiancée's desertion had wounded him this deeply.

She saw the implication of that realization with scalding clarity.

He loved her, too.

And now it was too late. Her spying had turned his love to hate.

All the reasons she'd told herself anything long-lasting between them wouldn't work came back to punch her in the belly. Maybe he did want her for herself after all, but the other reasons were still valid. He was a wealthy CEO, an international businessman who fit into a world she never could. And now he'd never trust her again.

Her heart throbbed, then fell like a lump of coal low in her chest.

Tomorrow they had to work together. From somewhere inside her, she had to find the courage to work beside him. To finish their mission.

And then to walk away.

"You don't seem with it this morning, Wade," J. T. McNair said. He carried the laptop case stuffed with money and paper. "You sure you're up for this meet?"

They walked to the garage, where Nick waited for the drive to Arlington. Vanessa glanced at her watch. Four o'clock exactly. Forty-five minutes before the meeting with the New Dawn leader or his agent.

She knew she looked like hell. Her eyes were red and puffy to match her hair. She'd had no sleep. Caffeine and adrenaline had to power her through. "I'm ready. Let's roll up this slime."

For the first time in weeks, she carried a weapon, the S&W 640 in the ankle holster concealed by her navy pantsuit. Practical brogans, not sexy slingbacks, were on her feet. Her hair hid the tiny mike in her ear, and she had a cell phone for emergencies. She felt herself. Less vulnerable.

Except to one man.

As they entered the garage, Nick looked up from the newspaper he was holding.

On the surface, he looked better than she must. Handsome and potently male in his charcoal-colored wool suit and white turtleneck. Harder and more unreachable than she'd seen him, with an edge of pain that scraped her heart. Determination defined eyes as black and deep as the inside of a cave. His jaw could cut glass.

"I'm gonna miss driving this car today." A white grin flashed in McNair's dark face. He stashed his burden in the trunk. The case as well as the car had been fitted with tracking bugs. "You up on the drill?"

Nick's gaze skipping over her, he skewered the officer with a menacing stare. "ATSA cars stationed along the route to make sure we're not ambushed. Arrive at the cemetery ten minutes ahead of the meet. Leave the car in visitor parking and take Roosevelt Drive directly to the Tomb of the Unknowns and wait to be contacted. As soon as I'm approached, your people will move in." There was a pregnant pause. "Satisfied?"

"You wearing a wire? Mike work okay?"

"Affirmative. Checked everything out earlier. Let's go." Nick sauntered around to the driver's side as if going to a picnic.

Vanessa slid into the passenger seat and buckled up. If for no other reason, she needed clamping down to keep her somersaulting nerves in check.

Their erstwhile driver spoke into the headset he wore. "Fiancé's headed out." The code name made Vanessa wince.

McNair bent to speak to her. "I'll be here at the command post. Byrne's already in place at Arlington. Harris heads your escort, in one of the cars en route."

"Got it." She pressed the button to roll up the window.

In silence Nick and she drove into D.C. on Connecticut Avenue. He steered the powerful automobile along the mapped-out route and took no apparent notice of her presence. Tension rode between them, a thick wall more impenetrable than the stones Ray would slather with mortar on Monday.

As they proceeded around Tenley Circle to continue on Wisconsin Avenue, she noted the ATSA vehicles stationed at intervals, but didn't acknowledge them. The sunny Sunday offered barely any traffic to impede their progress. They left their escort behind as they crossed into Virginia and onto the George Washington Parkway. To Vanessa, the short drive had lasted eons, but twenty minutes put them ahead of schedule.

"Nick, I know you're angry with me, but we have to talk to each other for this op to work." Heart racing, she clenched her hands in her lap. They were icy beneath a film of sweat.

She saw his jaw tighten. He expelled a breath as though from a burst balloon. He jerked a nod at the dashboard clock. "We're early. What do you suggest?"

The tension wall seemed to thin and waver. She allowed herself to relax a bit. "Pull up ahead. We can wait awhile."

The Mercedes rolled to a stop in the small rest stop she indicated. No one occupied the five parking places or the lone picnic table.

"You're right," he said, still gripping the wheel as if it might fly away, "We have to set aside our differences. That's only part of what's tying me in knots."

"If you still think something smells of trap in this arrangement, why go through with it?"

"Not trap. Al-Din wants that money, and there's no reason to harm either of us if he thinks he has it."

"Then what?"

"They chose the day and time for more reason than dusk. Byrne has found nothing to suggest that, but my gut warns otherwise. I'd like to be wrong. That's another reason to go ahead." He reached for the *Washington Post* he'd tossed to the back seat. Multiple sections made the Sunday edition thicker than a New York deli sandwich. "I was looking in here for what else might be scheduled for today." He began leafing through a section, skimming headlines.

Vanessa trusted his instincts, even if he didn't. Working together felt wonderful. Temporary, she reminded herself. "Give me a couple of sections. I can search, too."

Nick watched her over his pages as she scanned the features. Last night had exacted a heavy toll on her. She must not've slept any more than he had. He'd tried to ignore the effect of his fury, but the image of her, pale and shaking, had haunted the rest of his night.

Her translucent skin held a pallor as white as the newsprint she held, and exhaustion smudged violet beneath her eyes. The sight of her, brittle and hurt but undaunted, speared him with remorse.

But they had to get through this damned meet first before he could fix the damage. He had to put himself in the zone and stay focused until the danger passed.

As he turned a page in the Capitol news section, the photo of a familiar building caught his attention. He read the caption and the accompanying story with mounting agitation. "I found it."

"What? We don't have much time."

The dashboard clock read four-thirty.

He shoved the paper between them so she could read it. "Remember at the Hirshhorn, the Yamari sculpture?"

She nodded, peering at the page. "The pedestal was covered with a tarp when we were there." Her eyes widened, and she gripped the paper's edge as what she read sank in. "Ye gods, the dedication ceremony's today. *At exactly five!*"

"The Yamari president will take part—is probably already there—along with the ambassador and several U.S. diplomats including the U.S. Secretary of State."

She looked up from the story. He could see the implications clicking in her intuitive mind. "Our money exchange is a decoy to distract ATSA. They must be on to us. New Dawn's real objective is that gathering."

"The money meet may be legit. Or they sent an expendable agent for ATSA to grab." He tapped the photo of the draped sculpture with the Hirshhorn Museum in the background for emphasis. "I'm betting the new Yamari democracy is their real target. Not the U.S. president on Veterans Day, but the new Yamari president today."

"Two days *before* Veterans Day. The ceremony'll have only the normal Diplomatic Security detail." The State Department provided security for foreign diplomats.

The knots in his shoulders eased at her acceptance. "So you buy my logic?"

"Your logic is flawless given the timing of both events. No way it's coincidence." She straightened in the bucket seat and dug her cell phone from her jacket pocket. "If they kill Ambassador Khalil as well, Husam Al-Din and New Dawn could carry out a coup with little opposition."

Nick waited as she hit speed dial. She reached the command post in seconds and explained their discovery. Moments later, she disconnected.

"What?"

Vanessa bit her lip. "McNair alerted Byrne and Harris. In case we're wrong, Byrne will continue to stake out the cemetery. Harris and the escort are on the way to the Mall. Capitol Police and Diplomatic Security will evacuate the Hirshhorn ceremony site."

Nick turned the key, and the engine purred to life. "What about us?"

Her pulse jumped, then slowed. He didn't mean *us* in that way. "We're to drive around for a while, shake any tails, then return to Chevy Chase. Byrne doesn't like the feel of Arlington, no matter what else happens."

From the furrows on her brow, she didn't like her orders any more than he did. Had his suspicions screwed up any chance they had of snaring Al-Din and stopping New Dawn? Or did his hunch hit a bull's-eye? He had to know.

"How far are we from the Hirshhorn?" He pressed the accelerator and rolled to the Parkway entrance.

He waited as she studied his face. Then her shoulders slumped. "We can't. Our New Dawn tail would know ATSA was on to their plot."

He slapped the steering wheel in frustration. "I hate to admit it, but you're right. Dammit, I need to know."

Her approving smile ratcheted up his confidence. "Your hunch has to be right. There are no coincidences. Simon or Gabe Harris will let us know."

"Okay. Our not going to Arlington might abort the money meet, but that can't be helped." The car's quick response soothed his nerves as he pulled into Parkway traffic. Too long since he'd driven his own car.

He drove along the winding road as Vanessa used the map to guide him in taking exits and reversing direction. They had just detoured for the third time when her cell phone jangled.

From her side of the conversation, Nick could tell it was Simon Byrne. She listened intently to his sit rep.

When she disconnected, she said, "He's on his way to the Mall. Something's going down at the Hirshhorn. They evacuated the diplomats already. He wouldn't say anything more."

Nick rolled his shoulders, tension drawing his muscles taut. "Did anyone show up at Arlington?"

"Just as you figured, Al-Din sent a close advisor. ATSA has him at HQ now. The general himself is grilling him."

"Not Husam Al-Din after all." No surprise. The terrorist leader was no fool. "Who is he? Does Byrne know his name?"

"And his voice. So do you. Abdul Rashid was your phone buddy. The shop employee Alfieris identified him as his contact."

"What else?" Nick said, hearing something in her tone.

"Rashid works for the Yamari prince as his secretary. Officers are on their way to talk to Prince Amir."

The possibility of Prince Smarmy's complicity in this affair should please Nick, but he felt no satisfaction. Only a tight knot in his belly about what was going down at the Mall. Had anything happened? Was this all a monumental waste of time? His heartbeat clattered. But all he could do was drive. And wait.

Vanessa said, "I still see familiar headlights behind us. Take this turn. We'll shake him before we head home."

"Husam Al-Din might call since he didn't get his money."

Now that darkness camouflaged them, Nick took the Chain Bridge exit across the Potomac and back into D.C. Somewhere after the Chain Bridge, as they zigzagged through a maze of streets, they lost whoever was following them.

Vanessa directed Nick to Massachusetts Avenue. Tense silence reigned as the Mercedes wound north to Chevy Chase.

When they reached the house, Nick intended to remedy last night's mistakes. He glanced sideways from time to time at Vanessa. In the gathering darkness of twilight, he couldn't see her clearly, only the halo of her bright hair. Wisps freed from her braid floated out like sunbeams.

Her gaze focused ahead. The occasional thinning of her mouth said her professional bearing was wavering. No wonder. Her case of nerves must match his Capitol-dome-size one.

As the car neared the D.C. line, Vanessa said, "You need to know what I've found about your mission in Somalia. I uncovered the last piece of the puzzle only this morning."

He waited for the old pain to surface from its dark burrow, but guilt gave his heart only a minor pinch. "I told you before it won't make a difference."

"The officers I tracked down were less than forthcoming, as you predicted. Then I accessed your original report, buried in army archives. And I talked to the other man who survived."

"Cruiser?" Guilt had kept Nick from keeping in touch. After all these years maybe he'd contact the man.

Smiling, she tsked at him. "Among other things, he told me your nickname, but I could've guessed. 'The Greek.'"

He steered around the circle and into the tree-lined streets of the wealthy suburb. "Turns out you didn't have all the facts prior to the mission in the Karkaar Hills. The brass orchestrated the cover-up to protect a general's son."

"Smitty?" The news threw him for a loop. He knew the team's exec was an officer's brat and his old man had pulled strings to get him promoted. But the guy had appeared to do his job. "How?"

She shifted in her seat to face him. "Smitty was responsible for obtaining the surveillance photos. Seems he fell into a stupor of hashish and other drugs, cheap in the village markets. He spent a lot of time out of it. He never sent out helicopters. He passed old footage to you. The old tape didn't show the warlord's troop buildup. He also faked other reports to keep superiors off his back.

"Nick, you can hang on to your guilt if you want, but the burden should fall on lots of others instead. Smith paid the price. He died of a drug overdose five years ago."

"Thank you for digging that out. You didn't have to do it. Plenty of mistakes and blame to go around, not all on these shoulders. The truth eases my mind, but I'll always see the faces of those men."

Vanessa smiled. "You said you and Cruiser escaped, but not how you took care of the warlord."

He knew what was coming. "It doesn't matter."

"Oh, but it does. You patched up your comrade and then single-handedly eliminated the bad guy and his men. Nick, you're the hero, not the goat."

"I did what was necessary. But thanks." Even without that weight lifted from his heart, one of the day's events helped. His hunch had panned out. The captured Rashid might lead them to the New Dawn leader.

"We still know nothing about New Dawn's plot on the Yamari leadership. If there is one. Nailing my brother's murderer would sure feel good. It would redeem the rest of my honor and that of my family." And maybe give him back his life and a chance at a future.

She started to reach a hand out to him, but pulled it back. "Simon should've scoped out the situation by now. Once we get in the house, I'll call him. Okay?"

"Thanks." He turned into the driveway and saw the spotlights in the front of the house. He pulled into the lighted garage and lowered the door behind them.

Vanessa started to open the passenger door, but he stopped her. "Wait. The security panel. No light."

"Power's not out. Something's very wrong."

Alarm skittered down his spine. "What the hell are the surveillance people doing?"

"I think there's only a skeleton crew next door. Mostly techs. McNair's downtown with the rest of the team. They must've alerted HQ." When she opened the door, she had her S&W in her hand. "I'll go inside to check it out."

"Somebody could be in the house. Husam Al-Din's agent. Or the man himself. They must've heard us enter the garage." He knew her capabilities as a government operative. Skilled and tough as she was, he wouldn't allow her to face this danger alone. "Vanessa, don't be a hero."

She bit her lip, and her brow pleated as she thought. She nodded. "We do it together."

In moments they had a plan.

Vanessa called Byrne on her cell while Nick sneaked around to the back. When she figured he was ready, she crept to the front door in case Al-Din or one of his fanatical thugs waited in ambush at the garage entry.

The arched panes over the door showed no light. The foyer was dark. Was that good or bad? She gripped her weapon.

Slowly she opened the door.

Lights flashed on. She blinked in the sudden glare.

A man stood in the center of the foyer. He pointed a silencer-equipped Beretta at her heart.

# *Chapter 18*

*P*rince Amir.

Fear tightened her stomach in a cold knot.

The prince took a step closer. His lips curled in a leer. The cruel blackness in his eyes sent chills down her spine.

How had she ever thought he was charming?

"My dear Danielle," he said with oily smugness, "put that dangerous toy on the floor. We would not want an accident."

She couldn't let panic weaken her. As long as he thought she was Danielle, he might underestimate her. She bent to lay down the S&W. When she stood, her hand flew to her throat.

To the mike in her collar. *Please somebody be there.*

Her mind raced. The man sent to Arlington worked for Amir. Amir knew all her and Nick's social activities and the Yamari government plans. His declarations of praise for the new democracy were pretense. He was Husam Al-Din's man.

Or else… "Husam Al-Din, I presume."

The Beretta wavered a fraction before he recovered. He

made a small bow. "So you and Markos figured out my game." He glanced behind him. His eyes narrowed at her. "Where is your doting lover? Not sneaking up on me from behind, I trust."

She let her chin tremble a little. "He…he was hurt at the cemetery. The doctor put him in the hospital." She hoped he didn't know they'd never gone to Arlington.

"Pity. I would have liked to have seen him one *last* time. But his absence makes this job easier. And more pleasant. Too bad I don't have time to thoroughly enjoy your…charms before I say adieu. But time is of the essence."

His slimy insinuation slid nausea into her throat. The thought of his paws on her roiled in her stomach more than his other implied intent.

Amir meant to kill her. That truth had hit her at the sight of him. She had to get him talking, had to get him moving toward the back of the house. "How did you get in?"

"Pah, the house's security system was hardly a challenge. Your government conveniently taught a group of Yamari's finest officers clandestine techniques. Helpful of them."

He said nothing about the hidden cameras. Hope that the techs had seen him enter bolstered her courage. "What do you want…Your Highness?"

His mocking laugh grated on her eardrums. "What I wanted from the beginning. My money."

She glared at him. "Blood money. Money to set yourself up as sole ruler of Yamar. More money than you need for that."

"My dear, one can never have too much money. Yamar is a small country with vulnerable neighbors. And I have spent the last few years building up the Yamari forces. Soon Yamar will be a formidable presence in the region."

Dear God, he had plans for an empire. And he had as good as admitted his intention to overthrow the Yamari president. If she pushed him further, she'd know the rest. "But your assassination plan has failed."

His features drew together in fury.

She was right!

"Pah! I am surrounded by incompetents. And that fool Rashid has talked. I cannot return to Yamar. The ten million will buy my escape." He smiled, a croc's toothy display. "But I fooled them all. You included, dear Danielle."

"What do you mean?"

"Husam Al-Din is a holy man, a recluse who is unaware of anything outside his retreat. I merely co-opted and refined his religious ideals, shall we say, to a greater purpose."

"A greedy purpose. You set up the attacks at the embassies?"

"And a few other bombs in strategic places."

"Including the bomb at Alexei Markos's funeral?"

He laughed. "That poor fanatic rode in my limousine trunk."

She longed to punch him in his smug expression. "You sent suicide bombers who thought they were dying for a religious cause. Instead it was for your despicable ambition and greed."

His good humor vanished. He waved the black pistol at her. "Your opinion has no consequence. Now where is my money?"

She shrugged. "You won't get away. What does it matter if I tell you? I locked the money in the safe before I went to the hospital with Nick."

"Ah, how convenient." He gestured again with the gun. "After you, my dear."

Head high, she swept past him to the sunroom. She showed Amir the small safe behind a wall panel. She had no idea what was inside, but it sure wasn't ten million dollars. If he tried to open the safe, his back would be to the outside door.

She chanced a quick glance in that direction. No sign of Nick outside. A blanket of darkness hid any movement.

*Where is he?*

"Open it." Only a foot away, Amir regarded her with an unyielding hardness. His musky cologne nauseated her.

She shrugged. "I don't have the combination."

"Wrong answer." He slammed her cheek with the pistol. Pain exploded in her head.

She crashed to her side on the floor. She tasted blood, hot and coppery. Dazed, dizzy, she was too stunned to move.

Crimson hate ripped through Nick in a deadly ray. He clenched his fists and stayed hidden in the kitchen. He had to wait for his chance.

Byrne and five other ATSA officers had arrived soon after Vanessa went in the house. They waited outside. Nick had given no quarter on who would go in to her. She'd saved his life and his honor. He had to tell her he loved her. He couldn't let the damned prince hurt her.

He wouldn't let himself consider a worse possibility.

Edging closer to the archway between the two rooms, he peered into the sunroom. He crouched, ready.

Amir jerked Vanessa to her feet. He yanked her hard against him. He jabbed the pistol against her throat and turned toward the terrace door. "Come inside, Markos. You wouldn't want to see your lovely fiancée's blood flowing all over this valuable carpet."

Nick itched to pound the bastard into the damned carpet. *Help me,* latrea mou, *give me an opening,* his mind called.

"I saw you looking out there. Your hospital tale was a trick." Staring at the night-blanked windows, the prince lowered the gun. He shook her like a rag doll. "Where is he?"

"Oh, I'm so weak. I'm dizzy." Vanessa sagged, becoming a dead weight.

Nick rushed in from the side.

Amir swung the pistol toward him.

"No!" Vanessa shouted. She heaved herself in front of her captor. She aimed a knee and threw up an arm.

Amir fired. The crack of the shot filled the room.

She reeled and dropped to the side. She didn't move.

Armed ATSA officers in flak vests burst in through the terrace and the front doors.

Nick slammed into Amir with his full weight. They rolled onto the floor, both struggling for the pistol. Nick smashed the heel of his hand into Amir's nose. Blood spurted as cartilage crunched. His grip on the weapon slipped.

Nick knocked the pistol away.

Byrne picked it up.

Nick hauled back a fist. "You bastard, I should kill you, but I want you to suffer like all the people you hurt. Just killing you isn't good enough."

"It's over, Markos," the ATSA officer said. "I know how you feel. I'd like a piece of him myself. After questioning, the U.S. will turn him over to his government. In that part of the world, they don't treat traitors gently. He'll wish you'd killed him."

Nick saw the panicked fear in Amir's eyes at the idea of what they'd do to him in Yamar. He let his fist drop.

"Cuff that man. Shackle his feet, too," Byrne ordered.

Leaving the broken-beaked prince to them, Nick crawled to Vanessa. His hands shook. He lifted her gently and cradled her still form in his arms.

Her eyes fluttered open. "Nick…you're all…right."

He breathed again. "Thank God you're alive."

Blood soaked the side of her jacket. He tore off his sweater to staunch the bleeding.

"Call 911," he rasped out past his tight throat. "She's been shot."

Vanessa woke from a restless sleep. An elephant sat on her chest. Every breath stabbed pain in her side.

Then she remembered. Amir. Nick. The gunshot.

It was finally over.

At a noise beside her bed, she turned her head. The dim

glow from a bedside lamp showed Nick asleep in a chair. Dark bristles shadowed his jaw. He'd combed his thick, dark hair with something like a garden rake. Both hands had swollen knuckles as if he'd gone ten rounds without gloves.

For her.

He looked so beautiful to her greedy eyes that for a moment the pain receded. Her heart swelled with love for him, and ached with sorrow for what would never be.

He stirred. His eyes opened. His Aegean-blue eyes studied her. Worry crinkled fan creases at the corners. "You're awake. How do you feel?" His normally smooth, deep voice cracked like an adolescent's.

Her mouth tasted like the inside of a vacuum cleaner, and an ache radiated through her as if she'd been stunt double in a kickboxing movie. "Hurts."

He came closer and helped her sip ice water through a straw. His familiar scent floated to her above the antiseptic and medicinal odors.

"The IV beside you is pain meds. The self-dosing kind. All you have to do is squeeze the control by your hand."

"In a minute." With her right hand, she lifted the flowered hospital johnny. A white bandage covered the entire right side of her torso and wrapped around her chest beneath her breasts. "How bad?"

"The doctors said you were lucky." His mouth flattened. "Lucky is a matter of opinion. The bullet cracked a couple of ribs and tore muscle. But no organ damage. You'll recover. No thanks to me."

He hadn't learned yet. "Not your fault, oh responsible one. You can't stop a bullet." The long speech provoked the elephant to squash her a little harder. Her breath hitched.

"I should've gone in the front, not you."

"Twenty-twenty hindsight."

She heard his sigh of resignation. "You never give up," he said. "Get some rest. Take care of the pain."

"Not yet. What happened at the Mall?" From his grim expression, she expected the worst.

"The unveiling ceremony was to be an assassination all right. A setup. Al-Din aka Prince Amir's fanatics had rigged a bomb to blow when the tarp was pulled from the sculpture. C-4. It would've collapsed that wing of the museum and killed dozens, maybe more. Hundreds of people were there, including the U.S. Secretary of State. One of the fanatics tried to trigger the explosion, but an ATSA officer stopped him."

So why wasn't he jumping for joy? Her breath caught at the sharp pain as she tried to turn toward him. "You are vindicated, Nick. Your hunch saved scores of people and prevented a coup. If ATSA saved the day, why aren't you celebrating?"

He covered her hand with his. His blue eyes bored into hers. "The ATSA officer who stopped the bomber was Gabriel Harris. The New Dawn man had a knife. He stabbed Harris before a sniper could take him down. Harris…didn't make it."

"Oh my God, Gabe!" Vanessa gasped. "Poor Janna. They've only been married a year." Hot tears filled her eyes.

"Byrne was going to see her after they took Amir into custody. He apologized for not trusting me. Said General Nolan'd be contacting me."

"We should all apologize for not trusting you. You're a hero."

"I appreciate that, honey, but Harris is the real hero of the day. I'm sorry about him. I understand he was a good officer."

"A stand-up guy. Hero Harris is truly a hero this time," she said, blowing her nose in the tissue Nick had handed her. "He'll probably get a medal. Too bad it'll be posthumous."

"Enough talk. Do I have to pump those meds into you myself?" Nick stood by her with his arms folded.

"I can do it. I'm ready to rest now." Moving her left arm provoked a spasm of sharp pain like a tusk in her side, but she pressed the control.

A languorous fog gathered in her body and blurred her vision. The meds were fuzzing the rest of her system. The elephant went on a diet. "Sleep now. You leaving?"

The cool hand that brushed her forehead trembled. Or it could've been her imagination.

His last words put a smile on her lips as the fog bank closed around her.

"You couldn't get rid of me with a forklift."


At noon the next day, Nick drove Vanessa back from the hospital. He'd left in the morning to meet with the ATSA director, of all things. She'd expected J. T. McNair to show up, but Nick had apparently taken over.

During the ride she talked about the wrap-up of their mission, anything but "It's been great, but so long, babe."

The surviving bomber at the Mall had been the one who had pushed the statue over on Vanessa and Laura. Emil Alfieris had identified Prince Amir's secretary, Rashid, as the man who'd paid him for the house plans. And Rashid himself had revealed all of the Yamari prince's recruits, people whom he'd convinced he spoke for the New Dawn leader.

When Director Nolan finished briefing Ambassador Khalil, the ambassador had thanked him profusely and vowed to root out the rest of New Dawn. An enlightening conversation with the holy man himself should put an end to their terror campaign.

In the garage, Nick opened Vanessa's door and offered a hand.

"Guess I'm still a bit weak," she said, accepting it. The warmth and support of his callused hand reminded her of what joy she'd found in his arms. Going back to her solitary life was too painful to contemplate.

"You look four hundred percent better." His gaze, full of tenderness, captured hers.

Normal human concern, she reminded herself with a sharp pang of regret, after what they'd been through. No more. She'd disappointed him, deceived him, so they were done.

"I feel better. Like I fell off a fifty-foot cliff, but I'm mobile. And clean." A newly plaited braid draped her right shoulder, and she wore clean slacks and a pullover. "Laura Stratton breezed in this morning with stuff from my apartment. And she did my hair."

"I'm glad you don't have to conceal your friendship any longer."

"Me, too. They're adopting another child, a two-year-old from Romania. I can visit anytime since I'm on medical leave for a few months."

She stopped her chatter. Their words were small talk, meaningless. The conversation of two people who have nothing to say to each other. That saddened her more than ever.

She ought to explain about her final search of the desk. Afterward she'd ask McNair to drive her to HQ to do her report. They were probably packing up the command post.

Then she would go home to her studio apartment. Alone.

"Vanessa, we need to talk about the other night. I overreacted, but it hurt that you didn't trust me."

"I did trust you. I felt lower than a snake, but I had orders." By snooping and not finding anything, she could prove to ATSA that he *could* be trusted. But she didn't say that. "A former soldier should understand."

His hands hovered over her shoulders as if he feared hurting her. Lowering them to his sides, he said, "After a long night of soul searching, I figured out a lot of things. For one, that you had no choice. Security was paramount. But I needed to hear you say it again."

She realized she'd been holding her breath. What? Hoping for declarations of love? No more foolishness.

Her gaze snagged on the library door. "Nick, did you ever look at the two papers? The ones I had when you came in?"

He shook his head. "I stuffed them in my briefcase and shut down the laptop. Haven't been back in there since."

That didn't surprise her. They'd been a tad busy. "But they're not *your* papers. I found them in the desk jammed to the back of a drawer."

"Then what the hell are they?"

"They show what Alexei did with the ten million dollars."

"Say what?" Ray Lincoln scratched his head, making his short dreadlocks bounce like springs. "You want to pry off this gizmo. Y'all sure?" The wry cant to his mouth and the look in his eyes clearly said his new employer was nuts.

"I'm sure," Nick said, restraining a grin. "Go ahead and do your work. Just let me use a crowbar."

Ray shook his head in disbelief. "A crowbar? You better let me do it. You'll trash the good part of this here wall."

"Do your worst. I'll pay you for the extra."

Ray went at the medallion with a hammer and chisel.

Nick joined Vanessa, buttoned in a corduroy jacket, at the wrought-iron table and chairs. Her cheeks glowed with the excitement of treasure hunting. She was poring over the two sheets of paper, the keys to Alexei's stash.

"I think the ATSA searchers either missed these or thought sketches of the stone medallions and descriptions of coins were of no importance. Who would?"

"They weren't looking for ten million dollars." He cast an anxious glance at Ray's progress. From the slow work chipping at the medallion's edges, it would be a while. Alexei must've anticipated he'd have to hide his thefts from New Dawn. He'd converted the stolen funds to valuable coins. A quick check on the Internet had located the dozen coins on the list. Two—a 1913 Liberty Head nickel and a Colonial American silver sixpence—had each sold for over a million dollars within the last two years to an anonymous bidder. Damned clever of Alexei, Nick conceded.

Then he'd mortared them behind the second medallion from the house. But after committing murder, he'd fled in such a rush that he'd left behind the coins. And the papers. By a fluke they'd lain stuck in the desk drawer for months.

A crash and a crack like a lightning-split boulder pulled Nick from his cold seat.

"Here you go, Mr. Markos." Ray dropped the crowbar with a clatter. He mopped his brow with a red bandana.

Nick knelt beside the medallion, split in three chunks. The pale November sun caught on shiny spots in the crumbled mortar. He picked up the trowel lying on the terrace and chipped them loose.

"Oh, wow," said Vanessa behind him.

Nick levered to his feet. He held out the twelve coins in his palms.

"Holy sh—, um…damn!" the young mason exclaimed. "All that for pocket change?"

"You'll think I'm a couple of inches off plumb, Ray, but these are the key to your future."

They hurried inside, leaving Ray scratching his head.

"What did you mean by the key to his future?" she said.

"The charitable fund," he said as he put the coins in the safe. She should be part of this decision, as she would be in all his future ones. If she let him. Fear that she might not want him chilled the warm glow from finding the coins.

"What have you decided?"

"What do you think of low-interest loans to help deserving disadvantaged people start businesses?" He turned to see her reaction.

The color in her cheeks brightened almost to match her hair. Her glowing smile reached inside him and hugged his heart. His throat was tight, and his eyes burned. Maybe he still had a chance.

"Oh, Nick, that sounds perfect. Like a hard-working guy who needs a truck and tools for a landscaping business?"

He knew she'd catch on quick. He ached to hug her, but her injury restrained him. "You got it. Or a great cook who wants to own a restaurant."

Moving gingerly, she unbuttoned her coat. When he offered to help her off with it, she shook her head and kept it on. He was afraid she'd leave, but she followed him to the kitchen.

Vanessa geared up to be flip and casual about saying good-bye. She squared her shoulders. What she wanted to do was to cry and howl. The pain whacking her chest had nothing to do with her cracked ribs.

She couldn't help staring at Nick, memorizing the exact shade of his eyes, the proud blade of his nose, the sexy cleft in his chin, the ebony hairs curling above the V-neck of his cream-colored sweater.

"You'll be able to sell those coins for more than your brother paid," she said, tamping down emotions that threatened to overflow. "That and the proceeds from the house sale will set up the charity fund."

"Dwight Wickham finally came through with a reasonable offer for the import business, too. He and Abdul Nadim have some scheme to enlarge. So that's done."

He opened a cabinet door and took out the bag of coffee beans and the grinder.

"Don't make any for me," she said, hoping her voice sounded normal. "I have to get going. Write out my report."

Slowly he turned, his wide shoulders impressive in the clingy knit. Something like fear or anger flitted across his features before his expression gentled. He took her hand and pulled her closer.

"Honey, your report can wait. We have something much more important to sort out. Our future."

# Chapter 19

*O**ur future?***

In his eyes she saw desire…and something softer. His dark velvet voice stirred heat and hope within her.

"I…thought we…it was done." She didn't trust herself to say more than that. Another word and she'd blurt out her love, lay her crumbling heart at his feet.

He cupped her shoulders, kissed her nose. "If I have my way, 'we…it' will never be done. I don't want to lose you, Vanessa. I love you. And I think—hope you feel the same."

His words branded her brain and jumpstarted her heart. The heat in his eyes held her in thrall, and she could say only, "Nick."

He curled a hand on her nape and massaged. "I'm climbing out of the darkness I've wallowed in for years. A few sessions with a shrink should help me the rest of the way out. I'm starting to trust myself. You're responsible for that."

"Me? How?" The gentle pressure of his hands mesmerized her, drugged her more than the Demerol had.

"Honey, you've prodded and challenged and supported me ever since we met. You helped me deal with my anger at Alexei. You made me examine my marriage plans and realize I'm not my father. I've been trying to prove my family honor and redeem my own. Without your tenacity on Somalia, I'd still be in that dark pit. You mean more to me than I have words to express."

"You were suffering. I knew from the first you were a good man, an honorable man who'd find his way. But you don't know me, not really."

"I know enough, and we have time for the rest. I know your warmth and generosity, your wit and your humor. I know you brought sunshine and laughter into my empty life." He lifted her hand and kissed the palm. "Besides, you're so damn cute I can't keep my hands off you. Marry me."

He surprised her so much she gasped, and the sudden twist cinched the elephant's trunk around her ribs. After a couple of shallow breaths, she slipped from his hold. "Marriage? What kind of marriage? I want no part of your corporate contract. I want a real home and family."

"Vanessa, I want that, too. I've been hiding from my problems by filling the hours with work and social obligations. I didn't think I could have a home other than a pad to crash in. I want the woman I love, not a contracted hostess. I want my best friend to make that home with me." Intensity glowed in his dark eyes.

She'd hurt him once. She couldn't hurt him again by denying she loved him. "Oh, Nick, I tried not to fall in love with you. I had something to prove, too, that I could go undercover without getting involved."

He smiled with affection. "I'm glad you blew uninvolvement."

"I wanted you to be the hard-nosed CEO, but you weren't. Your kindness and honor beat down my defenses. And you seemed to want me for myself, not for who I pretended to be or for an ulterior motive."

"And I know that you wanted me for me, not for my money."

"I guess we've both missed knowing what it's like to be loved for ourselves. We have that in common."

"Unless you want me for those ten-plus-million dollars worth of coins."

"What?" Then she saw the mischief in his eyes. Love softened his gaze and seeped into her soul, tempting her to believe. But doubts lingered. "You. Me. It would never last."

"And why not? We love each other. Everything else can be worked out." He bent and nuzzled her ear.

She dredged up courage and backed away. "Nick, I'd never fit in your social circles. All those sophisticated jet-setters and important diplomats and tycoons." She twisted her hands in front of her as if that could soothe the panic racing an Indy course in her stomach.

"*Latrea mou.* Sweetheart." He crossed his arms and leaned against the counter. "You have been doing exactly that for the past few weeks. Fitting in with jet-setters and diplomats."

"But that was like in a play. Inside I knew I was just a cop's daughter. It wasn't real. I was just playing the part of Danielle."

He shook his head. "Danielle LeBec, European fashion editor for *Adorn,* isn't real either."

She frowned, confused. "Well, she's a bit shallow and egotistical, but—"

"She changed her name. She was Twyla Zickafoose from Pork Chop, West Virginia. Didn't think the fashion world would take her seriously."

She burst out laughing, then choked to a halt when her throbbing torso reminded her of her wound. "Really?"

"Really. Cocktail parties, business luncheons, receptions. Everyone plays the part they make for themselves. Myself included. You think I don't still feel inside that I'm just that kid selling sandwiches on the docks?"

"Truly? Old insecurities come back to jab you, too?" She swallowed. Hard. Was it possible? She chanced a step closer.

"Besides, with you to come home to, high society doesn't have the appeal it used to."

He drew her against him, cradling her gently so he wouldn't hurt her wound. She closed her eyes at the thrilling feel of his body, the intoxicating scent that was uniquely Nick, the needy hope that raced her heart.

"Marry me, Vanessa. Build a life with me. I can set up an office in D.C. if you want to continue with ATSA. N.D.M. has plenty of accounts in the area."

The conflicting emotions swirling and eddying inside her flowed into certainty in her heart. "You'd do that for me?"

"If you promise to leave undercover work to others."

"That's an easy one. I plan to tell the director I'll resign before I do another undercover assignment."

He laughed. "As long as you stay involved in this one."

She ran a finger down the crease in his chin. His skin felt warm and real. Not a figment of her dreams. She closed her eyes, and uttered a silent prayer of thanks for this incredible man who loved her. "ATSA has a division in New York City, you know. I could transfer."

He flashed a grin that nearly blinded her. "You'd be going home."

"Home will be wherever you are."

"Then it's yes? You'll marry me?" He sought her gaze, as if trying to see her answer.

"Yes, Nick. I love you so much." She pressed a hand on his chest and felt the steady beat of his heart.

He cleared his throat and covered her hand with his. "I have something else I need to tell you."

Tilting her head to peer at his worried expression, she thought she knew. "I know General Nolan was extremely impressed with your—how did he put it? Ah, your 'contribution to the mission.' Did he want more than to thank you?"

He shook his head. "More mind reading. You amaze me."

"The general?" she prompted.

"He asked me to work for ATSA as a part-time consultant."

"A consultant? Like on foreign threats?"

"Exactly. All the travel I do can serve double duty."

"Oh." She tried to feel pleased and proud, but knowing he had to leave her behind carved a hollow place inside her.

He tilted up her chin. "I agreed on one condition."

"Yes?"

"That you can come with me as my advisor."

"You didn't!" At his wide grin, her heart overflowed with happiness. "Nick, I love you so. Kiss me before my heart beats right out of my chest."

His hands cradling her head, he bent to capture her mouth in a kiss of compelling delight and caring warmth. She'd never felt so cherished.

Raw sexual hunger shot through Nick so he could barely breathe. He burned to seal their love in the fires of passion. But it would be weeks before she was well enough. "I guess we'll have to wait awhile for more than that," he said ruefully as he lifted his head.

"I heal fast."

Chuckling at her incurable optimism, he settled for holding her hand. His gaze caught on the engagement ring.

He tapped it with his index finger. "Shame to ship this back to Danielle. I've grown used to seeing it on you."

"This old thing?" She twisted off the ring and tossed it over her shoulder. The ring bounced across the kitchen floor and came to rest in a corner. "Who needs it?"

"What are you doing?"

A teasing smile curved her lips. "Nick, it's only a paste copy. Danielle has the real diamond. I don't need a ring."

"Maybe you don't, but I need to proclaim to the world that you're mine. I'll have the fluorescent diamond made into a ring for you. Its fire is no match for you, but it's the best I can offer."

"Oh, Nick, it's perfect," she said, tears shimmering in her beautiful green eyes.

"Not by a long shot, honey." He tilted up her chin. "*We* are perfect. This is perfect."

He drew her into a kiss that celebrated their promise and spoke of forever.

\* \* \* \* \*

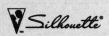

*Signature Select*™

# THE

*Signature Select*™

## SERIES

will bring you more
of the characters
and authors you love.

**Plus, value-added Bonus Features
are coming to a book near you.**

- Your favorite authors
- The characters you love
- Plus, bonus reads!

### SIGNATURE SELECT
Everything you love about romance and more.

~ On sale January 2005 ~

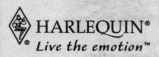

If you enjoyed what you just read,
then we've got an offer you can't resist!

# Take 2 bestselling love stories FREE!
# Plus get a FREE surprise gift!

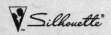

# INTIMATE MOMENTS™

## and award-winning author
# VIRGINIA KANTRA
## present
# STOLEN MEMORY
### (IM #1347)

**The next book in her exciting miniseries**

# TROUBLE IN EDEN

**Small town, big secrets—
and hearts on the line!**

Dedicated cop Laura Baker is used to having all the answers. But when reclusive inventor Simon Ford wakes up on the floor of his lab with a case of amnesia and a missing fortune in rubies, all Laura has are questions. As her investigation heats up, so does her attraction to the aloof millionaire. Can she find the missing jewels...before she loses her heart?

*Available February 2005
at your favorite retail outlet.*

And look for the other electrifying titles in the TROUBLE IN EDEN miniseries available from Silhouette Intimate Moments:
**All a Man Can Do (IM #1180), All a Man Can Ask (IM #1197),
All a Man Can Be (IM #1215)**

# COMING NEXT MONTH

SIMCNM0105